ACRE

J. K. SWIFT

Acre
Hospitaller Saga Book 1

Published by UE Publishing Co.
Vancouver, BC, Canada
Copyright© 2016 by J. K. Swift
All rights reserved.

ISBN-13: 978-1533478771
ISBN-10: 1533478775
Print Edition

Cover design by C. Ryan

www.jkswift.com
New Releases Mailing List
http://eepurl.com/hTAFA

Book Description

A doomed mission. The Kingdom of Jerusalem hanging by a thread. One Knight Justice must face his greatest fears or die trying...

Brother Foulques de Villaret just wants to stay in Acre and perform his sworn duties. Instead, the young Hospitaller Knight must undertake a dangerous journey from the Holy Lands to a remote village nestled in the Alps. His mission: buy 500 peasant boys and return them to Acre to be trained as Soldiers of Christ. Pursued across the Mid-Earth Sea by slavers, Brother Foulques and his small band of Hospitallers are about to be thrust into a confrontation with the greatest warriors the East has ever known: the Mamluks. To survive, Brother Foulques must turn to risky alliances... and pray that his choices do not lead them all to destruction.

For Mom. You wouldn't have liked this one.

CHAPTER ONE

W HEN VIGNOLO DEI Vignoli forced his eyes open, the
world remained dark. The sounds of the city were
muffled, the air around him damp and stagnant, with not a
trace of the cool breeze always present in Acre's Mid-Earth
Sea harbor. It was not the first time Vignolo had had a sack
tied over his head. In a way, he found the blackness
comforting, once his breath had returned from being struck
in the abdomen, and he had managed to spit out the moist
cloth of the hood he had sucked in and out of his mouth as
he struggled to regain his wind.

He tottered along with a captor at each elbow, his hands
tied before him, and tried not to think too much. No sense
in attempting to figure out who had hired these men or
where he was going. Sadly, it could have been any of a
number of people. Their information was good. They had
been thorough in relieving him of his weapons, even finding
his boot knife without much of a search. This was no chance
abduction.

So, he relaxed his shoulders, blew the coarse material out
of his mouth once again, and allowed himself to be led

through the narrow side streets of Acre. For a time he found himself almost enjoying the freedom of letting someone else dictate his course, but that initial thrill soon wore off.

A door squealed open. His toe caught on the threshold as he was pushed through and he almost fell. They weaved in and out of rooms and the sounds of the late night denizens of Acre were shut out. Another door opened and they were back outside. A woman's voice cursed them and a man grunted in surprise as they pushed past.

"Oi, watch yourselves!" the woman said. The smell of sweat, alcohol, and sex found its way inside Vignolo's hood.

"Excuse us, my lady," Vignolo said, turning his head back to the couple. "Might I have your name for future—"

A fist pounded into his stomach and he found himself sucking on sack cloth yet again.

His breath returned faster this time. I must be getting better at this, he thought.

"My father is a rich man. I can get you double whatever they are paying you."

A hard palm or maybe an elbow smashed half onto his nose and upper lip. Pain registered immediately and Vignolo cursed. He hated being hit in the nose for the eye-blurring pain always had a way of making him instantly angry. Still, it had been worth a try. You never knew who was going to turn at the opportunity to make a better profit. Vignolo had once bribed his way out of a fix when he was caught in bed with a noble man's sister. The man was rich, but the prospect of being even richer was more attractive than his sister's honor. Of course Vignolo had never actually paid the man.

"Dead men cannot spend coin," a rough voice said in Italian with a strong Milanese accent. "And we know your father hates you."

Milano? Oh, this is not good.

"Hates me? That is an exaggeration. I am his only heir, the last of his blood. I assure you, he could not bear to see harm come to the last of the Vignoli line."

The man laughed. "And what if we already work for him? Who would pay us then?"

That was a prospect Vignolo had not considered. But no, his father would never hire Milanese thugs. Too unpredictable. They were cheap and you could get them to do anything for a bit of silver, however, they had a tendency to take matters into their own hands. Every time Vignolo had hired one he had regretted it. Of course rough work required rough hands, but a level head was required to lead those hands.

"Why so silent Vignolo?" The man pushed him stumbling into the side of a stone building, caught him as he rebounded, and shoved him forward through a doorway. Once again the sounds of the city died away as one of the men slammed the door shut and slid a locking timber into place.

Milanese. Who in Acre would be stupid enough to hire Milanese? Vignolo silently went down his list of French and English creditors and could think of no one.

Then it hit him.

Oh, Mary.

But not Mary. As far removed from the Blessed Virgin as one could possibly imagine, in fact. Provenzano. Francesca Provenzano. Only another Milanese would hire Milanese thugs. Albeit, she had married into a rich Venetian family and had been smart enough to publicly sever all ties with that world.

They brought him to a stop and someone ripped the hood off his head, taking with it more than a few of Vignolo's wavy dark hairs. He clenched his eyes shut, telling himself it was because of the pain and the sudden influx of lantern light. But the truth was, despite how easy she was to look at, he was in no hurry to see the woman standing before him.

"Open your eyes, Vignolo." The voice was flat, almost bored.

Vignolo opened first one eye and then the other.

"Ah, hello Francesca. What brings you to Acre?"

The man holding his left elbow leaned around and punched Vignolo in the stomach. "She said nothing about speaking."

Vignolo coughed and leaned against his captors until he caught his breath. He straightened up and looked at Francesca. She was a tall, beautiful woman with long, almost black hair carefully arranged to hang just off her shoulders and held in place with fine silk netting. She was perhaps ten years older than Vignolo. Even in his current state of distress he found himself admiring the length of her and wondered if there were any truth to the rumor that her late husband had expired in the throes of passion.

She caught him staring. Her eyes narrowed and she shook her head.

"You were about to say something?" Francesca said.

"I was under the impression I had another month."

Francesca's lips spread into a line. "You think I would bother coming all the way here for the likes of you and the paltry sum you owe? Your head is as big as your arse."

"Excellent. Then I will be on my way."

Francesca tilted her head and laughed. She ran her tongue over her lips once, giving them a luster that matched her eyes. Then she nodded to the man at Vignolo's side. He sunk his fist into Vignolo's guts so far Vignolo thought he felt knuckles bounce off his spine. He doubled over and black spots swam before his eyes.

"That is for looking at me with the eyes of a man."

Some time later, with his lungs only partially filled, Vignolo found his voice. It squeaked out, and he cringed at the sound of it.

"So, why are you here then?" At least he felt confident he did not have the *voice* of a man at the moment.

"Business, Vignolo. Honest business. But I would not expect a Genoan to know anything about that. Believe it or not, I have more on my books than treasure hunting no-goods like you."

"If the quality of your employees is any indication of your clients, I find that hard to believe." Vignolo was prepared for the blow this time, even though it came from the man holding his right elbow. He recovered quickly and spat on the floor.

"This conversation is going to take a long time if you keep letting your monkeys hit me whenever I say something."

"Yes, we do know how much you like to talk. And speaking of employees, I sent a man with a message for you before you fled Venice. But I am not sure you received it, for I have not seen him since."

Vignolo shrugged. "Venice can be a dangerous place. It is possible he was waylaid before he found me."

"I suspect there is at least some truth to that."

"So… What was the message?"

"He was to tell you not to leave Venice."

"Ah. Well now, that is an unreasonable request if you ever expect to see the money I owe you. I am a ship's captain. I make my living on the sea. And as you are well aware, the Venetians are not always hospitable to Genoans. Or anyone for that matter."

"Maybe I do not expect to ever see that money again."

Francesca had a point. It was not a great deal of coin to someone of her means.

"You will get your money. I swear it. I have something in the works as we speak."

She shrugged. "I will, or I will not. But that is a discussion for another day. Right now, I have someone here that wishes to see you."

Francesca twisted her head and spoke over her shoulder, but kept her eyes fixated on Vignolo. "Giacomo. Bring him in."

A red curtain, heavy enough to be a carpet, slid aside

behind Francesca. A tall, gaunt man backed through dragging a limp form along the ground by one booted ankle. He let go of the man's leg and it bounced twice before settling on the floor. His hooded head lolled to one side. Other than that, he did not move. The gaunt man wiped his hands on his breeches and, as he looked into Vignolo's face, a slow smile creased his angular features.

Vignolo's stomach turned. He had never seen this man of Francesca's before, but he had known a handful of men like him over the years. Men from the docks of Genoa who worked not for gold or glory, but for the simple thrill of violence. Perhaps he was not from Genoa; he could have been from the streets of Milan or the public squares of Venice. It did not matter, for these men were all the same. They shared a lust not for life, but rather, the absence of it. Those who were disciplined enough, sometimes managed to find a place within one of the elite Genoan Crossbowmen mercenary troops. Life amongst the soldiers of the red and green offered a steady salarium, along with a healthy measure of respect from the world's fighting forces. But for some men that was not enough. Vignolo understood this well, for he himself had served three years as a Genoan Crossbowman while in his late teens, but his restless nature soon had him turning in his crossbow and pavaise and taking to the seas.

"Remove the hood," Francesca said.

Squatting low over the body, Giacomo did as she bid, but he kept his eyes on Vignolo's face lest he miss something fascinating. He yanked the coarse material away in one swift motion, like a magician revealing a vanished rat.

Vignolo raised his eyebrows at Francesca. "Am I supposed to know this young man?"

Francesca's eyes lit up and laughter bubbled out of her. She put a hand to her mouth and, for a moment ever so brief, Vignolo thought a lady stood before him. That was before she slapped him.

She grabbed his chin in both hands and turned his face to hers.

"Oh, Vignolo. You are one of the best liars I have ever dealt with."

Vignolo licked at a cut on the inside of his lip. "I am not sure how to take that. I imagine a woman like you gets lied to more than even you would think."

Francesca leaned in close. Vignolo could smell orange blossoms.

"A woman always knows when a man is lying." She pushed Vignolo's head back and jerked her hands away. Then she turned to Giacomo. "Get him up."

Giacomo sloshed a full chamber pot, of what Vignolo hoped was water, onto the face of the young man. He came to coughing and bucking, his face heavily bruised, bloodied, and swollen.

"Andrea Moresco. Second son of your much older sister. Deny his identity again and I will have Giacomo slit his throat before your eyes."

Vignolo thought he saw Giacomo stand a little taller, the furrow in his face that passed for a smile grow a little deeper.

"Ah, Nephew. Is that you? I suppose I failed to recognize

you with all the recent beatings you have received about the head."

"The fool boy swore up and down that his dear Uncle Vignolo could help him. I pray for his sake he is right."

Vignolo did not like the sound of Francesca's words. It was not what she said but rather how she said it. Her voice had a bored, monotonous ring to it.

Andrea coughed and rolled onto his side as he dragged one hand across his face to clear his vision. He gave Vignolo a weak look, and when he spoke there was little air in his words. He kept his elbows pressed tight against his ribs to lessen the pain there.

"I am sorry Vignolo. I had no other choice."

"Nonsense!" Vignolo said. "We are family, are we not?"

Andrea nodded eagerly, perhaps too eagerly. The sudden movement made a fresh grimace appear on the young man's boyish features.

Vignolo looked at Francesca. "What is the boy's sum?"

"A week ago it was ten thousand. Today it is twenty."

Vignolo allowed himself a private sigh of relief. It was a large sum, but not unworkable.

"That is rather aggressive interest. Are you not concerned for your soul?"

Francesca laughed. "Usury is the least of my sins, I assure you. Now, the situation here has grown old. Can you help the poor boy or shall we just move on?"

Her eyes moved slowly around the room until they came to rest on Giacomo, who leaned against a wall directly above Andrea.

"Can I have a moment alone to confer with my nephew?"

"I will give you two," Francesca said. She smiled and curtsied before leaving the room through the heavy curtained doorway. The men holding Vignolo's elbows deposited him roughly on the floor beside his nephew and followed their mistress. Giacomo stared at Vignolo for a moment longer and then he pushed himself off his wall and followed the others.

"Thank you for coming, Uncle. You have no idea how relieved—"

"Shut up!" Vignolo leaned in close so his words could not be overheard in the next room. "Do you not realize how much trouble we are in? Francesca Provenzano is the most notorious money lender in all of Venice. She regularly executes her least profitable clients just to keep her reputation up. And when I say execute, I do not mean in a 'stab you through the heart and be done with you' type of way. Oh, no. It is always slow, with many witnesses present to spread the word about how long and how hard you screamed."

Andrea's eyes grew wide and he reached out a hand to claw at Vignolo's sleeve. "Please, Vignolo. There must be something you can do. I have heard that you deal with her regularly. That is why I sought her out in the first place."

"Why would you need the likes of her? Your brother is the Governor of Rhodes for God's sake. Why not go to him if you cannot pay off your gambling debts?"

"This is not about gambling. I needed the money to buy

a ship."

"A ship?"

Andrea nodded. "A small galley with two banks of oars. She is a beauty. You would have approved, Uncle. I tried to get my brother to buy her for me but he accused me of living out some boyhood trader captain fantasy on the seas, when I should be helping him rule Rhodes for the Byzantine Emperor."

Vignolo leaned back. This is not what he had expected to hear. He had assumed the boy had spent all the money on whores and gambling. That would have been the more sensible thing to do, what with all the Venetian and Turkish pirates prowling the waters these days.

"So, let me guess. You got your beautiful ship loaded up with silks from Damascus and set sail to make your fortune. Unfortunately, you were set upon by pirates and they took everything."

"How—?"

"And probably, at some point during your flight from these pirates, your ship had an unfortunate mechanical failure, which resulted in your capture."

Andrea cringed, but not from any physical pain he might be experiencing. "Our rudder pin sheared off leaving us unable to maneuver. It does sound almost too coincidental. Are you saying someone on my crew was one of the pirates?"

"They were no common pirates."

"How can you be so sure?"

Because if Vignolo had been in Francesca's position, he probably would have done the same. A naive young captain with rich family connections would have been too much for her to resist. Now she had his cargo, as well as his original debt, and whatever Vignolo was about to promise her to spare the lad's life. Of course Vignolo was not one of those rich family members, but he suspected Francesca knew that.

"I know this because you are alive. At the very least, you should be living the miserable life of a galley slave right now if your attackers had been true pirates."

"Then who—?"

Vignolo cut him off. "Look, Andrea, you can puzzle this all out later. We have little time. I may be able to get us out of here alive, but you have to trust me and do exactly as I say. Understood?"

"Of course, Uncle! You and my brother may have issues, but I have always admired how you carved your own way through this world. Whatever you can do."

"Very well. Do you still own your house on Rhodes? The one in the valley with the orchards attached?"

"I do…" Andrea said, his eyes narrowing.

"The second we get out of here, *if* we get out of here, I will take you to a scribe I know and you will sign over the house and lands to me."

Andrea pushed himself up on one elbow. "Are you mad? My brother would kill me if I gave you that house! It was a commission from the Byzantine Emperor himself."

"Oh, come now. You exaggerate. Your brother would never kill you. But Francesca Provenzano will, of that you can be sure. And without your house under my name I will never be able to secure enough credit to satisfy her."

Vignolo watched the light in Andrea's eyes dim as he lowered his gaze to the floor. No doubt he was hearing his brother and father talking about what a scoundrel Vignolo was and how it was no wonder his own father had disinherited him. When the boy looked up again his eyes were set, hard. They had lost every last bit of adulation Vignolo had always seen in them. That was good, Vignolo thought. He was nobody's hero. Heroes belonged in songs and children's stories, and the sooner the boy understood that, the sooner he could get on with living.

"All right, Uncle. I will do as you say if you get me out of here, and my debt to Francesca is cleared."

Vignolo's eyebrows twitched. "I did not say anything about clearing your debt to her."

"No, but I know the value of my house."

The boy was a faster learner than Vignolo thought. "Very well. I will try."

Vignolo stood and as he was straightening his clothes, Francesca entered the room. A step behind her was Giacomo.

"I trust you had a nice reunion," Francesca said.

"Very nice, yes. Thank you. I feel I understand the situation much better now," Vignolo said.

"Good," Francesca said, her eyes as cold as her voice.

"You have the boy's ship somewhere near?"

Francesca shrugged. Vignolo took that as a 'yes'.

"All right, we are prepared to give you his ship as payment of his debt."

"The ship is damaged," she said.

"Surely you know someone who could repair that damage?"

"In fact, I do. But he is not cheap. My investors would not be happy if we had to pay the cost of repairs."

"I do not suppose you know exactly how much your shipwright would charge?"

"As a matter of fact, I do. He could do it for exactly the same amount as your own current debt to me."

"I see. Well it just so happens that I have a contract coming up that will see me with enough funds to repay both my debt and the cost of the shipwright's repairs, as well. Would that prove satisfactory to your investors?"

"It depends. Tell me of this contract."

Vignolo held up his hands and smiled. "Now, Francesca. What kind of business would I be running if I talked about my clients so openly? I am sure you of all people understand."

"I understand that you are Vignolo dei Vignoli, liar, cheat, adulterer, and pirate. Did I leave anything out?" She stepped toward him and raised up on her tiptoes to brush at a patch of dirt on his shoulder. His shirt was freshly torn there and he felt the heat of her slender fingers brush along the skin near his collar bone. "And if you cannot convince me of the legitimacy of this contract you say you have, then you are worth far more to me dead than alive."

Vignolo had often wondered just how high a position he held on her overall client list. Apparently, it was quite low. Disturbingly low.

He cleared his throat and caught her eyes with his own.

They sparkled with the thrill of the hunt, and they both knew Vignolo was the one up the tree.

"I suppose there would be no harm in a little sharing between friends. On one condition, of course."

She raised her eyebrows and took a step back. "Condition, Vignolo?"

He held his arms out wide to display the poor state of his shirt. "My chemise has suffered at the hands of your men. I see it only right that you contribute toward a new one. I know a good tailor in Acre, but perhaps you have a source that could supply him with a bolt of silk. Damascene silk, preferably?"

CHAPTER TWO

FOULQUES DE VILLARET, the youngest man ever appointed as a Knight Justice of the Order of Hospitallers of Saint John, stood motionless, except for his blue eyes, which glinted from under a black tangle of hair as they darted around the small room. The heavy posts and beams of the small community hall, square-hewn timbers blackened with age, seemed to close in on him with every passing second. Three men and one woman sat behind a rickety trestle table. In front of them was a bag containing more coin than any of them had ever seen in their lives, yet their eyes avoided it and they kept their hands at a distance, as though it were filled with vipers.

"It is not a simple thing you do, but rest assured you have chosen wisely in putting your faith in my order, and in God," Foulques said.

The woman stood so quickly her chair shot out behind her and toppled to the floor, causing everyone to jump, including the young knight.

"Desperation is not faith," she said, leveling a thin finger at Foulques. "We put no faith in you or your kind, only in our own people." She jerked her head toward the door, her eyes never leaving his face. "Go now, before we come to our senses."

Upon becoming a Knight of the Order of Saint John, besides taking vows of chastity and poverty, Foulques had sworn to accept the poor as his lords, but until this moment he had no idea just how difficult that would prove. Having been born into a noble French family, he was unaccustomed to being dismissed by a peasant, nevertheless a woman. He hesitated and looked to the men seated at the table. Their downward cast eyes told him who held sway in these lands.

He willed his clenched hands to unfold. He was no student of diplomacy. He was a soldier of Christ and was sure God had better uses for him than this. His sword was needed somewhere at this very moment and the constantly nagging image of a defenseless caravan or pilgrim being set upon by Mohammedan raiders gave rise to a pain behind his eyes so intense that he came close to cursing God. But then, it was not God who had sent him from the Holy Lands to this cold, shadow-haunted place of mountains and rock. The order had come from Grandmaster Villiers, himself, but Foulques suspected it had begun as a whispering in the Grandmaster's ear from Marshal Clermont.

Foulques took a deep breath. It mattered not. He had carried out his orders and would be back in Acre, the city of his birth and the only home he had ever known, soon enough. He bowed his head at the woman, ever so slightly, and without a word strode to the exit, his mail making a metallic rustle. He threw open the door and stepped out into the summer's early morning light.

The quiet was disconcerting, unnatural, for it should have been deafening.

Spread before him, overflowing the town square, were five hundred children lined up in flawless marching formation. They varied in age from five to twelve years old, all orphans or second sons sold by their families or villages Fifteen of Foulques's fellow Hospitallers, seven knights clad in the same black surcoats and cloaks, and eight grizzled sergeant men-at-arms dressed in brown, all with white crosses displayed on the chest, were interspersed amongst the orderly group. The few men stood out like giants as they were head and shoulders above even their tallest charges.

Without a backwards glance into the village hall, Foulques strode to take his place at the front of the column, next to Alain, a tall knight leading a string of pack mules, aware with every step that the woman's eyes were still locked upon him. Burning, boring deep into his being.

The column began its long winding journey toward Saint Gotthard's Pass. It was the fastest route Foulques could take to cross the treacherous Alps, jagged abominations the Devil himself had placed in the middle of the world in his continuous efforts to divide faithful Christians. Eventually, God willing, they would descend into northern Italia, and make their way to Genoa and the shores of the Mid-Earth Sea. There, he would load his new charges onto a ship and set sail for the Holy Land.

For home.

✠

THOMAS HAD NEVER been so weary in all his short life. He stared at the ground while he forced one foot in front of the other yet again. He carried a stick slung across his shoulder with a small bundle of clothes and a tin cup tied to the end. The stick bit further into his shoulder with every moment.

He was five, at least that was what the trapper had told him, but no one knew for sure. Thomas had liked living with the trapper after the black fever took his parents. He, too, was alone and insisted the boy call him Uncle. He was a soft-spoken man who laughed often and never raised his voice in anger. That is, until the men from Schwyz came to take Thomas away. The trapper had shouted at them and had a brief scuffle with one, but in the end Thomas joined the men. He could still see the trapper's scraggly face with a thin line of blood running from a cracked lip disappearing into his white beard. He stood in front of his cabin holding a hand up in farewell as the men led Thomas away. Thomas never cried, but he often worried about the old trapper being alone.

The men led Thomas slowly over the Alps, collecting other children along the way, until finally they met up with dozens of other small groups in the village of Schwyz. Thomas had never seen so many people gathered in one place. And there were so many children, many his own age.

In the town square, tall, black-robed men herded the children like sheep into lines. They shouted things Thomas could not understand but when one lifted him up by the shoulders and deposited him next to a boy a few years older, Thomas knew better than to stray. As they marched out of Schwyz on the south road, several children broke into tears. Villagers lined both sides of the road and anguished screams of women occasionally drowned out the sound of shuffling feet. A child in front of Thomas broke ranks and tried to thread his way back to his mourning parents, but one of the black-clad knights was there to bar his path. He snarled something in his strange tongue and pushed the boy back into line.

Eventually, the sounds of the villagers died away as the group plodded along the dusty road, the Lake of the Four Forest Regions mocking them all with its cool greenish-blue waters visible in the distance. Thomas was a quiet boy and did not make friends easily, but it comforted him to be part of so large a group. He was just another boy amongst a sea of children; no one paid him any attention, leaving him feeling protected, yet anonymous.

A blond-haired, scowling boy walked beside Thomas. He was older, perhaps eight, but already his stocky build hinted at the massive man he would become. At his side, walked the biggest working dog Thomas had ever seen. She was short-haired and largely black, with a powerful white chest and snout, and a square head with a mask of black surrounding even blacker eyes. She would have been terrifying if it was not for the rust-colored thumbprints above her eyes that softened her expressions. The draft dog was hitched to a cart she pulled effortlessly with a nonchalant grace, as though trying to pretend it was not there.

While most of the emotional outbursts from the children had ceased, a tall, thin boy walking in front of Thomas continued to sob intermittently. The sounds were an obvious annoyance to the boy with the dog, and finally, with an exasperated sigh, he shouted at the boy in front. His words were laced with an accent Thomas had to struggle to understand.

"Shut yer fae yer skinny, heavin' foal!"

The boy never looked back but, although he stifled his sobs, his shoulders still bucked with an occasional tremor.

The stocky boy rolled his eyes and looked at Thomas. "We are all of us feelin' black, but nay cause t'whee like a runt."

Thomas did not reply. He stared at the older boy and tried to make sense of his strange-sounding dialect. His speech was slow and flowing, one word rolling into the next, almost like he was singing. The big boy squinted at Thomas and looked him up and down, as though trying to decide whether or not he was worth wasting words on.

"Yer fane and yer half of that one. Wha's yer name, boy?"

"Thomas."

"Toomis? Strange name, that. Well, I be Pirmin. Pirmin Schnidrig of Tasch. Wha's yer father's name?"

Thomas shrugged and said, "You talk funny."

The bigger boy glared at Thomas for a brief moment and when he decided he was not being made fun of, he smiled and shook his head. "Me family's from Tasch, in Wallis. Is how w'all speak." He reached down a hand and nuzzled the dog pulling the cart. "This 'ere is Zora."

At the mention of her name the large dog straightened up and turned her head to look at Pirmin. In his strange way, Pirmin explained how they came from the land of the Matterhorn, a rugged mountainous area where the people and animals had to be as strong as the mountains themselves to survive. Even their houses were made from stone. Zora used to be a sheep dog on his father's farm but now was used as a draft animal to haul milk and cheese because she was getting too old for rounding up sheep on the sides of the steep hills. This last he whispered to Thomas behind a raised hand so Zora could not hear, then he took Thomas's hand and told him to give the dog a pat. The rust eyebrows arched as Thomas reached out his hand but the old dog seemed to enjoy the small boy's attention, even though she continued to stare proudly ahead.

"She is too warm," Thomas said.

Pirmin frowned and nodded. "Poor Zora's long far from home. Should be in the mounts and snow. Nay on a dusty forest road."

Shortly after, the marching column came to a halt and the gruff black knight Thomas had come to recognize as the leader, announced in stilted words the boys could understand that it was time for a rest. The children collapsed on the ground. The black knights moved efficiently throughout the large group. The leader wandered throughout the seated crowd and shouted that no one would receive food or water until every boy had removed his footwear and massaged his feet and calves for three minutes. The announcement brought many strange looks from the children but the promise of food had everyone's shoes off in seconds.

As promised, food and water was unpacked from the mules and the black knights distributed a generous piece of dark bread and a slab of strong-smelling cheese to each boy. Other knights milled through the mass of seated boys filling outstretched cups from dripping water skins.

Thomas drank half of his water then held his cup out for Zora. The panting dog lapped it up in seconds.

Thirty minutes later, the black knights and brown-robed sergeants roused the children from the ground and inspected their marching formations. When the leader was satisfied, the column once again began its slow, snaking progress along the forest-lined road.

Thomas grimaced and shifted his stick bundle from one shoulder to the other. It offered no comfort so he tried to move it back, but Pirmin stretched out a hand and plucked it away. Without a word to the smaller boy, he put the stick with its tiny attached bundle in Zora's cart on top of his own things. Zora did not balk, nor even glance back at the added weight. Her stoic gaze remained locked on the road ahead.

CHAPTER THREE

THE ISLAND CLIMATE was comfortably warm, but humid, so when the summons found him in his quarters, Badru Hashim was dressed in only sandals and cotton breeches held up with a wide leather belt. He hastily pulled a sleeveless, Tartar-styled blue shirt over his head. It was loose fitting, but the embroidered hem that went from his his left shoulder all the way down to his right hip still strained as it crossed his massive chest. His corded shoulders and arms were left bare. As an Emir of thirty warriors, it was his right to wear shirts with long and wide sleeves, but he preferred the freedom of movement over the distinction of class. He did not even consider taking up his sword or donning his armor, but he did pause long enough to tuck his scabbarded khanjar into his belt.

As Badru strode toward the twelve-foot-high double doors leading to Madame Veronique Boulet's private chamber, they seemed to pivot open magically on silent hinges. He entered, catching the eye of the servant working the right hand door. It was Yusuf. The smooth-skinned young man smiled thinly and then lowered his gaze.

"Hello, Badru. How I have missed you," Veronique said. She stood with a delicate crystal glass of wine in one hand and an elaborate silk fan in the other, which she used to stir the humid afternoon air around her in slow, lazy movements. She wore a matching bath robe cinched tight at the waist and her face was still flushed from her recent cleansing. The robe clung to her small, yet undeniably feminine, frame. Badru averted his eyes as he went down on one knee and bowed his head.

"Welcome back, Mistress. I did not expect you for another few days."

Veronique stepped lightly over to a small table at the end of her bed and refilled her glass from a matching crystal pitcher. Her pale skin and flaxen hair reflected the light just as well as the fine glassware. Anyone that did not know her would assume she was as fragile as the exquisite crystal, but that would be a mistake. She put her lips to her glass and eyed Badru over its rim as she sipped.

"Yes, a shame really," Veronique said. "It is not often I get to visit Acre, and you know how I love that city. It is the exotic jewel of the East as far as I am concerned. Do you not think so?"

Exotic? Acre was a melting pot of the dregs of humanity. Jews, Christians, Muslims—all clamoring over one another to be heard by their respective deity in a fetid city that no true god would give a shit about. Badru had been relieved when Veronique instructed him and his men to remain in her family estate on the island of Candia while she sailed to Acre on business.

Veronique took a drink of wine and raised one of her sculpted eyebrows at Badru, apparently waiting for him to respond to her question. "The city has a good port," Badru mumbled. Then, in hopes of changing the subject, he said, "Will we soon be departing for Marseilles, then?"

Veronique's main estate was there, along with her husband, so she made it a point to visit once every two years. The rest of the time she split between Venice and the Kingdom of Candia, which some years past had become an official Venetian colony. If Monsieur Boulet did not approve of the situation, Badru had never heard him complain. Most likely that was because the income Veronique earned through the lucrative slave trade far exceeded anything he contributed to the relationship. Of course, her husband was also intimidated by Badru and his Mamluk warriors, so he avoided them whenever possible. So, while it was possible that the husband did not approve of his wife's lifestyle, Badru saw no need to concern himself with the man's feelings. The man was a mouse and he deserved no one's respect. Not even his wife's.

"In time we will go back to Marseilles. But not yet. I must take another short trip to meet with a supplier."

"Where will we be going? I shall ready the Wyvern," Badru said.

Veronique shook her head. "I will take a few of your men, but you will not be going with me. You have become too well known in certain circles and I do not wish to resort to harsh bargaining practices with this supplier. It is a little early in our relationship for that."

"As you wish, Mistress. I will hand pick the men myself."
Badru's pulse picked up a beat at the thought of being able to
remain here with Yusuf for a few days more. Yusuf was a
common house slave bound to the Candian estate, so it was
not often that Badru got to spend time with him.

"However, I do have a task that calls for your talents,
Badru," Veronique said. "In Acre, I met with Francesca
Provenzano and she presented me with an opportunity that
we should address."

At the mention of Francesca's name, Badru's quickened
heartbeat died to a slow *whump*. "The Venetian money
lender? She is not one to be trusted," he said.

Veronique waved his words away with her fan. "For
most, that would be sound advice. But who do you think
introduced her to her now deceased, and very rich, husband?
She owes me far more than she will ever be able to repay in
this lifetime, I should think. At any rate, she only presented
me with half the opportunity. The rest I was able to discover
on my own."

"She knows of a cargo. What is it, Mistress?" Badru
asked.

"The breathing kind. One of her clients has undertaken a
contract for the Hospitallers. Her client told her it was a
troop transport from Genoa to a secluded port a few hours
march north of Acre."

"Troop transport? I am not sure we have the men to
attack a ship full of Hospitallers."

"Ah, but this is where the story gets interesting," Veronique said. "After making some inquiries, it turns out the

Hospitallers have purchased a few hundred slaves and the ship will have only a handful of Black Knights guarding it."

"A few *hundred* slaves?" That was indeed a valuable cargo. Badru's mind started going over the logistics of how he would acquire them. First off, he would have to hire some mercenaries, for his men were Mamluk warriors. They would not appreciate sullying their hands with the stink of slave collars, and he would not ask it of them. But how many could they realistically handle? A hundred? Perhaps two?

"It gets better. They are all young children," Veronique said.

"That simplifies things," Badru said.

She set her glass on the table and walked around behind Badru. He turned his neck to follow her but her head barely reached the center of his back, so she was lost from his sight. "What color is their skin?" Badru asked.

"White," Badru heard her say. Then he felt the softness of her breasts at the small of his back. "But they are peasants from the German speaking Alps, so they will need a good scrubbing to remove the odor of pig sausage and mud." One of her small hands glided around his side and grasped his belt knife. She slid the still-scabbarded khanjar from its spot at the front of his hip and let it drop to the floor. It hit the tiled floor with a heavy, but muffled, thump. She pressed herself against Badru and somehow made the giant man pivot around so he looked down on her face. She still had the red glow to her cheeks, but it looked out of place next to features that could have been freshly chiseled out of quarry rock.

"And not a one of them is female," Veronique said. Her voice was husky with drink and something else Badru knew only too well. She turned her head and spoke toward the servants at the door. "Leave us."

Badru heard the servants shuffle. He could have looked up to see the doors easing silently closed, but that would mean he would have to look at Yusuf. He chose instead to focus on the khanjar lying on the cold, hard floor.

LATE THAT NIGHT, when Yusuf came to Badru's sleeping chamber, the usually talkative and animated young man was quiet and subdued. Badru ignored him, thinking that it would pass. It did not.

Yusuf separated himself from Badru's embrace and pushed himself up off the Mamluk's pallet. He dressed silently in the pre-dawn darkness by the light of a tiny candle in a brass holder he had brought with him. He grabbed the door handle and just when Badru thought he would leave without saying anything, Yusuf turned back to Badru.

"Why do you let her do that to you? Is it because you like it?"

This was the exact conversation Badru had hoped to avoid. He let out a deep breath. "You know women have never held any attraction for me."

"Then why do you let her use you like that?"

"*Let* her?" Why was it that Yusuf always wanted to have these talks so late in the night? "What kind of question is that? She is my master. I am hers to do with as she will. That is the way of the Furusiyya."

"You always talk of your code as though it were so much more than it really is," Yusuf said.

Badru laughed. "And what would a manor slave know of the Furusiyya?"

"I know that you are as much a slave as I am. But where my master uses the whip to keep me in line, yours tricks you into doing her bidding by having you follow some ridiculous set of rules."

Badru sat up. "Ridiculous? You know nothing of life in the Citadel. Those rules are all that kept the one thousand Mamluk warriors in my tabaqa from killing one another. Yes, we were forced to study the Quran and Sharia, but it was the Furusiyya that truly ruled our lives."

'To live by honor and for glory'. That was the rule that came unbidden to Badru's mind after all these years. He could of course recall all of them if need be, such as *'To serve Allah in valor and faith'*, or *'Never to refuse a challenge from an equal'*. He had no memory of arriving at the military barracks of the Cairo Citadel, the training ground for the Sultan's Royal Mamluks, but he knew he had spent twenty-one years there. They were granted leave from the Citadel only to visit the city's public bath houses.

His education began first with unarmed combat, then fencing, mace, and lance work. Special emphasis was put on the short, powerful, recurve bow. A Mamluk warrior was expected to hit a three-foot target at a range of two-hundred fifty feet, and be able to loose three aimed arrows in one-and-a-half seconds. Once proficient with all those weapons, he had to relearn everything from the back of a galloping horse. And not one of the clumsy, barrel-shaped cows the Franks called horses, but an agile, hot-blooded steed descended from the finest stock in Egypt. And finally, before his training could be considered complete, he had to be familiar with all the common sicknesses and injuries that might befall his horse, and be able to treat them.

The last three years of his training, he slept with his mount in its stable and learned to recognize every sigh and wheeze that he produced. When he had not eaten enough hay during the day, he would pace all night long. If he had too much grain, he would do the same, but his steps would be lighter. He would breathe heavily when his hooves needed a trim. If he had been worked too hard he would never complain, but in the darkness of the night Badru would listen as he set his muscles to quivering every few minutes to relieve the fatigue. And sometimes, it would be Badru who had been worked too hard, or injured in training. In those times, it would be the stallion who would watch his master carefully, his eyes mirroring Badru's pain.

When Badru was sold to Madame Veronique Boulet's household, he was given his horse and favorite weapons as a celebration of his completed training and liberation from the tabaqa. It was she who had promoted him to the rank of Emir. Over a period of several years, she had managed to buy thirty Mamluk warriors for an exorbitant sum, and they needed a general. Though many were high-ranking warriors of exceptional skill, none had been trained at the Sultan's Citadel. Badru was her prize acquisition. Shortly after arriving in Marseilles for the first time, the young daughter of a business associate of Veronique's saw Badru mounted on his stallion and commented on the magnificence of the beast. Veronique told Badru to dismount, took the horse's reins and pushed them into the tiny hands of the ten-year-old girl. She thanked Veronique over and over, and in her offhanded way, Veronique dismissed her. "It is nothing," she said. The girl's servant led the horse away. The stallion had been a large part of Badru's everyday life for over twelve years. He felt as though someone had cut off his arm. His training had required him to undergo extreme periods of suffering that most could never imagine, but that day had caused him far more pain than anything he had ever previously experienced. Though he was not a praying man, he swore to Allah that night that he would never become attached to anyone or anything like that again.

Yusuf seemed to sense Badru's moment of reflection, for his next words lost their cutting edge. "Do you not see, Badru? That is why you need to stand up to the Mistress. You are no house slave, you are Mamluk. As was the great Sultan Baybairs. But, he realized when it was time to throw off the yoke of his master."

"Stop that talk. If someone hears, your life will be worthless."

Yusuf held up the tiny candle in front of his face and looked at Badru for a long moment. "Is it worth so much now?"

Badru knew he wanted to hear some words of comfort, but he had none to give. That had not been part of his training. *'To obey those placed in authority,'* that was the only path he knew of that led to anything resembling comfort.

A dog patrolling the grounds outside howled. Yusuf blinked and took a deep breath. "Good night, Badru. May your journey be swift and without peril." He eased open the door and stepped softly into the hall.

Badru cast aside the linen sheet covering his legs. The night had grown hot and humid. He remained sitting on his pallet, his back pressed against the stone wall, and listened to the cries of the dog until, eventually, he drifted off to sleep.

CHAPTER FOUR

VIGNOLO AND HIS first mate, Vagelli, leaned against the
railing at the stern of the ship, their eyes focused far
away on the horizon. They had first spotted the sails a few
hours ago. The ship had gradually grown in size and now
they could make it out as a small galley.

"What do you think?" Vignolo asked, handing Vagelli
his compact looking glass. In his middle years, Vagelli had a
tight, compact build with wavy, dark brown hair and sun-
creased skin the color of hazelnuts. Hailing from the island
of Rhodes, Vagelli, like many Rhodes-born natives, had
seawater for blood. There were no better sailors in Vignolo's
experience, and it was one of the reasons he had been so
eager to get his nephew to sign over his house on Rhodes.
Having access to Rhodesian crew members and ships was a
necessity in Vignolo's line of business. Of course, it took
some time to get used to their incredibly placid demeanor
and single-speed work ethic.

Vagelli's forehead wrinkled as he looked at Vignolo's
offered looking glass. He shook his head, turned away, and
walked over to a long, oiled leather bag tied fast to the stern

railing. He flipped open the bag's flap, untied the drawstring, and hand over hand, removed a long looking glass. Once he had it in his hands, he gave it a twist and the instrument telescoped out even further. He ambled back to where Vignolo stood and polished the eyepiece with his shirt.

"If you had one of these," Vagelli began, as he carefully worked his way down the instrument and wiped the end glass, "you would not have to ask my opinion."

"If I had one of those, it would be in a thousand pieces before week's end," Vignolo said.

Vagelli did not acknowledge Vignolo, but bent to one knee and hefted the looking glass up to rest on the railing. He leaned into the eyepiece. Vignolo tried his best to be patient. He pushed away from the railing, took a deep breath of the salty air, turned in a complete circle while counting the sea gulls floating above the ship, and then grabbed the railing again with both hands.

"Well?" Vignolo finally asked.

Vagelli kept his eye to the instrument. "It is a galley."

"Uh, huh," Vignolo said. We know that, he thought, but dared not say it out loud lest it interrupt Vagelli's process and he had to start all over.

"It is English," Vagelli said.

"Pirate?" Vignolo asked.

Vagelli leaned away from the eyepiece. "Most definitely. I believe it to be Hob Miner's crew."

Vignolo thought about that for a moment. "That makes sense. Last I heard old Hob was plying the Venice-Genoa lanes." If it was Hob Miner's ship he definitely was not looking at them just to say hello. Hob had never hauled an honest cargo, as far as Vignolo was aware. Vignolo looked at the gulls above them once more, and then back at Hob's ship.

"He will never catch us before we reach Genoa," Vagelli said, echoing Vignolo's thoughts.

"That would be best," Vignolo said. Hob had a good name among mercenaries, so he was always able to assemble a top notch boarding crew. The Englishman was almost close enough to tell they were empty, so that meant they might wait out here until Vignolo's ship left Genoa with cargo. But Vignolo did not care if he caught them after they left Genoa. He would love to see old Hob's face when a few hundred fully armed Hospitallers crawl out of the hold to confront his boarding party.

"We will have to watch for him on our return," Vagelli said.

Vignolo smiled. "That we will, Vagelli. That we will."

CHAPTER FIVE

THE ENGLISH GALLEY changed course and, ever so gradually, began to close in on the Wyvern.

"They are curious, Emir," Hanif, the helmsman, said. A middle-aged man with dry, leathery skin, Hanif was not a Mamluk. Nor was he a slave. Like his father and his father's father, he had been a fisherman once. But that was long ago, before Veronique discovered him and offered to change his life. It was difficult to find good seamen in the Arab world as they had a natural distrust for large bodies of water. Hanif was not one of these.

Hanif looked toward the rear of the ship with one hand resting on the wheel handle and the other on the pommel of his sheathed scimitar. "Curious, but not yet committed. They are too far away to know who we are. Shall I put us before the wind?"

"Let them get a little closer," Badru said. "I am not in the mood for a chase."

"We will board them, then," Hanif said, nodding in approval.

When Badru felt the winds shift, he gave the order to

tack around and point the bow at the English ship. As the Wyvern came about, the English ship's captain finally realized something was wrong. His ship floundered as his crew scrambled to get her turned away from the Wyvern. But that cost him precious minutes, and when you were running before a ship with the lines of the Wyvern, it was a game of seconds, not minutes. Badru unsheathed his khanjar and dragged it across a stone he kept tucked into his belt for that purpose. The short, gracefully curved knife's edge was already keen, but the Furusiyya demanded he care for the tools of his trade with a dedicated fervor. Not even the most despicable enemy of the lowest class of human beings imaginable deserved to be cut down with a dull blade.

Twenty minutes later the Wyvern pulled alongside the English vessel. Badru had two dozen of his thirty warriors on board. He estimated the English crew to be forty-five or more. He could tell by their clothes and weapons they were no more than hired swords, so he knew they would not put up a coordinated defense. He ordered his men to crouch behind the side rails of the Wyvern with their bucklers held in front of their faces. As one, they shouted and stood, and then immediately ducked behind cover once again. A volley of arrows, and a few crossbow bolts, thudded into the Wyvern's low railing wall or arced harmlessly over the deck to disappear into the sea. Ten Mamluks twirled grappling hooks over their heads and launched them, while the rest of Badru's men dropped their shields and picked up their powerful horn bows. They let their arrows fly at will and the mercenaries on the other ship ducked for cover. Each archer clutched a fistful of arrows in the same hand that held his bow. This enabled the Mamluk archers to nock and release shafts in rapid succession. Under the barrage, the helmsman of the English ship went down, an arrow protruding from his eye. Another man screamed when a wooden missile penetrated straight through his thigh and pinned him to the deck. More men fell as they attempted to bring up their own bows from behind cover.

Heaving on the grapple lines, the Mamluks pulled the two ships close enough to drop wide planks across the gap. Once they were locked in place, Badru gave the command to board. The archers dropped their bows and drew scimitars or falchions, a few opting to fight with their cherished tabarzin, small axes with thin metal handles designed to be wielded from horseback, but just as effective when used on foot. The Mamluks charged across the planks. Since they were lightly armored, the first men leapt over the heads of the defenders standing at each plank and cut them down from behind, opening the way for their brothers. Mamluks poured onto the English ship. In seconds, there were no more defenders, only terrified men running for their lives. Unfortunately, on a galley, there are few places to run, and nowhere to hide.

Some Mamluks scrambled around the bases of the masts that still flew sails and cut their lines, dropping them to the deck in rumpled heaps, while others rounded up the survivors and shoved, dragged, or kicked them into the center of the main deck area. Badru stood watching his men force the mixed lot of mercenaries and sailors to their knees.

He counted fourteen men, most of them pink-skinned English. As Badru approached, the stench of spoiled fish stung his nostrils. He pulled a silk cloth from a pocket underneath his sleeveless mail and used it to cover his nose. The English always stank, as does a beach a few hours after the high tide retreats and leaves the remains of thousands of half putrefied sea creatures.

"Who is your captain?" Badru asked, pulling the cloth away only long enough to get the words out. No one said anything, but a few sets of eyes gave the man away. Badru pointed at a tall man with a crown of gray hair ringing an otherwise bald pate. He showed no signs of having been in a fight, even his shirt was still tucked neatly in his tailored breeches. "That one," Badru said. "Make the cross."

"Yes, my Emir," the Mamluk nearest him said. He needed no further instruction. He gestured to three other Mamluks and together they pulled up one of the planks joining the two ships. They grabbed the captain and threw him flat on his back. Two men stretched his arms straight out from his shoulders, then two others dropped the plank across his chest and tied his arms to it by wrapping thick ropes around limbs and wood.

He cursed as the rope bit into his flesh, but other than that, he put up little fight. Badru had expected as much. The man had let his men fight for him. Die for him. His end would reflect how he had lived.

"Get him up," Badru said.

Badru's men tied long ropes to either end of the plank and threw the other end over the boom of the main sail.

They heaved on the ropes, hoisting the captain to his feet. He cried out as he came off the ground and then groaned as he hung suspended with his feet off the deck.

Badru nodded to his men to tie off their ropes. He walked around to the front of the captain. His chin rested on the plank and his face was flushed.

"Why do you cry out?" Badru asked. "Are you not Christian? It should be an honor to die on the cross as your Christ did."

Badru wanted the man to spit at him, to curse his Mohammed loving soul, to make some show of defiance. But he only stared at Badru with wide, pale blue eyes while his lower lip trembled. Badru suspected he knew what the problem was.

"Do you know who I am?" After a long moment, the captain's head nodded once. Badru stepped in close and, even though the man was suspended off the ground, he still had to look down at his face.

"Say my name," Badru said. The captain's nostrils flared and both lips quivered. "Say it!"

"You are the Northman," the captain said. His voice sounded as small as his courage.

Badru nodded. "Then you know what is about to happen."

"Please! I beg you. Take my ship. I have gold hidden in my cabin. I can get more…"

Badru let him plead for only a few seconds before he cut him off with a disgusted shake of his head. "You can give me nothing. Hold him." Badru walked around behind the man as a Mamluk each grabbed one of his legs.

Badru could not remember the first time he had been singled out as something different. In Cairo, he had begun life as the 'barbarian child'. At first, when he was very young, his hair had been lighter, so that combined with his gray eyes, earned him countless nicknames from the other children. Then his hair grew darker and he had been glad, but he also experienced a growth spurt at about the same time. The barbarian child became the barbarian boy, and some time later, the Norse-ling. He hated the names. They marked him as an outsider, but eventually, he came to learn all the Mamluk children in the Citadel were outsiders. None of them were Muslims born in Egypt. How could they be? A Muslim could not enslave another Muslim, so they had all been bought in far off lands. They were Kipchak or Cuman Turks, Circassians, Armenians, Georgians and countless other peoples Badru had never heard of. But he was the only half-blooded, gray-eyed Norseman. He would never come to embrace his heritage, for that would imply a sense of pride he did not feel, but he would learn to use it to his advantage.

As he entered his early teens, Badru was taken by the sense of curiosity that many boys that age experience. He began to ask himself questions about where he came from and why he was so big and light of skin. When he could not provide the answers himself, he began to question his teachers: What is Danes' Land? Why do they have such white skin? What is snow? He soon realized he had more questions than his teachers had answers, and so he turned to reading scrolls and books whenever he had the opportunity to access the royal libraries. It was not difficult, for all Royal Mamluks were required to be as well-versed in writing and reading as they were in the code of the Furusiyya. He devoured all the writings of Ahmad ibn Fadlan, an Arab chronicler of the tenth century who lived amongst the Northmen for a time. Then he turned to the Sagas, mostly oral stories of the Norse written down by Arabs a hundred years ago. When he could find nothing else, he read Arabic translations of the Norsemen's poetry.

It was in a poem about Ivarr the Boneless that he first discovered the blood eagle. Badru took it for what it was, a poet's embellishment. An attempt to instill fear and morbid fascination within his audience. The poet succeeded so well others soon followed. Though he doubted the blood eagle was an actual method of execution commonly used, he found it interesting in its potential to instill fear, and a grudging respect, in an audience. He stowed it away in his mind as something that may one day prove useful. That day would come shortly after joining the house of Veronique Boulet.

Badru tore the captain's fine linen shirt from his back, eliciting a fresh round of pleading from the Englishman. He drew his khanjar, checked its curved edge against his thumb, and then went to work on the man's skin. The captain screamed non-stop as Badru lightly traced the shape of an eagle with outstretched wings on either side of his spine. "Hold him tighter," he commanded, as he peeled the skin flaps away with the point of his bade. The captain bucked and screamed but the combination of the cross and the

Mamluks hanging off his legs held him in place.

According to the poet, Ivar the Boneless would have then used an ax to hack the ribs away from the spine, but Badru knew that would make an unnecessary mess. Instead, he used the keen edge of his khanjar to slice through the connective tissue holding each rib in place. Once they were all separated from the spine, starting at the top, he grasped each one firmly and yanked it outward. Some snapped, a few assumed their new position with little effort. The captain had stopped struggling, and his screams lessened with each adjustment, but he was still very much alive. And that, after all, was the goal. The victim should live through the creation of the eagle's wings. Death would come later, when his exposed lungs were pulled from his chest cavity and placed over his outstretched ribs. Then, onlookers would be treated to the sight of one last bird-like flutter of the organs as the victim died.

The last step, pulling the lungs from the body, was something Badru had never done. The release of a quick death was not his intention.

He stepped back to appraise his work. It would do. He turned his eyes on the remaining prisoners. They were all pale, even for Englishmen. Several had their eyes closed, their hands clasped so tightly in prayer their nails drew blood.

"What do we do with the others?" the Mamluk at his side asked.

"Execute them," Badru said.

"How would you like it done, Emir?" The Mamluk was

unable to stop his eyes from wandering to the hanging mess in front of Badru. His distaste was evident. Perhaps, he was worried Badru would order him to blood-eagle all the remaining prisoners. He should know his Emir better than that. It was not that he could not have done it. He had witnessed Badru perform the ritual often enough.

"Behead them," Badru said.

One blood-eagle would suffice to keep the legend of the Northman alive.

CHAPTER SIX

T HREE DAYS LATER the army of children and their black knight guardians crested the Pass of Saint Gotthard and began the descent into northern Italia. From there they would make their way to the port city of Genoa, where Foulques was to meet up with a Genoan captain by the name of Vignolo dei Vignoli. He was unknown personally to Foulques but he was familiar with the Genoan's name, as the Order had used him on occasion to transport troops and supplies. He had been told that Vignoli could be depended on to get Foulques and his cargo back to the Holy Lands in the shortest time possible.

At the top of the pass, movement far below on the winding trail caught his eye and Foulques motioned for a halt. He reached into the pouch at his side and removed a telescoping looking glass he had received as a gift from his childhood friend, Najya, on the day he was knighted. "Since you do not always see what is right in front of you," she had said. He was sixteen, and she a year younger but always seemed much older. When Foulques joined the Order of Hospitallers shortly after, he was expected to surrender all his worldly possessions to the Order and take back only three sets of clothing in exchange. With his uncle Guillaume de Villaret at his side, he did not hesitate in signing over all his rights and titles as a French nobleman. The looking glass, however, found a place in his simple wooden trunk, squirreled away in the folds of his heavier black woolen cloak.

Holding it to his eye, he could make out thirty or forty riders on the road snaking their way up toward them. From the colors they flew, a red lion on a field of gold, he marked them to be an Austrian patrol from the house of Habsburg, probably on their way home. Foulques cursed silently at his ill fortune.

He had been eager to put the Alps behind him and as much distance between his new charges and the Austrian controlled lands as possible. On behalf of the Order, his uncle had gifted a large sum of gold to Rudolf I of Habsburg, the current German King, for his permission to recruit new members into the Order of Saint John from territories the Habsburg family exerted influence over, even if the people in those high, remote lands did not always recognize them as their rightful rulers. Rudolf was said to be an ambitious ruler who had not only amassed extensive possessions in Aargau, Elsass, the lands of Lucerne, Schwyz and Unterwalden, but also distant territories in France and Spain. He appointed counts and bailiffs over his lands to see to the daily govern-ing while he focused his energies on expanding the family's holdings further afield in more profitable regions. When he was not acquiring more lands for the Habsburg family, he spent a great deal of time on winning the support of other

German lords to ensure his son Albrecht would succeed him to the German throne. From what Foulques had been told, the young Albrecht had apparently proved himself capable and made quite the impression in noble circles, attracting a great deal of envy from more than one German prince.

Foulques had been warned by his uncle that he had been intentionally vague when it came to the number of subjects he had intended to recruit. The mountain people were poorer than Foulques could have imagined, and the gold that the Order had entrusted to him had gone far. Rudolf would not be pleased on hearing the Hospitallers had reduced his future workforce by a full five hundred men. Foulques had been counting on Rudolf's attention being turned elsewhere while he slipped in and out of Habsburg controlled lands. He had hoped to make it to the Milanese Castelgrande on the southern side of the pass before being spotted, but that was no longer possible.

The young knight collapsed the looking glass between his calloused palms and replaced it in his pouch. A nod to Alain, the knight at his side, had him leading the mule train to the back of the procession and within seconds, six black-clad knights were marching next to Foulques, the white crosses on their surcoats glinting in the afternoon light as they led the five hundred children down the road into Milanese lands.

Twenty minutes later the two groups met where the road leveled out for a time before continuing its gradual spiral down to lower elevations. The riders pulled up their mounts within fifty paces and three riders trotted out, one holding aloft the red lion pennant. Foulques halted his column and walked out to meet them alone.

Foulques turned his soldier eyes on the men as they approached. Unlike the heavy mail of the Hospitallers, the Austrians all wore leather armor, well made and splendid to behold, but designed to provide comfort in the saddle rather than protection in actual battle. By his dress, the youngest of the three was in command, but the haunted eyes of the massive, bearded young man at his side told Villaret that he was the only one of the three who had been on a battlefield. He too was young, but there could be no doubt the man had been raised as a professional soldier.

The leader reined in his mount, sitting high in the saddle. He held up his hand, and smiled. His high-bridged nose would have dominated his clean-shaven face if not for the piercing eyes. Even before he spoke, Foulques had the sinking feeling he knew who he was.

"Hail Crusaders. I had heard the Holy War was going badly, but I did not know the Saracen infidels had pushed your armies all the way back to Austrian lands! I am Albrecht, the recently appointed Duke of the lands you are just leaving. To whom do I have the pleasure of addressing?"

He spoke in High German, a language that Foulques found much easier to understand than the incomprehensible local dialect of German spoken in the mountain lands he had just left.

Foulques bowed and said, "Brother Foulques de Villaret, Knight Justice of the Order of Saint John's Hospital of Jerusalem. On our way back to carry out His will in the Holy

Lands, and on leave in your lands, by your father, his majesty King Rudolph."

The young man did not seem to be listening as his eyes skipped over the knight in front of him and scanned the large group of children standing far behind Foulques.

"And is this God's army, Hospitaller? Children? I see now why I hear the Crusades are finished in the Levant. Tell me, is it true even King Henry has fled Acre but still attempts to rule the Kingdom of Jerusalem from the island of Cyprus?" The flag-bearer laughed at this but the bearded man at Albrecht's side only shifted in his saddle and looked away from Foulques's smoldering eyes. Foulques was caught unprepared by the Austrian's flippant disregard for the men and women struggling to maintain a foothold in the Holy Lands. Did he not realize they fought for all of Christendom? He had been told that the ruling classes outside of the Levant had become so engrossed in their own petty squabbles that they had lost sight of the Holy Quest to reclaim all of the sacred sites from the Infidel, but to call the Crusades finished in front of one of God's soldiers was beyond blasphemy. It was unwise, to say the least.

"Henry still rules the Kingdom of Jerusalem," Foulques said. "It matters little where he does it from. And even if our king were to desert the Holy Lands it would not affect the calling of the Knights of Saint John. Our Lord is the true King in the Holy Lands and as long as there are poor, sick, or wounded Christians in Outremer, my Order will be there to care for them. We have a long journey ahead and would be on our way now. Please pass on my regards to your father."

"I do not recall my father mentioning a French man would be coming to take so many of our serfs away. When is it that you spoke with him?"

Foulques shrugged. "It was not I, but my superiors. Three months past? Perhaps he did not think it important. I imagine ruling the German Empire leaves much on a man's mind."

Now Foulques had Albrecht's undivided attention.

"Be careful the tone and words you use with me, French Knight. For as Duke of these lands, it is my decision alone which can mark you a liar and a thief of Austrian property." Albrecht rose up in his stirrups and surveyed the army of youngsters. "Where do they hail from?"

Foulques did not like where this was going. "Most are from the forests and mountains surrounding the Great Lake between Lucerne and Schwyz."

At this Albrecht laughed and said, "The land of rocks, mountains, and stubborn peasants? All that water and not a fertile field anywhere to be seen. Yes, I see now the logic in how those villagers think. The only valuable crop they can raise is their own offspring. Pity harvests are so many years apart."

And not much of a crop at that, Foulques thought. He wanted to say how ridiculous it was that the two of them were standing on a road at the end of the world arguing about something neither one of them really wanted. But, with effort, he managed to still his tongue by reminding himself that he was only a soldier following orders.

"We will be on our way again, Duke Albrecht," he said,

then wheeled around to walk back to his men.

"You do not have my leave, Hospitaller," Albrecht said, with no sound of mirth in his voice.

Foulques stopped in mid stride and turned back slowly to face the Duke.

"Nor do I need it. We are not on Austrian land and by decree of His Holiness the Pope, no King or Queen may command a Knight of the Order. We are subjects of the Holy Father and by divine law are to submit to his rule alone."

Albrecht's face reddened. "Your politics are misguided. My men outnumber yours three to one, Hospitaller. It matters little whose land we stand upon."

The eyes of Albrecht's bearded sergeant grew wide and he leaned brazenly forward to place a cautionary hand on his young lord's sword arm. "My Lord…" he said.

The Holy Wars had been fought in Outremer for nearly two hundred years and although rare in this part of the world, the man may have seen black knights on occasion. He had enough experience to recognize the dispassionate looks of trained killers, men who lived with death forever hovering over them. It mattered little that they called themselves Hospitallers, caregivers to the poor and sick, or soldiers of God. Mercy did not live in the houses of men such as these.

Albrecht immediately yanked his arm away and withered him with a reproving look.

"Heed your man, Duke Albrecht," Foulques said. As he spoke, he shrugged his cloak aside, clearly revealing the white-crossed linen surcoat and the sword at his side.

Twenty paces behind him the other black knights and brown-robed sergeants swiftly formed two rows. The eight sergeants in front dropped to their knees, pulling loaded crossbows from beneath their cloaks and trained them on the Austrians, while the seven knights stood behind with their hand-and-a-half swords drawn, their shoulders relaxed, eyes clear and looking straight ahead.

"I may not look much older than you, my lord, but believe me when I say I have seen horrors that you will never know if you live to be seventy," Foulques said. "That is the way of it for someone brought up in the Holy Lands. Each of the men behind me long ago lost count of the lives he has taken in the name of God. They have faced the Saracen hordes, time and time again, defending the faith of our Lord Jesus Christ, and while men fell around them by the hundreds, the Almighty has seen fit to allow these few to survive. I doubt God has been saving them all these years so that they may die today, so far from the Holy Lands they have faithfully defended." Foulques made eye contact with the flag bearer and then the Duke's sergeant before looking at Albrecht again. "But, being only a simple servant of God, I do not presume to know His plans for my men. Or your men. Or yourself, for that matter."

The main host of Austrians cast nervous glances amongst each other and waited for a command from their leaders. Albrecht seethed as he looked at the crossbows pointed at him and his patrol, but he made no sudden movements. Foulques had a feeling Albrecht understood the destructive power of the weapons. At twenty yards an iron-tipped bolt could tear through three men and embed itself deep into a tree beyond. After a moment's consideration Albrecht seemed to come to a decision.

"I trust you paid good coin to the families of this rabble? I will not allow my serfs taken advantage of," Albrecht said, sitting tall.

The Duke was young and bold, thought Foulques, but he was no fool. The threat of the crossbows aside, his words rang surprisingly true with actual concern for his people. This surprised Foulques and he was not sure how to reply.

"Of course," said Foulques, lightening his tone somewhat.

"Perhaps my vogt will be able to collect some tax revenue from those rock peasants, now that they have fewer mouths to feed. I do not expect I shall ever see you on Austrian lands again?"

Foulques shook his head. "I expect not."

Albrecht nodded. "As it should be. There are no pilgrims here that need your protection. Tell your brethren the black knights are not welcome on Habsburg land."

Without another word, Albrecht walked his horse toward the children. The knights opened up the children's ranks and, under watchful eyes, allowed Duke Albrecht and his Habsburg patrol to ride through in single file.

Foulques stared after the patrol. One of the dogs amongst the mass of children began barking at the Duke's party. A tall, stocky boy and a much smaller one struggled to hold it back. The Duke's sergeant trotted his horse between the dog and his lord and locked eyes with the children. His hand was on his sword. The seriousness with which the man acted struck Foulques as a gross overreaction. They were only children, but the man kept his eyes on them until his horse was well past and he could twist no further in the saddle.

After the Austrian host had retreated around the first bend in the road, Alain led the knights and children up to where Foulques waited.

"I honestly thought he meant to attempt to take back his serfs with force," Alain said, shaking his head in wonder. "Did you?"

"Not for a moment," Foulques said. "For that would have been a senseless waste and Albrecht does not strike me as a wasteful man. We brought much needed gold into these lands and left with a few hundred souls no one will miss. When he thinks it over, the young duke will be happy with his decision."

Alain's eyes narrowed. If he agreed with Foulques, or not, he did not say.

CHAPTER SEVEN

SEVERAL DAYS LATER, the bedraggled army of children camped within sight of the Mid-Earth Sea and the busy Italian port city of Genoa. Foulques knew it would be impossible to keep this large a group secret from all prying eyes, but he saw no reason to attract any unnecessary attention. He consulted with the other knights, and they decided it prudent to rest until well past nightfall. Under cover of darkness, they marched everyone into the city. They passed through the gates two hours before dawn, with no more resistance than a disproving nod from the sentries. His uncle had promised there would be no questions asked when they entered Genoa, but Foulques had not expected it to be quite so easy. They weaved through the twisted streets and alleys of the sleeping city until they came to the docks.

"That went better than I had hoped," Alain said.

"It was not for free, I am sure," Foulques said. "I am told the Genoan captain hired to transport us has strong connections with the city watch."

They stood on the seawall looking out at the darkened hulks of a hundred ships lit by the waning moonlight. Some were tied up to births, other larger ships were anchored out in deeper waters. Lanterns hung off masts, and sterns of a few, and occasionally, a voice drifted over the water mixing with the sounds of lapping waves. The smell of salt water was in the air and Foulques could feel moisture on his face. It made him anxious to be on his way. He had no love for the sea, but he knew once he was aboard ship his mission would be nearing its end. Soon he would be back in Acre, going out on regular patrols. Even a caravan escort mission would be welcome after this long journey.

"What now?" Alain asked.

No sooner had he voiced the same question that was on everyone's mind, than a lantern lit up on the dock two hundred yards away and began slowly moving closer. Two men materialized out of the darkness. One was short with curly hair and seaman's breeches that ended just below his knees. The other was tall and dressed more for a night out at the finest Venetian gambling dens than he was for the sea. His linen breeches were shaped and tucked into short suede boots that were tailor fit and had no need of laces. He wore a long-sleeved silk shirt open at the neck. It was so white it glowed in the moonlight and lit up the man's face to reveal a neat mustache contrasting with a few days of growth on his cheeks, which threatened to turn into a beard one day soon.

"Brother Villaret? Vignolo dei Vignoli at your service," the taller man said, giving a hurried bow. "This is my first mate, Vagelli. Actually, first mate, navigator, and conscience all rolled into one."

"This is not true," Vagelli said, his words heavy with the

accent of the people from the Rhodesian islands. "Everyone knows you have no conscience."

Vignolo ignored his first mate's joke, if that is what it was. His eyes flitted over the great crowd of children huddled in the darkness behind Foulques. "They are all children!" Vignolo's wide eyes turned back to Foulques and he shook his head. "How many fighting men?"

"Fifteen, including me," Foulques said.

"This was not our arrangement."

"This was precisely our arrangement," Foulques said. "You were to provide transport for several hundred members of the Knights of Saint John. Meet our newest recruits."

Vignolo shook his head, again, and he blew out a breath. He stared out over the children's heads, his mind struggling with something. Foulques thought that perhaps he was overwhelmed with their number.

"We are a few more than five hundred souls, but surely your ship has room for us if you were expecting all grown men," Foulques said.

Vignolo pulled his gaze slowly back to the knight. "Room aboard is not my concern. In fact, we will ride higher in the water than I had hoped. High enough to attract a lot of unwanted eyes."

"A lighter cargo means a faster ship and the sooner we board, the sooner we will arrive in Acre," Foulques said. "Lead us to your ship. I should like to leave the docks of Genoa behind us as soon as possible."

Vignolo cast another nervous glance at the shadows

around him. Foulques swore he could see the man's mind running through possible scenarios, none of them much to his liking. Finally, he said, "You have my agreement on that point. Have your *men* follow closely behind us."

The Genoan traded looks with his first mate, who shook his head several times. Neither man seemed happy about it, but they held up their lanterns and began walking toward the docking berths.

Minutes later they all began shuffling up the gangplank of a pot-bellied merchantman moored between two higher galleys. Once loaded, the ship maneuvered into the bay under power of a single bank of oarsmen slaves seated below deck, and by first light the ship's square sails filled with wind and they headed out to open sea.

By the time the morning sun was high on the horizon and the squawk of gulls filled the crisp salt air, the knights had most of the children settled in the cargo holds below deck. However, a dozen or so were wracked by the *mal de mer* and, since Foulques himself could not lose sight of the horizon for more than a few minutes without feeling his stomach in his throat, he allowed them to come above deck and huddle against the sides of the ship.

"What news from Outremer?" Foulques asked Vignolo as the captain joined him at the bow of the ship.

"Nothing has improved, if that is what you are after," Vignolo said. "You were gone a few months?"

"Sixty-eight days tomorrow," Foulques said, turning his head away from the sight of a boy losing his guts over the railing of the ship.

"Well, Lattakia fell while you were gone. The Sultan of Egypt sends army after army into the Levant and every day I hear of another city falling into their hands. They seem to be herding every Christian in the Holy Lands toward Acre where they can kill them, push them into the sea, and wash their hands all on the same day."

"Acre has a truce with the Sultan. As for the other territories, it is not the first time they have attempted to uproot us from the Holy Lands," Foulques said.

Vignolo shook his head. "These Mohammedans are different. The Mamluk Sultanate has turned the entire rich economy of Egypt to the task of expelling every last Christian from Palestine. The Mamluks are buying up everything they can get their hands on to support their armies. Prices are at an all-time high in Egypt, and I do not speak of only luxuries like spices and silk. A coil of rope is selling for twice the price of a good blade in Genoa! A trader like myself could make a fortune by sailing into an Egyptian port and cutting loose the sheets on my ship, coiling them up, and selling them to the Sultanate."

"And they would probably hang you right there with your own rope," Foulques said.

"There is that," Vignolo said, smiling. He paused, then said, "But maybe if I had something of more value to the Mamluks than rope. Something they could not get in their own country, and was becoming scarcer every year in the Levant. Let us say… something young, and fair-skinned. Something like that could earn good gold bezant, not just common silver or bronze coin, mind you."

Foulques turned to look Vignolo in his swirling eyes. "Vignolo, should I be concerned with you upholding your end of our deal?"

Vignolo widened his eyes in mock surprise. "What? The honest merchant Vignolo dei Vignoli balk on an agreed upon transaction with the pious Knights of St. John? Of course not. The Order is one of my best clients, as well as one of the few that always pays its debts. I was only giving voice to my thoughts. I am known for sometimes not being able to keep them to myself." Then, in a more serious tone, he said, "I just wish your Grandmaster had told me the new recruits you were bringing were young boys, not men. The slave markets in Cairo and Damascus have voracious appetites for boys. If I had known, I would have taken certain precautions."

Although he hardly knew the Genoan, Foulques sensed an uneasiness behind the man's bravado.

"You feel we may be in danger of a pirate attack?"

Vignolo laughed. "On these seas, my friend, you are forever in danger from pirates. Muslim, Christian, Jew, it matters not. Even if you are in a rowboat with nothing more than the boots on your feet, I guarantee there is a shoe-less pirate in a slightly larger skiff out there looking for you."

Despite Vignolo's misgivings, the rest of the morning proved uneventful. The knights and sergeants took the opportunity to catch up on some much-needed rest. There was a constant yammering down in the hold from the children, so Foulques avoided going down there as their guttural brand of German made his head hurt. Despite being susceptible to the occasional bout of sea sickness, Foulques usually felt at peace on the sea. The creaks of wooden masts, as their sails filled with wind, salt spray misting his face, the lapping of waves against the vessel's sides as she sluiced through the water; there was much to appreciate about being on the seas. Foulques found it relaxing, even invigorating at times. Perhaps this was because he had never been in battle aboard a ship. The Order's campaigns were all land-based missions to patrol the roads near their Hospitals, escort pilgrims and caravans, destroy Muslim and occasionally Christian camps of highway men, and in the past, to attack and drive out the infidel armies from cities in the Holy Land. But this last had not happened for some time. All of Christendom was in a defensive stance these days. The ideals of the Crusades were dying. Christians had been trickling out of the Levant back to Europe for the last forty years, ever since Muslim forces had taken back the city of Jerusalem. European Lords and Nobles no longer looked to the East as a way to acquire land and increase their holdings. It was now a time for Franks to band together and protect the few cities they still controlled.

In Foulques's mind, the most beautiful and strategically important of these was Acre. Its deep water port had no equal, making it the gateway between east and west for travelers, pilgrims, and merchants alike. But, perhaps he was biased. Acre was, after all, the only home he had ever known. He had been gone for far too long. If he had his way, he would never travel further than a day's ride from the city's Gate of Saint Anthony ever again.

A cry came from far above and behind Foulques, pulling him from his thoughts.

"Sail on the horizon!"

"Where?" Vignolo shouted.

"Forward port!"

Foulques shielded his eyes and peered ahead into the distance.

CHAPTER EIGHT

"**H**ER SAILS ARE down," Vagelli said. He stretched out his arm, and with the slow, languorous touch of a lover, adjusted the focus on his looking glass. "I see bodies on deck."

"Anyone still on their feet?" Vignolo asked.

"No. Wait… I think I see one." He lowered the looking glass and turned toward Vignolo and Foulques. "He does not appear to be alive."

"Is it old Hob?"

Vagelli shrugged and shook his head.

Vignolo was beginning to get one of those feelings. The kind that said *turn around and run the other way,* the type he wished he listened to more often.

"Are you sure?" Foulques asked. He had his own looking glass out. It was a Saracen piece and despite the immediacy of the situation, Vignolo could not help but admire its craftsmanship. Why did even a poverty sworn monk have a better looking glass than him? He patted the pouch at his belt for his own glass, with its battered wood and scratched, clouded lenses, but it was not there. He had left it somewhere else, again.

"I think I saw movement," Foulques said, holding his glass up to one eye.

That was enough for Vignolo. "Bear off southwest, Vagelli. Give them lots of room."

Foulques dropped his glass to his side. "You mean to desert them?"

"Desert who?" Vignolo said. "They are all dead."

"You do not know that. There could be survivors below deck."

"I very much doubt it," Vignolo said.

"What about the rowing slaves? They may still be chained to their posts."

"So? What does that matter to you? They would most likely be all Mohammedans, anyway."

"No man deserves to starve to death in the belly of a slave ship. Take us in. I would board that boat."

"That is not wise," Vagelli said. "Whoever attacked that ship is still out there somewhere."

Vignolo nodded eagerly in agreement with his first mate. "We have to think about protecting our own cargo," he said.

Foulques squared his shoulders to Vignolo. "That is a Christian vessel. It is my duty to investigate and offer my protection to anyone who needs it."

Vignolo threw up his hands. "Are you mad? Look around you! This is not Jerusalem and those corpses do not belong to pilgrims on their way to wash their faces in holy water. They were pirates. Scum that got what they deserved."

Foulques crossed his arms. "You are in the employ of the

Order of Saint John. Change your course, now, Captain. Get me on that ship."

Vignolo looked to Vagelli, but he offered no help beyond a sympathetic shrug.

"All right. But get your knights ready. The Devil himself could be waiting for us over there."

As they pulled alongside the English ship, it became clear the Devil was not lying in wait. He had already come and gone.

The headless bodies of the dead were piled neatly on deck. Holes had been punched through their skulls and a long rope was then threaded through each one to form something resembling a giant's gruesome necklace. The necklace was hung along the railing of the ship, so Foulques, Vignolo, and the other knights had to step over it to board. But the men paid it little attention, for their focus was on the splayed open corpse hung ten feet off the deck.

"Sweet Mary," Foulques said, crossing himself.

It was Hob, all right, Vignolo thought. But he had seen better days. Vignolo cast a glance back to his ship. Children's faces lined the railing, with the taller ones craning their necks from behind the shorter ones in front. Everyone wanted a better view of the carnage. Everyone except Vagelli. He stood at the helm, looking around nervously at the open water all around them. He had refused to accompany them, and Vignolo knew why. Vignolo had never seen the Northman's work up close like this, but he had heard the stories. He knew what to expect before he set one foot on Hob's ship.

Foulques crossed himself, again, and then clutched a tiny crucifix on a chain around his neck for a few seconds as his lips moved in silent prayer. When he was done, he looked at Vignolo. "What happened here?"

"I told you. Pirates."

A breeze tickled Vignolo's scalp, and the long plank Hob was tied to shifted and creaked. Vignolo and Foulques looked up and Hob's eyes snapped open. His head twisted to look at them as his lips, purpled and crusty with dryness, forced themselves open. Behind him, his wings of bloodied ribs and skin shimmered against the clear blue sky.

"Holy, Jesus," Vignolo said, surprised to hear the sound of the Savior's name come from his throat. He froze at the sight of Hob, or what had once been Hob, struggling to speak. He wanted to look away, but some unseen force would not allow it. They should never have come here.

There was movement to his left and then he heard a clicking sound he knew well from his days as a Genoese crossbowman. A bolt tore through Hob's heart from below and exited where his back should have been. Its leather vanes whistled as it left the body and receded into the distance, disappearing into the horizon. Hob's head immediately dropped.

Vignolo's breath came back and he was able to turn away. Beside him, Foulques lowered his crossbow to his side. He motioned to one of the knights.

"Alain. Let us gather the bodies and heads together. You can say some words. No soul should leave this world unshriven." He looked at Vignolo. "Even a pirate deserves the chance to make peace with his maker."

Vignolo watched as Foulques and Alain cut down Hob's corpse and carried him over to the other bodies. He wanted to get back on his ship and get as far away as possible, but he said nothing as he watched the Hospitallers go about their grisly work. He could give them a few more minutes. But that was all, for there was no doubt in Vignolo's mind that Hob's ship had been left as a warning to other would-be pirates. A message that said Vignolo's ship, its crew, and its cargo had all been marked as the property of the Northman.

CHAPTER NINE

"CAPTAIN! SAILS AFT!"

Foulques was standing on the bow deck when he heard the cry. He turned his head skyward, in the direction of the crow's nest. A sailor stood on a narrow plank of wood, one hand wrapped around a line on the main and his other arm stretched toward the horizon behind the ship.

On the midship deck, Vignolo raised himself up on his toes and stared off into the distance. He cursed, and immediately began shouting orders as he strode in a direct line toward the helm. The ship came alive and sailors seemed to materialize out of nowhere. They shouted to one another relaying Vignolo's commands and immediately busied themselves with hauling on ropes and adjusting sails. Others ran from one side of the ship to the other, some carrying coils of rope, others with no discernible mission as far as Foulques was aware. Foulques squinted across the shimmering blue water. The late morning sun was at his back and it glinted off a tiny, inconspicuous, white speck far away on the horizon.

Vignolo was at the helm now. He took control of the

rudder wheel from the helmsman and continued barking orders. The words were Italian, a language Foulques spoke as well as his own, and yet he had no idea what the Genoan shouted to his men. Foulques saw two of his fellow black-robed knights look to him with confusion spread openly across their faces. Foulques became keenly aware just how out of his element he was here on the open sea. He needed to find out what was going on.

Foulques began moving toward Vignolo, but just then, the sails snapped as they filled with wind, and the ship turned and lurched ahead. The wood beneath his feet groaned, protesting the sudden direction change, and Foulques nearly lost his footing. He caught hold of a railing with one hand and steadied himself. Gliding his hand along the wood for support, he continued moving toward Vignolo at the helm.

"Vignolo! what is going on?" Foulques asked when he finally reached the Genoan.

"Nothing to worry about," Vignolo said, staring up at the sails as he made minute corrections to their heading with the wheel.

"Then why the sudden change of course? Who is that behind us?"

"No idea. And I would like to keep it that way."

"But you suspect they mean us harm," Foulques said.

"I assume everyone means me harm. I find it makes for a less complicated lifestyle." Vignolo nodded to himself and finally took his eyes off the sails bulging with wind high overhead. He lashed the wheel in place with a leather strap attached to its column. The two men climbed the few steps to the lookout on the aft deck and stared at the far-off speck.

"Do you know what kind of ship it is?" Foulques asked.

"She is a galley," Vignolo said. "The kind of ship I wish I had brought instead of this pot-bellied merchantman."

Foulques did not like the sound of that. "Are you saying we cannot outrun that ship?"

Vignolo shrugged. "If the wind stays like this we have a good chance. That galley has three or four times as many oars as we do, so in calm waters she would be on us in no time. But running before the wind like this? Dipping oars into the water will just slow her down, so they have to rely on their sails."

"And if the wind fails?"

Vignolo let out a mirthless chuckle and looked at Foulques. "Well, if you were a praying man, now might be the time to ask for wind."

Foulques crossed his arms over his broad chest. "Why did you hire such an inferior ship? My Order has agreed to pay you more than enough."

Vignolo's eyes narrowed. "Do not put this on me, Hospitaller. I was told I needed space for three or four hundred fighting men and their equipment. Who in their right mind would attempt to pirate a ship with that many Hospitallers? Instead you show up with a bunch of children! And after marching them past every slave market from here to the spine of the world you balk when someone takes an interest?"

"And how much did you save by hiring a merchantman

over a galley? You increased your profit at our risk," Foulques said. "If we get to Acre I will make sure your payment is cut in half."

"What? You are mad! With terms like that you make me not want to try very hard to get you anywhere."

Foulques stepped in close and lowered his voice. His hand drifted down to rest on the pommel of his sword.

"Know this, Vignoli. If we are boarded, you will not live through the battle. That is another of my terms, and it is not negotiable."

Vignolo held up a hand and leaned as far away from Foulques as the cramped observation deck would allow. "Hold up, no need to go saying things like that. We are not boarded yet."

Foulques nodded. "And I will pray that we are not. I suggest you do the same."

A FRANCISCAN MONK had once told Foulques that prayer was a tricky thing. The key to having one answered was to phrase the prayer so as to make out the benefactor to be someone other than yourself. If you wanted money, pray for your father's success in business. Then, someday, you would inherit your father's money. One should never appear greedy in one's own prayers. Foulques had told the man he was a fool and when he needed, or wanted, something for himself, he would ask God and it would be up to Him to grant the request or ignore it.

But this day, Foulques decided the situation did not warrant a divine intervention. He did not pray for the winds to continue, and if Vignolo did, then God was not listening. By early afternoon the wind had died to half what it had been in the morning. From that point on, it decreased little by little with every hour. The speck on the horizon had become a sleek galley with three lateen-rigged sails and two long rows of oars on either side. Every now and then the wind carried with it the deep boom of rowing drums. Foulques thought he could make out figures moving about the bow deck and as the dying sun fell from the sky, it set off metallic glints and shimmers all over the pursuing ship that Foulques knew only too well. The way the sun reflected off weapons and armor was no different at sea than on land.

Foulques and Vignolo stood together again on the aft observation deck. The last bit of the sun had descended below the horizon but its light continued to flood the sky behind the galley, turning its white sails black and casting the ship itself into shadow.

"Can we lose them in the darkness?" Foulques asked.

Vignolo shook his head. "Unlikely in these waters. Running at full sail as we are, I do not dare order all our lanterns extinguished. At the very least we need one under the main. I could sail dark for a short time, perhaps, but the moment we light up a single wick, it might as well be a signal fire."

"Very well," Foulques said. "How many fighting men do you have on board?"

"Fighting men? You were supposed to bring those. My men are Rhodesian seamen. The best sailors you will ever find, but do not try to put a weapon in their hands."

"What about the oar slaves? Since they have not been

rowing, they should be well rested. Can you convince them to fight?"

Vignolo laughed and shook his head. "Most of them are Musselmen. They will not fight for your Holy Order. Safest thing to do is keep them chained up below deck."

Vignolo had become uncharacteristically quiet the nearer the galley had approached. "You know that ship. Is it the one that attacked the English?" Foulques asked.

Without taking his eyes off the galley, Vignolo nodded. "I know of her. Its captain is a man they call 'the Northman'."

"Northman? That is no Norse ship," Foulques said.

One of the crooked, self-sure smiles that Foulques had begun to associate with the Genoan flashed across his face. But there was something almost empty about the expression this time.

"The Northman is no true Norseman. He is a Mamluk slaver. They call him that because of his size and the color of his eyes. He is supposed to be the offspring of a Danes' Land princess and some giant Turkish warrior, or god, or what have you. You know how stories go."

"Have you seen him?"

Vignolo shook his head. "No. And I would like to keep it that way."

Vagelli, the first mate, joined them. He nodded toward the growing blackness following them at an uncomfortable distance. "It is the Northman," Vagelli said. "We should not let him catch us."

Vignolo nodded. "I have to agree with you on that one,

my friend. To that end, how many skiffs do we have on board?"

"Eleven," Vagelli said.

Vignolo gripped the railing with both hands and looked out over the small expanse of black water separating the round merchantman from the sleek galley closing in on them.

"I suppose it will have to be enough," Vignolo said.

Foulques did not hear him. He was staring down at the foam in the small wake their ship created as it slipped through the water under power of their sails. It was so quiet, peaceful even. He looked up and could no longer see any ship. Though he knew better, Foulques allowed the relief of the moment to wash over him. However, the feeling lasted mere seconds, for in the darkness behind them, closer than he thought possible, tiny pinpricks of light began to appear as the pursuers lit their lanterns.

CHAPTER TEN

BADRU HASHIM TOOK the stairs down to the rowing decks two at a time. As he pulled open the door and ducked his head to step through onto the upper rowing deck, humid air thick with the stench of human toil rushed past him. He pushed his way around the drummer, a heavy man naked from the waist up with a base drum strapped to his chest, and stepped onto the catwalk between the long lines of rowing benches. Two men labored side by side on each narrow bench, working hard to avoid the lashes of the guards walking up and down the walkway.

Badru spotted the slave-master, who was attempting to fork a piece of bread dipped in wine into the mouth of one of the wretched galley slaves. Naked as the day he was born, the emaciated man craned his head and lapped at the bread with a blotchy, white-coated tongue as he bent at the waist and pushed his oar forward, clearing the back of the man in front of him by only inches. The slave-master saw Badru approach and he stood up abruptly, thwarting the slave's attempt to get the bread into his mouth. The man groaned, and in his misery he fell out of rhythm. The oar behind him slammed into his back and he cried out. Immediately, a man was at his side whipping him across his shoulders and back until he was moving once again in unison with the other rowers.

"My Emir," the slave-master said, bowing his head. "You should not have to sully yourself down here."

"I would not have come if you would have followed my last messenger's orders to increase the beat," Badru said.

"I did so, my Emir. Twice now we have increased the pace, but the rowers are beyond exhausted. They have been rowing all day and are weak."

"And how many have you lost?"

"Three men have died. Two more are yet alive, but they cannot row."

"Three? We can afford to lose a dozen. Increase the beat again but give them more bread and wine. Especially the Christians. It will lend them strength."

"It will be done, my Emir."

Badru turned and left as quickly as he had come. He paused only for a moment to take in several deep lungfuls of the fresh night air when he reached the top deck, and then he was moving again. His long, thick legs carried him unerringly to the helm, situated on top of his own cabin at the rear of the ship.

Hanif was there, peering ahead in the darkness. The low light of the lanterns cast shadows around the helmsman, and the way he hunched over the wheel added another ten years to his already forty plus.

"They have gone black," Hanif said.

"Maintain our course. They will show a light soon enough and if they try to veer off to a new course, the wind will only hinder them. We will be on them in minutes."

Hanif nodded, but his evasive eyes told Badru that he was not so sure. They should have had them hours ago. The Wyvern was one of the fastest galleys on the Mid-Earth Sea. Badru knew of only two others that could rival her speed in open waters and neither one of them was shaped like an overloaded half-walnut shell.

Badru had underestimated the merchant ship, or rather, her captain. If he had made one mistake during the course of the long day, one slip of the wheel to spill one of her sails of even half its wind, the Wyvern would have been on her like a wild dog on a chicken with clipped wings. But his hand had been steady, his heading true, and now Badru's crew was avoiding their own captain's stare. When they caught the merchant ship, Badru would have to make an example of its captain. The code of the Furusiyya demanded it.

He was lost in thought, contemplating various methods of execution as a means of regaining his lost face, when a cry went up from a sentry midship.

"Light spotted, starboard!"

"Starboard?" Hanif said, his brow wrinkling.

"They have dropped their sails then," Badru said, "and changed course. No doubt hoping we would glide right past them in the dark."

Hanif pointed to starboard. "There. I see them, Emir."

"Hard to starboard," Badru said. Then he raised his voice and shouted down to an officer standing at the stairwell leading below decks. "Raise starboard oars. Double time on port!" The command was relayed throughout both rowing decks, the drums skipped a beat and then resumed at an increased rate. Within moments, Badru felt the galley shift beneath his feet and the bow began to swing toward the light.

They closed the distance quickly. Too quickly, Badru thought. Something was wrong. A minute later, they came alongside a dinghy with a sole occupant. The small boat was a runabout, used for ferrying men and supplies between shore, or a dock, and the larger merchant vessel. It was fitted with a small mast, but the sail was noticeably absent. However, a lit lantern had been hoisted to the top of the mast by the lone man in the dinghy, who was reed thin and dressed in ragged clothes. He stood in the boat waving his arms and shouting.

"Get me that man. Now!" Badru said. The order was relayed, and once the ship was close enough, they lowered a rope ladder off the side of the ship. The man jumped into the water, splashed his way to the ladder, and hooked his arms in the ropes. He was too exhausted from his short swim, so the crew of the Wyvern hauled up the ladder with him dangling in it like a trapped crab. He fell to the deck, rolled onto his knees, and began bowing at Badru's feet.

"May Allah preserve you captain. Thank you, thank you…"

The man had obviously been a slave aboard the merchant vessel. Badru turned to one of his Mamluk officers. "Question him. Find out if he knows anything useful and report to me on the helmsman's deck."

"Yes, my Emir."

Badru made his way back to Hanif. Just as he reached him, a lookout called out. "Light spotted! Port bow!"

"Adjust course," Badru said, but before Hanif could spin the wheel another shout rang out.

"Light spotted! Aft starboard!"

Hanif gritted his teeth and looked at his Emir for guidance as more shouts came from the crew.

"Light spotted! Port!"

"Light spotted! Bow starboard!"

The shouts kept coming, one after another. "Captain?" Hanif asked.

"Maintain current course, helmsman," Badru said. A metallic taste had taken over his mouth. He spit on the deck as an officer appeared at the top of the stairs.

"The man we picked up is a Muslim from Aleppo, my Emir. He has been a galley slave for three years and only recently was put to work on the merchant vessel. He does not know much."

"What did they tell him when they set him free in the dinghy?"

"The captain, a Genoan by the name of Vignoli, gave him flint and steel and said that he was being released in a very remote part of the sea. If he did not manage to light his lantern and attract our attention, there would not be another ship for weeks. He would most assuredly die."

"He said the captain's name was Vignoli?"

"Yes, my Emir."

At least he had a name to go with his disgrace, Badru thought. He looked out over the darkness and counted nine or ten lights mocking him from afar.

"Emir. Which one should we follow?" Hanif asked.

Badru took a breath. "None. They think they escaped. But we know where they are going so today has just been an inconvenience. I will give you a new heading."

"And the man we picked up? What shall we do with him, Emir?" the officer asked.

"Send him to the master of the rowing decks. He lost a few men today."

Badru watched the man carefully for any sign of hesitation, but the officer bowed and hurried away to carry out his Emir's order. If he thought the treatment of a fellow Muslim harsh, he said nothing.

Vignoli. Badru repeated that name over and over again in his mind as he stared ahead into the darkness.

CHAPTER ELEVEN

THERE WERE TOO many pirates plying the lanes leading into the busy port of Acre, so the Grandmaster's plan had arranged for a discreet disembarking at an uninhabited cove north of the city. Since Vignolo's merchant ship had a shallow draft, they were able to anchor just a short distance off shore. However, since they now possessed only a single skiff, it still took most of the night to ferry all five hundred children ashore. They broke their fast at first light and soon after, Foulques led his army of children away from the sea while Vignolo pulled anchor and headed back out to open waters to lead anyone away that may have followed.

They were less than three hours from Acre, central Christendom, on a scarcely used road that wound between tall rock formations offering shelter from the unforgiving sun of the Levant. The canyon road was narrow, stretching the column of five hundred children and the few knights thin. The going was slow as the children were not accustomed to the heat, but Foulques continued to push them. He and his men were just hours away from the end of a long, grueling journey, so it was no wonder their minds were wandering to the soft comforts of a bed and warm food awaiting them in the great Hospitaller fortress in Acre when the rock slide hit the rear half of the group.

An avalanche of boulders and smaller rocks careened down the steep hillside, crushing a knight and the handful of children in its path. A deafening rumble echoed all around them and dust billowed up and choked the gorge.

Foulques drew his sword and looked back over the heads of screaming children, their eyes wide with panic. Looking to the front again he saw a flicker of movement ahead, and immediately realized they were under attack.

Divide and conquer, he thought. The landslide was a diversion to split the large group. But where would the main attack come from? In answer to his question, a group of men appeared on the road ahead and began moving toward them slowly, shouting and yelping in Arabic. This was the diversion, he thought, but there were still too many. He signaled to the handful of knights that could see him to remain where they were and protect the children from the front of the column, and then he pushed through the throng of children and began moving toward the avalanche debris and the rear.

Foulques heard screams and the sounds of fighting on the other side of the rocks almost immediately. He ran for the lowest point of the debris wall, scrambled up it, and slid down the loose scree on the other side. Using the momentum from his slide, he raised his sword with both hands and brought it down hard on the helmeted head of a raider, cleaving both head and helmet in two.

All around him was chaos. Dust hung in the air like smoke, and children were running, screaming, trying to escape the slavers who seemed to be everywhere with ropes and leather collars. Foulques saw one of his knights pinned to the ground with a spear, and two more fighting in the distance. He pulled his sword free from the corpse at his feet and charged after a man leading three children away by ropes around their necks.

✠

THOMAS PRESSED HIS back up against the rock wall, trying to disappear, as he watched Zora savage the throat of one of the slavers, who moments before had been dragging the boy away by his hair. Pirmin snatched up the dead man's war ax and leveled it at a heavyset man with a full beard and dark, fleshy circles under his eyes who stalked warily towards the snarling dog. He raised a heavy crossbow and shot an iron bolt into Zora's side, lifting her up and throwing her away from the dead man. She yelped, her feet scrambling briefly to find purchase on the rocky ground before her strength gave out and she toppled over on her side. Zora raised her head once, to bite weakly at the leather-vaned shaft lodged deep between her ribs. Shaking with the effort, she was unable to reach it, and finally her head dropped hard to the ground, as though it were made of stone. She panted a few times. Then, with a whole-body shudder, she died.

Pirmin, eyes wide and chest heaving, charged the man with his ax while screaming something in his strange accent that Thomas could not comprehend. The heavy man dropped his crossbow, sidestepped, and caught the ax shaft, twisting it out of the young boy's hands. Then he whipped the butt-end across Pirmin's face. To the man's surprise, the enraged boy took the blow, threw his arms around the slaver's upper legs and drove his head into his stomach, knocking them both to the ground. Pirmin straddled the man and rained blows down upon the man's face and chest. Although big for an eight year-old, Pirmin was still just a boy and his adversary out weighed him by at least a hundred and some pounds. His blows were ineffective, and once the man recovered from the fall to the ground and the surprise of the boy's ferociousness, he rolled Pirmin over and beat him without mercy, until the boy's hands fell limp at his side and blood flowed freely around his eyes, mouth, and nose.

The slaver stood up quickly, as though embarrassed, and produced a length of rope from his belt with several leather collars strung along its length. He kicked the stunned Pirmin over on his stomach and knelt to slip one over Pirmin's head, cinching the metal buckle in place at the back of his neck. The boy coughed into the dusty ground and moaned, but other than that did not try to fight back.

Thomas stared at the big dog's still form, and memories of a cold cabin with two lifeless forms holding each other came unbidden to his mind. Not much time had passed since the fever took his parents, but already their faces were blurred and indistinct. He knew Zora was dead and what that meant. It meant that as soon as she was out of his sight, he would never see her again. And somehow he understood, without the smallest doubt, the man kneeling over Pirmin intended to take Thomas's friend far away, to a place Pirmin did not want to go. He eyed the large ax on the ground next to the man, who was sweating freely from his tousle with Pirmin. The small boy pushed himself away from the rock wall and walked slowly forward.

✠

FOULQUES FOUGHT BACK to back with Alain. Although a learned man who had once studied to be a priest, Alain was a vicious warrior. He fought with a long, sleek war hammer, which he wielded faster than most could use a sword, and the sheer impact of its strikes penetrated even the heaviest of armor. Not that heavy armor was a concern for the knights this day, since the slavers were dressed for mobility, not combat. Their aim was to strike fast, overwhelm the knights with their numbers, gather as many children as possible and then flee. Everywhere Foulques looked he saw dozens of his young charges being carried away, slumped over men's shoulders or being dragged with ropes and collars around their necks.

Foulques and Alain stood guard over forty or fifty children they had herded into a large gap in the rock wall. In front a dozen slavers eyed their charges hungrily, but were wary of the heavily armed knights guarding them. A single Hospitaller was dangerous enough, but two working together in the coordinated fighting style they were famous for, were deadly. Already several of the slavers' comrades lay at the feet of the knights, their bodies cold and eyes unseeing.

A tall raider with a leather helmet shouted and bravely lunged forward swinging his falchion, a wide-bladed weapon that was half sword, half ax. Foulques deflected the blow into the ground and almost simultaneously, Alain smashed his war hammer into the man's unprotected thigh, breaking his femur. The man screamed but before he could fall, Foulques brought his sword down between the man's shoulder and neck, splitting him open to his sternum. The corpse toppled over and the group of slavers stepped back. A few drifted away to find easier prey.

Children were still running everywhere, but Foulques could do nothing for them without endangering the group he and Alain were protecting. Out of his peripheral vision, he noticed a small child with his back up against the rock wall opposite him. A large slaver knelt over another boy, fastening a collar about his neck. He considered making a run for the boys and bringing them back to this group, but that would mean leaving Alain here alone with still close to ten men surrounding them, looking for an opening. He had no choice. The boys were on their own.

Though he was preoccupied, Foulques could not keep his eyes from straying to the plight of the two boys. He watched, even though he knew what the outcome would be.

The small boy was moving now and it looked like he might escape, as the slaver had his back to him and was busy with the other one lying on the ground. But instead of fleeing, the boy walked right up to the slaver.

Was he mad? What are you doing boy? Get out of there.

He stopped in front of an ax and a crossbow lying on the

ground, and hesitated for a moment. Then, he squatted and gathered up the crossbow in his arms, straining under the weight, and slowly backed away from the slaver. The little hope Foulques had for the boy was extinguished when he saw the limbs on the crossbow were straight. Its bolt had already been fired, and even if the boy had another arrow, it would take a strong man to lever the bowstring back into place. No mere boy possessed the strength.

Fool. Why did you not take the ax?

When the boy once again had his back pressed up against the rock wall, he screamed so loud Foulques heard him clearly, even though the sounds of chaos were all around. It was not a high-pitched sound like one might expect to come from a boy his age, but deep and primal. A wail that combined fear and anger into one long outburst.

The slaver heard it too. He looked up from his captive, and though Foulques was too far from the man to see his face clearly, he saw the man eye the unloaded crossbow and sensed him smile. He stood up and strolled toward the boy, shouting and gesturing with his hands. The boy hefted the crossbow up to his shoulder, bending back into the wall to support the heavy weapon. He said nothing, but seemed relaxed. Confident. Maybe the earlier scream helped. The slaver drew a curved knife from his belt and fingered its edge. He said something to the boy, a question perhaps, or maybe he told him to put the weapon down. Whatever it was, the boy did not move. This seemed to enrage the man, for he yelled at the boy and whipped his knife across his face.

Even at this distance, Foulques could see the blood

spray. The boy screamed but he did not drop the crossbow. The slaver turned his face to the heavens in laughter. And then Foulques realized what the boy was doing. It was a desperate bluff.

Behind the slaver, a form pulled himself up off the ground and began moving toward the man's back, rope dragging from the collar around his neck. He stooped to lift the war ax from the dust, and with two quick steps followed by a ferocious woodsman's swing that utilized his whole body, the young boy buried the ax deep between the man's shoulder blades.

The way his legs gave out told Foulques the man's spine was severed. He may not have been dead at that point, but then the boy put his foot on the man's back and yanked out the ax. With another accurate swing, the boy planted the ax in the back of the slaver's head. He left it there and wiped his hands on his shirt as he ran over to the other boy.

The younger boy with the crossbow dropped it and fell to the ground, his hands cupped to his face.

Foulques shook his head in wonder and came to a decision.

"Alain. It is time to take the fight to them. Are you with me?"

Alain rolled his shoulders once. "Give the word."

Foulques let out a battle scream and the two knights launched themselves into the midst of the surprised slavers. Foulques closed on a man who could not backpedal fast enough, and thrust his swordpoint through the man's chest. Alain feinted at one and then brought his war hammer circling around to the side of the head of another. There was a loud crack and the man slumped to the ground. The group backed off to reform, and a few deserted completely. Foulques seized on the opportunity and sprinted toward the two boys.

He reached the boys in seconds. The large one jumped at his sudden appearance and Foulques was surprised to see him lift his hands like he was about to strike him.

"Easy, boy. Can you run?" Foulques asked in German.

A torrent of words flew out of the boy's mouth. Foulques had no idea what he had just said, but he figured the boy could not be too hurt the way he was flapping about. He sheathed his sword, scooped up the blood-soaked smaller boy in his arms, and yelled, "Follow me!"

Without waiting to see if the older boy had understood, he sprinted back to Alain and the others. Alain had killed two more men and was locked in battle with another when Foulques arrived. Without putting the boy down, Foulques lifted his knee high and thrust his foot into the man's back. He twisted at an odd angle and fell to the ground squirming in pain. Alain ended his discomfort with the pointed end of his hammer.

Foulques put the bleeding boy down against the rock face. He turned around and was pleased to see the older boy right on his heels.

"Come here, boy," Foulques said. He pulled his dagger and sliced, then ripped, a relatively clean piece off the boy's shirt. He pressed it against the side of the small boy's head and grabbed the other boy's hand. "You hold this here. You understand?"

The blond boy rolled his eyes and said something that Foulques took to mean he understood. That was good enough for him. He drew his sword and rejoined Alain. There seemed to be a break in the action, for Alain stood alone, his hammer in a low guard, and there were no enemy in front of him.

"What is happening?" Foulques asked.

"They are leaving, I think. But what do you make of that?"

Alain pointed with his chin to a group of men who emerged slowly out of the dust. There were seven or eight and they were heavily armed and armored.

"Those are no common slavers," Foulques said. It was not their arms that gave them away, but rather the confidence with which they carried them.

Alain nodded. "Mamluks," he said.

They walked slowly toward the two knights and the group of children huddled against the cliff. As they got closer, Foulques realized one man was incredibly large. He had a sinking feeling he knew who he was.

They stopped five paces away from Foulques. The men spread out in a casual yet obviously disciplined formation. The large man was the unmistakable leader and he stood a full head taller even than Alain. His scimitar was still sheathed, but Foulques did not doubt for a moment that it could be in his hand instantaneously. His mail did not extend past his shoulders, leaving his arms bare save for long leather wrist guards and metal bands that cinched tight around his bulging biceps. His skin was the color of wet oak, and it made the gray eyes in his clean-shaven face seem oddly out of place.

"Are you Vignoli?" the leader asked in very good French.

"And if I am?" Foulques said. What would he want with the Genoan? An ugly thought began to rear its head in Foulques's mind.

"If you are the man I seek, then I will wrap your intestines around my sword and roll them out of your belly as you watch."

Foulques suspected that the other Mamluks understood enough French to get the general idea of what their leader was saying, but there was not a snicker amongst them. Not even a smile. No one was joking here.

"You would have to take this away from me first," Foulques said, raising his sword. "And if you are successful in that, it will not matter what you do with me, for I will be with my maker."

There was a pause and then the man nodded. "You are not Vignoli. Where is he?"

"I am Brother Foulques de Villaret, Knight Justice of the Order of Saint John. I would know who dares to attack us and threaten our ten-year truce with the Sultan."

The Mamluk grinned, showing eye teeth that had been filed to a fine point. "How long have you been gone, Hospitaller? The Sultan owes your kind nothing." He looked carefully at Foulques and Alain, and then turned and surveyed the area about him. Now that the dust had settled, Foulques could see two other groups of children protected by other Hospitallers. Bodies were strewn about on the ground. Everyone stood on guard, ready to fight to the death.

The Mamluk looked at Foulques again. "Do you think you will die today, Christian?"

"No," Foulques said.

The leader nodded and crossed his arms over his chest. "I think you are right. You fought well today. I give you these children to keep as your slaves. But tell Vignoli that I will come for him." He tapped his belly three times with one hand and then made a coiling motion with his finger.

The Mamluk turned and began walking away. His men waited until he had gone a few steps, and then one by one, they wheeled around and followed like they were taking a leisurely stroll through the bazaar.

AFTER THE MAMLUKS were gone, it took the knights the better part of an hour to round up the terror-stricken children and tend to their injuries. Foulques sat on a boulder and looked at the sorry lot scattered in front of him.

"Three knights and four brother-sergeants are dead. Two more knights are wounded but they can travel," Alain said.

"How many children did the heathens make off with?" Foulques asked.

"Almost two hundred," Alain said. When he saw Foulques's face cloud over, he added, "But it could have been much worse, and they paid dearly for their prize."

Foulques did not look at Alain. Finally, he said, "Take

two men, bury our dead and provide services. They gave their lives for the Order and deserve better, but we are too vulnerable out here. I will push on to Acre with the children. Follow as soon as you can."

Alain nodded. "God be with you, Foulques."

He turned to go, but Foulques stopped him. "And Brother Alain."

"Yes?"

"See to it that dog over there is buried as well."

Alain's eyes widened slightly but he followed Foulques's gaze. A blond-haired boy held a big dog's head in his lap and wept uncontrollably. A younger, skinny boy knelt nearby, grimacing in pain as a brother-sergeant used needle and thread to deftly stitch closed a long, angry gash down the side of his face.

CHAPTER TWELVE

T HOMAS SMELLED THE city before he saw it. The road emerged from a low canyon onto a hill, and stretching in the distance before them, shimmering in the heat, were the fortified stone walls of the port city of Acre.

Atop the walls were crenelations the height of a man, with room for two men to stand between them and rain havoc down upon enemy attackers. Two massive towers flanked the main gate, but from his vantage point Thomas could see over a section of the two outer walls into the city below, and he did not like what he saw.

Everything was made up of hues of gray that clashed with the light sand color of the surrounding countryside, and in the distance, on the other side of the city, the azure blue of the Mid-Earth Sea. Narrow streets with minds of their own weaved between two- and three-story buildings and merchant stalls, and clouds of smoke rose high into the air from all parts of the city. Several pointed church spires rose up out of the smoky air, the crosses mounted on top stretched toward heaven in a vain attempt to escape the filth below.

The army of children dragged their sweaty, dust-encrusted selves forward without a sound, save for that of exhausted feet shuffling along rocky ground. Fortunately, the knights had recognized the difficulty they had adjusting to the searing heat of the Levant and had kept them well hydrated throughout their journey. Still, they were exhausted and too overwhelmed by the sights before them to speak.

Thomas, like all the children, gaped at the city in awe. He simply did not know what it was. Schwyz was the largest village he had ever seen and he had no concept of a city. There were no nearby mountains with gurgling streams, no trees, no grass. In fact, as they began their descent toward the main gate, there was a complete absence of the color green.

A two-hundred-yard killing zone had been cleared in front of the main gate, giving the tower archers a clear view in the event of a siege. The road lead through the cleared area, a few hastily erected merchant stalls on either side. Far to the left, a nauseating stench rose from a mountain of debris piled high against the city wall. Two workers struggled to dump a cart filled with refuse and night soil from the houses of those who could afford to have it removed. Several dead bodies lay on the ground. A priest pointed to those which were to be carted away for burial in the cemetery, and nodded with a scowl toward those which were to be thrown on the fire burning nearby.

As they neared the main gate, the sounds of the city became louder. A contingent of Hospitaller men-at-arms waited for them, and the city guards hastily parted to allow

Foulques de Villaret and his Hospitallers entry. They passed below two cages that held the decaying forms of criminals, entered the dim coolness offered by the twenty-foot-thick arch of the main gate, proceeded through another gate in the second set of walls, and then the city of Acre swallowed whole what was left of the army of children.

Once inside, they were met by a cacophony of city sounds and odors held in, and magnified, by the high stone walls. The sudden increase in noise was deafening to most who entered the city, but to country children from the Alps, it was terrifying. In a myriad of languages, all manner of merchants shouted in competition with one another, promising the best in the world at the lowest price. Poor people called out for alms, holy men preached, whores solicited, animals were slaughtered, and everywhere people shouted and screamed to be heard.

Pirmin's eyes were wide and darted wildly from side to side. Thomas's face was pale, the pain of his recent wound all but forgotten, as he held a hand over his mouth and nose in a futile attempt to keep out the city's stench. Without a word between them, the boys reached out to clasp one another's hand. They held on tight while the Hospitallers led the army of children through the winding streets of Acre.

✠

THE HOSPITALLER COMPOUND was in the western part of the city, near, but not on, the water's edge. Inside their own set of walls was the main keep, knights' quarters, hospital, church, monk and nun cells, barracks for the brother-sergeants, stables and training grounds for working with the destriers, forge shed, butcher, and a scattering of smaller lean-to buildings resting up against the walls. In short, it was a fortified village within a fortified city.

The first stop Foulques made after entering the fortress and allowing a contingent of brother-sergeants and monks to relieve him of the children's army, was to visit Donovan in the stables. Still covered in the grime of his travels, and several smears of dried blood from his fight with the slavers, he stepped into the coolness of the covered stables. His assigned destrier was in his regular stall and as Foulques opened his gate, the giant bay stallion reared his head in recognition and pranced in place. He was a beautiful animal with a lustrous black mane and tail setting off neat black points on his lower legs that accentuated the size of his massive hooves. Donovan dropped his head just low enough for Foulques to reach up and hug his neck.

"Someone is happy to see you," Kenneth, one of the chief stable hands said as he came up behind Foulques. He gave Foulques a slap on the shoulder and the two men clasped arms. "As am I. Welcome back, Brother Foulques."

Foulques ran his hand down Donovan's face and lightly stroked his velvety nostrils, something he usually loved. But today, he tossed his head in impatience and stared at Foulques with his large black eyes. "He is as anxious to be out on the roads as I am. Tomorrow, boy. All will be back to normal tomorrow." He noticed how his mane and tail had been recently combed out and his coat glistened in the light. "You have taken good care of him in my absence, Kenneth.

Thank you."

The groom shook his head. "That is Brother Everet's work. He has been taking him out on patrols since you have been gone."

"I will have to thank him, then," Foulques said.

Foulques stayed there with Donovan for the better part of an hour, then, with a sigh and more promises about tomorrow, he shut Donovan back up in his stall. He wished he could stay longer, but he knew he had put off his duties for as long as he could.

After a quick stop at his apartment to remove his armor and don a fresh robe, Foulques climbed the steps up to the Grandmaster's office in the keep just after midday. The guards at the door relieved him of both his sword and dagger and then admitted him without a word, all the while avoiding eye contact.

Foulques walked down a narrow hallway and stepped through the open door at the end into a large, high-ceilinged room. Adorning the walls were flags depicting the white cross of the Hospitallers, in all its varied forms. Suspended from the ceiling were the pennants of the Order's eight Langues: France, England, Germany, Provence, Auvergne, Aragon, Italy, and Castile. In the center of the room was the heavy slab table of the Knights Grande Cross, the ruling council of the Hospitaller Knights of Saint John of Jerusalem. Imported years ago from some forest across the seas, its impressive bulk glistened with polish and, despite all the flags and historical displays of armor and arms throughout the room, it was that simple piece of oak that caught one's eye and held it. Only as one drew near, did the scratches and dents appear, the chipped corners become visible, and if one knew where to look, they would see supports of cheap pine bolstering it from beneath.

There was sitting space for thirty people around that marred surface. Today only two men sat there, side by side: Grandmaster Villiers and Marshal Mathieu de Clermont, the high commander of the Black Knights' military forces. Both men wore black robes with the white cross displayed on their shoulders, and although they were dressed as monks, their respective statures hinted at something else entirely. Both were heavily bearded and well into their middle ages. But that is where the similarities ended. Grandmaster Villiers was short and thick with the neck of a bull. Marshal Mathieu de Clermont was tall, and as a young man, had earned the nickname 'the Mongoose' for his weasel-like appearance and ferocious fighting ability characterized by lightning fast lunges with his sword. Outremer was a land filled with knights, mercenaries, assassins, warriors, and desperate killers living on the streets. There was no shortage of opportunities for a man to test his skill with a blade, both within and outside tournaments. The Templars, the Teutonic Knights, and the Hospitallers sponsored a great number of these tournaments, claiming they kept their men sharp, but anyone witnessing the men of the cross battling one another in such brutal tournaments would be hard-pressed to call it sport. The tournaments had made Mathieu de Clermont a legend in Outremer. In twelve years he had never been defeated and when he retired as a combatant, his fame saw him rise in the ranks of the Hospitallers at a meteoric rate. The man was a celebrity, not only within the Hospitaller ranks but all the other fighting Orders as well. He had taken an early interest in Foulques when he was young. Whenever the boy's uncle was away in Europe on one of his frequent support-raising trips for the Order, Clermont trained Foulques in the ways of the tournaments. Under the Marshal's personal tutelage, Foulques had enjoyed some initial success and Mathieu de Clermont had been something of an idol to him. But, the tournaments were never something his uncle approved of. More than once, Guillaume de Villaret had voiced his opinion that they were a distraction meant only for the common knights, and were merely personal quests for glory not befitting a soldier of Christ. He was not alone in his beliefs, and even went so far as to bring a vote to council to ban Hospitaller brothers from entering any type of tournament. Apparently, Guillaume de Villaret had convinced others, for the motion was narrowly defeated. The experience created a rift between Guillaume de Villaret and Marshal Mathieu de Clermont, with a young Foulques caught in the middle.

As Foulques approached, he noticed the Marshal had a black flag in his hands. The older man made a point of ignoring Foulques as he floated the flag onto the table and busied himself spreading it flat with his palms. It was yet another version of the Hospitaller cross, this one rather unique as it looked like four arrowheads pointed at one another. Foulques stopped in front of a chair across from his superiors and waited for an invitation to sit. After a long moment of silence the Grandmaster beckoned and Foulques lowered himself into the chair.

"Brother Foulques," Grandmaster Villiers said, shaking his head.

Marshal Clermont was never one to mince words. "What happened, boy? The Order's treasury was spilled open and good men died for you. From what I saw march through those gates today, we have precious little to show for it."

"Let him speak, Mathieu. I should like to hear his thoughts on the matter," the Grandmaster said.

The Marshal grunted and waved his hand. "By all means. So, tell us Brother Foulques. How did a few slavers make complete fools of the Knights of Saint John?"

Foulques cleared his throat. "They were not ordinary slavers. I believe the attack was planned and carried out by a Mamluk Emir."

The pulsing veins in Mathieu de Clermont's neck squirmed like the body of a serpent whose head had been severed. His eyes narrowed and Foulques sensed his confusion. "Preposterous," he finally said.

"Mamluks?" The Grandmaster said, exchanging a sideways glance with the Marshal. "Why do you say that?"

"I exchanged words with the leader of the slavers. What he said would have me believe the truce Acre has with Sultan Qalawun is in jeopardy."

The Grandmaster let out a sigh. "The Sultan's army defeated the Mongols at a second Battle of Horns," he said.

"I heard the news in my travels," Foulques said, shaking his head. "Apparently they did not merely defeat them, it was a complete rout. The Mamluks grow stronger with every battle. But how does that affect our truce?"

The Grandmaster paused, and when he did not offer a response, Clermont said, "Because we sent a detachment of knights from Margat to ride with the Mongols! That is why."

Foulques was not sure he had heard his old mentor correctly. "The Hospitallers sided with the Mongols? Does Qalawun know this?"

"He sent us a half dozen Hospitaller heads. What do you think?"

Foulques was trying to make sense of all this. "Why? Why would you do this?"

"We had hoped to hurt the Mamluk Sultanate before it became too powerful," the Grandmaster said. "It seemed like the perfect opportunity. Who would have thought Qalawun could stand up to the Great Horde?"

"We must call an emergency meeting of the Grand Cross. We must prepare," Foulques said. They would march on Acre, he thought. It was the only Crusader target left worthy of a retaliatory strike.

"We have ordered an assembly tonight to vote on the Marshal's new flag," the Grandmaster said, pointing at the black flag spread on the table before Marshal Clermont.

"Flag?" Foulques glanced down.

"We are putting it to a vote before the Council. If it passes, we shall adopt it as the official trapping of the Order," Grandmaster Villiers said.

"What is wrong with our current one?" Foulques asked. What were they thinking? The Mamluks could be planning an attack on their home as they speak.

"It is time to go back to our roots, boy," Marshal Clermont said. "The number of new novices has been down every year for as long as I can remember. People on the streets confuse us with the Templars or the Teutonics, and being associated with those single-minded mercenaries bodes ill for the Hospitallers. No good can come of it."

"Marshal, they are all soldiers of the One True Faith. In speaking badly of them, you insult our Lord," the Grandmaster said.

"Fine. I take back what I said about the Teutonics. At least they can fight. But being a Templar these days is all about rank, title, and gold."

The Grandmaster crossed his arms. "I recall Master Guillaume de Beaujeu giving you quite the battle not that many years ago in a tournament. Perhaps not all Templars are as useless with a sword as you would have us believe?"

"The man is a pompous arse," the Marshal said. "But he has a steady hand when a blade is in it. I will give him that."

"The cross is different," Foulques said, pointing at the flag. "Have I seen it before?"

The Grandmaster nodded. "It is from the flag of Amalfi. It is similar to what the Blessed Gerard himself would have flown."

The Marshal nodded. "The Hospital was first established to care for merchants traveling to Jerusalem from the Amalfi coast, so when they founded the first Hospital in Jerusalem two hundred years ago, it stands to reason they would have used their flag to represent the Order."

Foulques could no longer even pretend interest. With all of the Levant wondering where the Mamluks would strike next, did they not have anything better to worry about than the accoutrements of the Order?

"Very well. When is the meeting? I will attend and tell what I know of the Mamluk I met," Foulques said.

The Marshal leaned back in his chair and laughed. "You will do no such thing. In fact you will not even be present tonight."

Foulques turned directly to the Grandmaster. "What is he talking about?" Foulques held the rank of Knight Justice, and as such, it was his right to attend any meeting of the Grand Cross that he wished.

The Grandmaster closed his eyes for a moment. "I am sorry, Brother Foulques. Your rank will be one of the topics tonight. Some members of the council feel we were too hasty in promoting you to the rank of Knight Justice. There will be a vote on rescinding your promotion and after the events of today, there is no doubt it will come to pass. As of this day, you will no longer be entitled to attend council proceedings unless invited."

Foulques felt like he had been hit in the chest with a war hammer. He could picture his uncle wordlessly shaking his head, as he did when severely disappointed. He looked from man to man. The grandmaster avoided his eyes, but the Marshal just sat there with his arms crossed and a thin smile upon his lips. "As I have said all along, you are simply too young for a position of responsibility, Brother Foulques," the Marshal said.

Foulques pushed his chair back and stood. "If that will be all?"

"Cut your hair. And let that beard grow out," Clermont said. "Why must you do everything against custom?"

Foulques ignored him and looked to Grandmaster Villiers, who nodded his permission. Foulques wasted no time in striding out of the room

CHAPTER THIRTEEN

F OULQUES THREADED HIS way through the narrow streets toward the harbor. His destination was the harbor marketplace, the main bazaar of Acre. It was situated in the south of the city, between the Venetian and Pisan quarters. In order to get there, however, he had to pass through the Genoan quarter, arguably the roughest section of the city with its brothels, taverns, and gambling dens. Most respectable citizens would skirt the outsides of the area to reach the bazaar, but Foulques wore the black tunic of a Hospitaller Knight. There was no criminal in Acre desperate enough to waylay a knight of any one of the Holy Orders, be it Hospitaller, Templar, or Teutonic. Even soldiers of the city watch would step aside when they passed.

The sun was still high, and though there were few shadows for the lower denizens of the city to haunt, they could still be seen in great numbers on the street and hanging out of doorways. A group of four men passed a clay flask amongst themselves and spoke in the raised voices of those whose courage had been lifted by drink. Yet they became tight-lipped as Foulques approached, and remained so until the knight rounded the next corner.

More than one doorway was filled with men sleeping off the effects of too much drink the night before, and Foulques paid them no notice. Then he came upon a young woman propped up against the side of a taverna. She looked injured the way she slumped there with her eyes shut. He stooped and placed a hand to her cheek. She sat up with a start and raised her hands to protect herself. Just then, the door to the inn opened and a full bucket of night soil splashed out into the street, narrowly missing them both. A woman's voice called out.

"Gwendoline! There you are!"

The woman threw her bucket back inside the taverna and scurried outside. She gave Foulques a dirty look as she reached down and helped the younger woman to her feet. She turned again to Foulques, her tone scolding, yet polite enough. "If you are done with her now, sir, I will be taking her home."

"I, ah—"

"You what? You think you paid for the whole night? Our girls do not work like that, even for a man of the cloth," she said. The two women ducked inside the taverna and slammed the door, leaving Foulques stammering in the street.

He did not know what bothered him more: the fact she had mistaken him for a priest, or her assumption that he had hired a prostitute. There was no leeway in the rules of the Order. To become a knight, one was required to will all possessions to the Order and take a vow of celibacy.

Foulques knew there were members of all the Holy Orders, Hospitallers, Templars, Teutonics, and priests, who regularly broke their vows of celibacy. But how the madame had spoken to him so nonchalantly suggested it occurred even more often than he had thought. In a way that did not surprise Foulques, for recently he felt the Order of Hospitallers had lost its way. Alliances and politics in Europe were a constant distraction that kept the Order from making any progress in retaking the city of Jerusalem. Sometimes he wondered if that was even their goal anymore.

"Your duty is to Christ," his uncle was fond of saying when Foulques first joined the Order. He would place his hand over Foulques's heart and say, "And He speaks to you from within here. Always listen to your heart before you pay heed to the will of others." Losing the rank of Knight Justice did not bother Foulques as much as it would most members, for he had always shied away from the politics of the Order. To him there was no higher calling than to be a simple soldier of Christ. He had no interest in telling others how they should fulfill their own oaths.

As he left the Genoan quarter, the winding streets straightened out, the smells of too many people living and cooking in too small an area faded from memory, and Foulques found himself standing on the edge of the merchants' square. Contained by the buildings surrounding the square, the sounds of the bazaar were a low murmur right up until the moment Foulques stepped into the large open area. All at once he was assailed with the shouting of merchants, the heady aromas of turmeric and pepper mixing with the saltwater air, and the wafting perfumes of Saracen men and women as they passed.

Ever since he was a child, Foulques had loved the vibrant energy of the bazaar. He pressed on through the crowd, his black robe giving him no special privileges here amongst the throngs of people of all races and nationalities. He allowed himself to wander, to soak in the multitude of merchants and their colorful displays. From farmers to slave traders, Acre had it all. Many of the stalls were familiar to Foulques, like Kas the Jew's bread stand. He stepped around a Bedouin family and put a coin into the baker's hand as the man took orders from two other customers. He winked at Foulques and thrust a dark, oblong loaf at him.

"Enjoy that one, Brother Knight. I have been saving it for you," he said.

"You mean it is not freshly baked today?" Foulques said.

Kas gave a cackle. "Oh it is fresh, Brother. So fresh the inside will burn your tongue and the crust will cut your mouth."

Foulques moved on past a wagon laden with bolts of cloth. He ducked under a line fluttering with silk and linen scarves, and when his vision was cleared of the blue and orange fabric, he was surprised to see the next vendor ahead was Najya.

He did not expect to find her cart here, in this spot, for this was not her usual place. She was almost in the exact center of the bazaar, no longer crammed into a low-traffic corner. The merchant guild must have allowed her to move. She had done well for herself, Foulques thought.

He stood there for a moment and watched his childhood friend ply her trade. The way she was dressed would lead one to think she was a dealer in exotic silks, but, in fact, she was a chandler. Her father had kept bees, only a hive or two at any one time, but it was enough to introduce his daughter to the candle making process. At an early age, she became infatuated with both honey production and the process of making beeswax candles.

Three men stood beside her cart. They were Franks, but their sun-darkened skin and loose, scruffy clothing marked them as laborers. They most likely spent their days on the docks picking up work unloading ships, and their evenings spending their meager coins in the Genoan quarter.

"Have you got any honey left?" one man said.

Najya shook her head. "All gone for today. You have to get here early in the morning for that." She was a pretty woman, and the gauzy head covering she wore would have been far too small for most Islamic purists, for it did little to hide her long dark hair. But that was Najya, Foulques thought.

"Show me some candles," another one of the men said, leaning forward and trying to come between his friend and Najya.

"Suet or beeswax?" Najya said, stepping away, the hem of her light lavender robe fluttering after her. She reached down and produced two candles, one a darker color than the other. "Or I have a mixture of the two, if you prefer." Her movements were slow and deliberate, almost like she was engaged in a dance ritual rather than a commercial transaction.

"I would rather have the honey," the first man said.

"I told you. I have none. Come back tomorrow," Najya said.

"You look like you have lots, princess," the man said. He took a step toward her side of the cart.

"Good day, chandler," Foulques called out. He walked forward and wedged his way between the three men. They reeked of smoke mixed with rancid body odors. He slapped his loaf of bread on Najya's cart in front of him.

"Give me a dozen of your finest beeswax tapers." His elbows bumped the men on either side, and he frowned at one and then the other. "What? Did I interrupt your purchase?"

One of the men dropped his eyes immediately, but the other gave Foulques a quick scowl. If Foulques had been a Teutonic Knight the man's lungs would be filling with blood by now, the Hospitaller thought. The Germans were known to kill a man for far less than a sour look. Foulques turned away from the man, but kept his elbow close enough to feel if he made any hostile move.

"A dozen?" Najya asked. "Are you sure that is enough?"

"You are right. Make it two dozen. But finish with this man's order. I will wait." Foulques turned to fix the scowling man at his elbow with a stare.

The man's lip curled for the briefest of moments but when he saw his two friends backing away from Najya's cart, he decided the numbers were no longer in his favor. He pushed away and mumbled, "Bloody Hospitallers... think

d in their relationship after that day. He felt like she
ow thought Sir Foulques was so much more than she
ever be. He thought that feeling would fade when he
p his title and joined the Order, but it had not. If
ng, it seemed to grow stronger.

does not matter how many men look for them,"
es said. "Those children are gone."

aybe. Or, maybe you just need to know where to

ney were taken by a slaver known as the Northman.
ear of him?"

e playful smile that had been on Najya's face fell away
e last grains of sand in an hourglass.

know of him," she said. "But little more."

ow about his real name?"

jya shook her head. "I know only the same rumors
he man that everyone else knows."

hat he is the offspring of a Northern shield maiden
Egyptian god?"

omething similar," Najya said. "Only his father was a
sh sorcerer and his mother a viking princess. I also
he is one of seven children who were each kept in their
parate box. The only time they were allowed out was
n in the warrior arts. When they became too tired to
hey were put back in their boxes."

ulques could not help laughing at this. The image of
ige Mamluk he had encountered on the road being
into a box was too ridiculous.

he Northman is not a laughing matter," Najya said,

the world should quake at your feet."

Foulques took a step toward him, but the man was already following the other two. In seconds they all faded away
into the crowd.

"You know you did not have to do that," Najya said,
when the two of them were alone.

"I did it for them," Foulques said. He scanned the crowd
to make sure the men had indeed moved on. He could see
no trace of them among the nearby stalls milling with
people. "If they only knew how close they—"

"No one can ever know, Foulques. Promise me," Najya
said.

Foulques turned back to Najya and saw the worry in her
eyes. Did she really think he, of all people, would betray her
secret?

"Of course. If that is what you want."

She passed him a bundle of candles tied together with a
piece of cotton ribbon. Their hands touched, lingered in the
contact for a moment. She smiled when he pulled away.

"And what brings you here today? Besides bread and
tapers, of course. Are you not afraid to be seen speaking with
me? Word could get back to your superiors."

Foulques took the bundle. "I do not care what they think
right now."

"I do not believe that for a moment," Najya said. She
shook her head, rested her elbow on her cart and put her
head in her hand. "Remember when we were children? Life
was so free of worry then. Do you ever think it will be like
that for us again?"

Foulques felt his face flush and he turned his eyes away.

Najya laughed. "No, not that! I did not mean it that way. We were young then, and you had none of your order's vows hanging over you. I just meant the carefree attitude, the bliss of not caring what others thought. The feeling of absolute freedom when your uncle and my father would turn to us and say, 'run along and play, now'. Those are the days I miss. And I know you do, as well."

She smiled weakly and Foulques felt his mouth go dry. "I remember," he said. "And I treasure those memories, as well."

"All of them?" Najya said, her eyes gleaming. "This time it is all right for you to blush, o' mighty knight."

It was Foulques's turn to laugh. "You see what I saved those men from? Torture, pure and simple. You are a master at it." Foulques regretted saying the words the moment they left his mouth.

Najya raised herself up to a full standing position. "Not as good as some," she said.

"I am sorry, Najya, I did not think—".

She held up her hand. "Say no more. Let us talk of other things, like, for example, what really brought you to the market today."

Their moment was over, and Foulques found himself wondering how it was that she found him so easy to read. "I needed candles," he said.

Najya crossed her arms. "And bread. Go on…"

"All right. I admit I needed a break from the compound and every one in it."

"That is more like it," she said. [...] she placed a hand over his. "I was so [...] what happened to those poor children [...]

Foulques pulled his hand away an[...] open. "How could you…?"

"The children?" Najya said. "It i[...] may be a large city but it is not eve[...] wounded Hospitallers limp throug[...] hundred frightened children in tow. [...] that loosens many tongues."

Foulques closed his eyes and he ra[...] his long hair. He had been naive to [...] known only within the Hospitaller co[...]

"What will you do?" Najya asked [...] voice was quiet, concerned.

"What do you mean?"

"What will you do about the child[...] soldiers to search for them?"

Her question caught him off gua[...] naive now?

"No," he said.

"Why not?"

"For one thing, I, myself, am onl[...] command or send other soldiers to do n[...]

"If you asked, I am sure many woul[...] help," Najya said.

Would they? Foulques shook his hea[...] seen him as something more than he re[...] was knighted, she had wept tears of joy[...]

change[...]
someho[...]
would [...]
gave u[...]
anythi[...]

"It [...]
Foulqu[...]
"M[...]
look."
"[...]
Ever h[...]
Th[...]
like th[...]
"I [...]
"H[...]
Na[...]
about [...]
"[...]
and a[...]
"S[...]
Moori[...]
heard [...]
own s[...]
to tra[...]
train, [...]
F[...]
the h[...]
force[...]

crossing her arms.

"So what happened to his siblings?" Foulques said.

"When they were old enough, their master had a box built that was large enough to hold them all."

Foulques managed to hold back another bout of laughter, but he could not stifle a smile. "Ah, much more economical than seven boxes. I do not suppose this story has a happy ending?"

Najya shook her head. "Weapons were thrown into the box and they were all told that the master had use for only one slave."

Foulques smiled again. "And at the end of the day, only the Northman walked out of the box."

"They say it took seven days for the Northman to be reborn," Najya said. Unlike Foulques, she did not smile.

Foulques waited for the first sign of one of her wry smiles but nothing came.

"Come now, Najya. You do not believe any of that, do you?"

"Not all of it, of course." Finally one corner of her mouth lifted and she cocked her head to look at Foulques out of one eye. "But all stories come from somewhere. There may be a touch of truth hidden in there."

"The man is a slaver. Nothing more. He probably started that story himself to bolster his own reputation," Foulques said. He saw the image of the Northman standing in front of his Mamluk warriors, magnanimously telling Foulques that he would allow him to keep the rest of the children.

"Perhaps. In any case, the man is smart enough to avoid

bringing the children to the Acre slave market. That is for sure. How many did he capture?"

"One hundred and eighty," Foulques said, his teeth clenching between every word.

"Oh, Foulques." She shook her head. "So many…"

"I do not need you to tell me this," Foulques said.

"No, what I mean is, that is too many for any one market."

Foulques did not follow her reasoning, and the expression on his face must have told her so.

"What I mean is, if he brought them all to one, he would sacrifice profits. With that many children of the same age put on the stage at once, it would drive the prices down. That is the very reason I only bring a few flasks of honey to market every day. Scarcity of goods is the merchant's best friend."

"These are people you talk about, not common goods," Foulques said. He was surprised to hear anger creeping into his words.

"You are wrong. In some cities, they are the commonest of goods and worth far less than a flask of honey."

"So what will the great Northman do then?"

"The children must be split up and sold at twenty or thirty different markets," Najya said.

"And if I were to send soldiers to find these children, how would I know which markets to go to?"

Najya shook her head. "How do you know which grains of sand will be washed up on shore and which will stay in the depths of the sea? I am sorry Foulques, but you cannot know. The Northman will sell the children to more than a dozen different brokers and they will take them anywhere from here to Africa, selling them where and when they see fit. They have access to thousands of slave markets. The children will simply disappear into the desert."

"It is over, then. As I said, there is no hope of finding them," Foulques said.

"I never said that. I know people I can ask. I cannot make any promises, but give me a few days and perhaps I can find out where some of them have been taken."

"You do not have to do this, Najya." He wanted to tell her it was a fool's errand, but he could not bring himself to say the words. The way her eyes lit up reminded Foulques of when they were children about to set out on some great, imagined adventure.

"There is very little in life that we *have* to do, Foulques," Najya said.

CHAPTER FOURTEEN

VIGNOLO TOOK A deep breath to clear the fog induced by breathing in the smoky, stagnant air of the small hazard den lit by nothing but cheap tallow candles and oil lamps. At least it kept the sour body odors at bay, he thought.

"I suppose this is just my lucky night," Vignolo said, trying not to grin too widely. Stephanos, the table master and proprietor of the *Frolicking Eunuch*, looked up at Vignolo from his stool, which was an untapped cask of ale placed alongside the long hazard table near its middle.

A heavy-set Greek, Stephanos peered at Vignolo from under a great, gray, curly mass of hair. "Must be due to the clean life you live," he said. He counted out a few coins and used a crooked olive branch whittled flat on one end to push them across the table toward Vignolo. It was a ridiculously unnecessary act, for the table was narrow and Stephanos could have just handed Vignolo the money.

Truth be told, his run of 'luck' was beginning to make the Genoan a little nervous. Things had started off slowly at the hazard table, so he slipped his own dice into the game.

But now that he had built up a nice stack of silver, Vignolo thought it best to dump the original dice back into the game, before someone noticed their weight was just a little one-sided. That could be a sensitive matter, however, as the table was now hot and had drawn a crowd. There were only a half-dozen players when Vignolo arrived, now there were over twenty.

"Same caster!" Stephanos shouted over the din.

Vignolo leaned forward and hovered his hand over the dice. He gave his arm a slight twist and felt the true dice begin to slide down his forearm inside his sleeve. Just as he was about to make the switch, a thick, calloused hand closed over his fake dice. The hand was missing one half of its index finger. Stephanos glared through his swaying, wayward curls at Vignolo. Vignolo had the sudden realization that maybe it was because of the missing finger people called him 'the Eunuch'. Or, perhaps, he really was a Eunuch. Hopefully, it was not because he enjoyed making others into eunuchs.

Stephanos was one of the few survivors of the Antioch massacre of 1268. No one knew exactly how he managed to flee the city before Baybairs put its population to the sword for refusing to surrender sooner. But, rumor had it, after losing everything, Stephanos joined King Edward's short-lived crusade and amassed a small fortune in war-captured treasure.

Vignolo cringed under the Eunuch's blue-eyed stare. A big Saracen stepped out of the shadows behind Stephanos, and Vignolo noted that neither he, nor Stephanos, looked too frolicky. Getting Stephanos off his keg of ale usually took a serious fight—one where weapons were drawn and there was a real threat of blood (or other bodily excretions) being spilled onto the hazard den's tamped earth floor. Stephanos kept careful track of how fast his customers consumed the wine and ale in any given night, and the drunker they became the more hazard tables he opened.

Stephanos picked up the dice and hefted them in his hand a couple of times, while all around the table, players slapped money down, making bets. Vignolo was still waiting for his flight instinct to take over when Stephanos leaned forward and, quick as a cobra, grabbed Vignolo by the wrist. He squeezed and Vignolo felt his hand pop open. Stephanos thrust the weighted dice into his open palm.

"Same caster! Same dice!" Stephanos shouted. He released Vignolo's hand with a subtle shove and eased himself back onto his keg. His eyes left Vignolo's own the moment he let go of his hand.

Vignolo swallowed and rolled the dice. He won, and so did most around the table. Cheers went up. Mugs were downed and topped up by serving girls, some veiled, some you wished were. Stephanos counted out silver and distributed it with his stick. Amid shouts of encouragement, Vignolo rolled again with similar results.

At some point Vignolo knew Stephanos would switch out Vignolo's dice. By the end of the night, the Frolicking Eunuch would empty every purse in the place, but not before each player had tasted victory. That small, delicious nibble would be enough to bring them all back tomorrow for more of the same. Vignolo looked across at Stephanos slouched over on his keg of ale, his arms crossed, a surly look on his sun-browned face. Two men appeared at the proprietor's side and he stood while they wheeled the keg away from underneath him. Stephanos pulled over a real stool and sat down, looking absolutely miserable.

It was time to go.

The sharp point of something that could only be steel suddenly appeared in his ribs behind his left arm.

"Hello, Vignolo," a familiar voice said. Though he could not immediately place the speaker, judging by the cadence of the voice, not to mention the cold pricking sensation below his heart, he suspected it was not going to be a joyous reunion. He pivoted his head to find a man about his height, thin as a candlestick. Looking into his eyes, he was glad he had not done anything rash.

"Ah. Hello. Giacomo, was it?" Francesca Provenzano's hired man. The last man you would want to meet on a dark street in Acre. Not that Vignolo felt especially good about seeing him in a dimly lit hazard den, either.

Vignolo made a slow, exploratory reach for the dice. The knife in his ribs followed, keeping just enough pressure to banish any thought Vignolo may have had of reaching for his own knife. Judging from the angle of Giacomo's arm and hand, it was a punch-blade. The kind you gripped with a fist, while the point extruded from between your fingers. Vignolo let out a sigh of relief. If Giacomo had wanted him dead, he would have already been dripping on the Eunuch's floor.

"Francesca has been asking about you," Giacomo said. "She was expecting to see you last week."

I know, Vignolo thought. Precisely why he was at the Frolicking Eunuch and not at one of his usual gambling dens. He had been careless. While it was true that he was not exactly in hiding, he had been sure to keep a low profile since returning from his Hospitaller contract. The Hospitallers had refused to grant him full payment, leaving him far short of the funds needed to repay Francesca. Grandmaster Villiers had given him only half of what was agreed upon since Vignolo had delivered only half the goods, and lost the Hospitallers several good men in the process.

"*Last* week, you say? I could swear it was *next* week."

Giacomo nodded. "A misunderstanding, then. No harm done." His thin lips flattened into a line. "Just give me what you were going to give her next week and I am sure she will understand."

"Ah," Vignolo said.

"Ah." Giacomo was perhaps as close to smiling as he had ever been in his life.

"About that," Vignolo began, "I was just going to come see her after I finished up here. As you can see, I am doing quite well."

"Time to finish up," Giacomo said. "We will continue this outside."

"Of course," Vignolo said. He looked across the table at Stephanos, who was gesturing for him to roll the dice. All eyes around the table turned to Vignolo, expecting him to roll. This might be a good time to pass on the dice, Vignolo thought.

"Here you are." Vignolo pushed the dice into Giacomo's

free hand. His brows creased, but his hand automatically opened to accept the proffered dice. "New caster!" Vignolo shouted.

Giacomo glanced down at his hand. "No time for games, Vignolo. We leave now." He let the dice fall onto the table. All four of them.

A squat, pock-faced man standing on Giacomo's left side was the first to notice there were two too many dice. "Hey! What are you up to?" The rest of the people on the table were seemingly too dim-witted, the fault of either drink or nature, to notice.

Vignolo decided to help them. "Cheat! This man is trying to cheat us all!"

He felt Giacomo's blade press into his ribs, but the table had begun to spring to life. Emboldened by Vignolo's loud outburst, the pock-faced man grabbed Giacomo by the shoulder and spun him. "You cheating us, boy? We—"

He had suddenly run out of words, but the pricking in Vignolo's side was gone. Even as Vignolo took a rib-heaving breath of air, the pocked man pressed a hand to his chest. Another man swung a blow at Giacomo's head, but he leaned to the side and snapped an elbow across the man's face, dropping him across the table and setting off a shower of coins. Two young men pushed at Vignolo's back to get to Giacomo. Vignolo slipped to the side and let them storm past him.

Vignolo looked at his mound of winnings on the table and tried to snake his hand through a gap in the bodies and limbs flailing around him. One of the young men screamed and fell to the floor as he clutched one hand over an eye, blood streaming from between his fingers. Vignolo tried a different angle of approach and could almost touch the table, but then he noticed the empty stool across from him. He looked up and saw Stephanos coming around the table, wielding a solid length of iron. He knocked people aside like he was beating chaff from wheat. The big Saracen was a step behind.

Vignolo realized this little ruckus was about to get sorted out. Promptly. And when it did, it would be best if he were not around.

Once again, it was time to go.

Vignolo weaved his way to the door. He stepped outside and took a moment to straighten his shirt and tuck it back into his breeches. Not because he was excessively rumpled, but because he was blinded; the afternoon sun was high in the sky. How long had he been at the Frolicking Eunuch?

The den was on the edge of the Venetian quarter, far enough from the Genoan slums to not scare off the odd noble, but close enough to the seedy areas of the harbor to pull in dock workers with fresh silver bits in their purses.

Squinting, Vignolo turned right and headed down the busiest street he could see. He did not run, as that was a sure way to draw attention and make himself memorable. Instead, he set off at a pace of leisure. It was another mistake.

"Vignoli!"

His eyes wide, Vignolo turned to see Giacomo striding toward him. His face was twisted with rage. It glistened with sweat and his hair looked stringier than ever. Blood had painted one side of his shirt a bright crimson. He lifted his fist and pointed it at Vignolo, the glint of steel reflecting between his fingers. In his other hand he had his sword drawn.

How had he managed to untangle himself from the mob at the Frolicking Eunuch so quickly? He had the feeling Giacomo would love to show him first-hand exactly how he did it... *if* he caught him.

Vignolo turned around and sprinted up the street. He took the first side street and then ducked down another even smaller pathway, hoping it did not suddenly end. He snatched a black robe hanging out a window as he ran past. He checked over his shoulder once, and to his horror, Giacomo was gaining on him. There were not many people in the streets, and those that were, leapt out of Giacomo's way when they saw him coming sword in hand.

The pathway poured Vignolo out into another main street, and up ahead was the domed shape of a mosque. He decided to put on the robe and hide in the mosque. It was not prayer time, so there would not be many people in there, but maybe it would work. He kept moving, pulling the robe over his head as he made his way down the street. He stood on the steps leading up to the entrance and realized the robe he had stolen belonged to a child. Its hem did not go past his knees. He stared down at his suede boots and knew he was not going to fool anyone. Frantically, he looked around.

Across the street was a public bath. Unlike the mosque, the hamam was most likely crowded right now. Vignolo dashed across the way, moving as quickly as he could in the tight robe. It was beginning to choke him, but he had no time to squirm out of it just yet. He glanced back the way he had come, expecting to see a sword-wielding figure hacking its way through the crowd, but so far so good. He ducked through the curtained doorway of the hamam and almost bounced off the chest of the biggest eunuch he had ever seen. A real eunuch, not some gambling den Greek.

Not surprised in the least, the almost naked man reached out a hand with cucumber-sized fingers and pushed Vignolo back. The only clothing he wore was a wrap around his waist that criss-crossed over itself and protected the world from viewing private parts that Vignolo was pretty sure were not even there. Thrust into that meager band of material was a huge, wide-bladed falchion. At first, his hand rested on the hilt, but then, once he had a good look at the Genoan, he crossed his arms over his chest. Steam from the baths in the next room wafted over the two men and Vignolo found himself sweating.

"You come for the bath?" The eunuch's voice was surprisingly deep.

"Yes. Yes, of course," Vignolo said. His hand fought its way inside his stolen robe and produced his depleted purse. The eunuch nodded toward a metal lock box strapped to the wall. Vignolo stepped over and dropped in a coin. He pulled out one more coin and then threw the purse to the eunuch. He caught it and one eye widened.

"That, my friend, is for you," Vignolo said.

"For what?"

"A little privacy. I come to the hamam to get away from my fellow Franks. Until I am done, the baths are closed to any other Frank that should enter." Strictly speaking, neither Vignolo nor Giacomo were Franks, but Vignolo knew that most Egyptians and Arabs could not be bothered to differentiate one barbarian from another.

"You forgot one," the eunuch said, pointing at the coin in Vignolo's hand.

"Come, now. This is for my scrubber. I would not have her beauty go unrewarded." Vignolo's smile faded as the eunuch took a much smaller coin out of the purse, put it in his hand, and made Vignolo exchange it for the coin he held.

"All right. You drive a hard bargain. But remember: no Franks."

The eunuch nodded. He pulled on a long cord that hung from the ceiling and Vignolo thought he heard a bell go off in another room. A moment later, a door slid open and a man who could have been the shorter, fatter brother of the eunuch appeared. He too was naked save for the middle wrap, and he held a bucket with an assortment of brushes and sponges sticking out.

"What is this?" Vignolo asked.

The eunuch shrugged. "He is all you can afford."

The fat, little man gave Vignolo a slight bow of his head. Vignolo opened his mouth to argue his case, but the eunuch was right. What little coin he had left from the Hospitaller contract was sitting on Stephanos's hazard table. He was now completely broke. Who knew the next time he would be able to afford a bath?

He gave the eunuch a resigned slap on the shoulder and followed his scrubber into the steam.

CHAPTER FIFTEEN

T HE HOSPITALLER FORTRESS was walled off from the rest of the city. A heavy iron portcullis was lowered over its gate every evening and raised at first light. Not far inside the gate was the *domus infirmorum*, Acre's large hospital that the knights referred to as the *Palace of the Sick*. Built upon an old Islamic inn that had once catered to merchants and other travelers, the *Palace* consisted of six parallel halls that opened onto a sunlit courtyard. It contained over one thousand beds, with one of the halls devoted to providing shelter to pilgrims traveling the Holy Land, and another reserved exclusively for treating the ailments of upper class patients. Surgeons and physicians were housed in another one of the halls. Some were members of the Order, others were hired for their particular skill sets. The surgeons were called *practici,* and were not as highly regarded as the physicians, the *theorici,* who were more knowledgeable in the areas of diet and herbal medicines. When the knights went on extended campaigns where there was a risk of a large battle, they would always take with them one or more of the 'practical men', the surgeons, to see to their wounded.

A narrow road led from the Hospital to the main keep, where the higher-ranking members of the Order lived and where business was conducted. Behind the keep were stables, a small church, and living quarters surrounding a large courtyard used for training the knights and men-at-arms in hand-to-hand combat. Near the stables was a riding ground long enough to practice cavalry charges and lance work, but it was too small to be useful for a large group. Therefore, every morning, after the church service of Matins, a detachment of Hospitaller knights and sergeants would lead their destriers out of the compound, down the hard-packed city streets of Acre, and through the Gate of Saint Anthony to drill out in the open, before the heat of the sun became unbearable.

Thomas awoke to the sound of a horn followed by the thunder of horses' hooves. The earth beneath him shook and he sat up to a flurry of activity all around him. A column of horsemen trotted into the courtyard. Riding four abreast, they did not slow their pace nor seem the least bit concerned that three hundred children slumbered on the ground in front of their destriers' pawing feet. Thomas was still wiping the sleep from his eyes when Pirmin pulled him to his feet.

"Time to rise, Thomi," he said and hastily threw their few belongings into his cart, the one that had once been pulled by his dog, Zora. Pirmin grabbed the wooden poles of the cart and pulled it behind him as he shouted at the younger boy to follow him. The children had spent a fitful night in the courtyard. Though Thomas was exhausted from the long journey, he slept little because of the suffocating, stagnant heat and the sounds and smells of the city that managed to permeate even the thick walls of the Hospitaller fortress.

The horsemen rode through the mass of scrambling boys, bringing to them the unmistakable smell of horse, man, leather and steel that had become their new life. The horses disappeared around the side of the keep, but the echo of their hooves was still in the air when the boys were set upon by dozens of monks wearing simple brown robes with the white cross of the Hospitallers of Saint John on their sleeves. They herded the children into a semblance of order and marched them to the far end of the courtyard where a long line of tables stood. Nuns clad all in black stood behind the tables with their heads bowed. The children were forced to their knees and a thick monk with prematurely white hair stepped up onto a low platform. He bowed his head and started speaking.

Thomas stared at the man's white hair until another man cuffed the back of his head. The cut on his face started throbbing and he turned to look behind him, but the monk grabbed a handful of his hair and pushed his chin toward his chest.

After the simple prayer, the monks efficiently moved the children through the nuns' tables where each child was forced to drink a full ladle of watered-down wine before being given steaming porridge scooped onto a crusty bread trencher.

The nuns and monks were calm and organized in their efforts, but discipline was strictly enforced, usually, by one of the many men-at-arms in the area. When one of the boys in front of Thomas and Pirmin refused to drink the wine-water, the nun holding the ladle shook her head and held up her hand. Seconds later a man-at-arms appeared wearing a brown surcoat with a large cross on the chest and a sword at his side. He glanced questioningly at the nun, who motioned at the ladle and the boy.

The man said something to the boy in French. When the boy did not answer, he repeated himself louder and grabbed the ladle from the nun. The boy glanced nervously around, unable to comprehend what the man was saying. Finally, the man seized the boy by the back of his neck and pushed him to his knees. He pulled back his head and force-fed him the ladle of water, while the boy coughed and sputtered, and then roughly pushed him in front of the nun again. The nun handed the boy his trencher full of porridge and ushered him along.

The event had frightened Thomas and he stepped in close behind Pirmin, his face almost buried in the small of the back of the bigger boy. Pirmin stumbled and looked back to see the small boy glance up at him sheepishly. Pirmin had not spoken much since the slaver had killed Zora, but something in Thomas's frightened look made him smile and set aside his own grief for the time being.

He put a hand on his friend's shoulder and said, "Do not worry, Thomi. Just do what I do and all will be well."

Thomas nodded eagerly. When the nun handed him his porridge and he said 'thank you' in an awkward attempt to copy Pirmin's sing-song Wallis accent, Pirmin laughed so hard he had to spit out a mouthful of half-chewed food, an action that earned him a slap across the cheek and an unintelligible lecture from one of the monks standing nearby.

After finishing their simple meal, the boys were lined up in a square formation and made to sit on the ground in the center of the courtyard. Soon, an older man with a bushy gray-black beard and an elaborate black robe with wide sleeves and white trim made his way to the low platform in their midst. A large silver cross hung on a chain around his neck and two black knights walked on either side, a step behind. Without preamble, he began to speak in high German. Though he did not seem to speak loudly, his clear voice carried to every corner of the large courtyard.

"Welcome children. Our Lord in Heaven has seen fit to deliver you upon us in our hour of need. Every one of you has talent of some sort, and it has fallen upon us, as your guardians, to uncover that talent and put it to work for the glory of God. Do not forget that it was God's ways that brought us together, and the future of your souls depends on how diligently you approach your new callings. Along with your new life, you have all been granted a new family name. Your Christian names shall remain the same, but from this day forward you will all be known as Schwyzer, the ones from Schwyz. Wear the name proudly and look after one another, for you are all brothers now."

Without any further closing remarks, he spun on his heel and set off toward the keep, the two black knights struggling to keep up.

The direct manner in which the man had spoken made Thomas think of the neat-bearded black knight with the fierce blue eyes who had led them on their long journey to this place. He glanced around for the man but he was nowhere to be seen. In fact, Thomas had not seen him since their arrival at the fortress the previous day.

The rest of the day was a competition of sorts. The monks, men-at-arms, and a few of the black knights put the children through all manner of tests. They pitted them against one another in foot races, wrestling matches, balancing drills, and feats of strength. At one station the children were even required to trace letters using ink and quill, which brought peals of laughter from one another as the monks looked on with stern expressions. At every station a brown-robed monk tabulated the results on sheets of parchment.

At the close of the day, the mass of children bedded down once again in the courtyard, and this time the heat and city noises seemed less noticeable. Thomas lay awake listening to Pirmin and the other boys complaining about everyone being given Schwyzer as a last name.

"I do not care what those monks scratch in their books. I am born of Tasch, not Schwyz! My name's Pirmin Schnidrig and that is that."

A thick boy with small eyes, named Maximilian, agreed with Pirmin. "You have that right. My father would whip me if I gave up my family name so easily."

"I doubt that," another boy said. "He is the one that gave you away, so I think it safe to say he does not care one way or another what you go about calling yourself now."

"Shut your *fae*," Pirmin said, his words coming quick and angry. "No one wanted to give any of us away. It was a hard choice. My Papi did what he had to for the family, and I would wager yours did no different. Quit feeling sorry for yourself."

The boy grunted, but he did not risk making Pirmin angrier with a response.

Schwyzer. Thomas Schwyzer.

In the darkness, Thomas whispered his new name to himself a few times. He did not understand all the fuss. It sounded like a fine name to him.

CHAPTER SIXTEEN

F OULQUES ROSE BEFORE dawn, eager to return to the life he had known before he had been sent on his journey to the Alps. His day began with a morning prayer, kneeling at the edge of his sleeping pallet, before he even donned his lightweight black robe. He wore no mail underneath the thin fabric, and he had spent so much time in his armor of late, that he had a difficult time leaving his room without it. Feeling half-naked and more than a little uncoordinated, he made his way to the church for the daybreak service of Matins. The church was not large enough to accommodate both knights and sergeants at one time, so the knights entered first, while the sergeants waited outside.

A peace washed over Foulques as he stepped inside the church with his fellow knights. He had never thought he would have missed services so much, but it felt surprisingly good to kneel in prayer with the other knights in the humble church of the Hospitallers of Jerusalem. His mood was buoyant when he exited the service and passed the sergeants still awaiting their turn. As with the church, the knights were also the first to sit down in the covered mess area to eat their breakfast. It was a simple, yet hardy fare of porridge, eggs, and cheese, with a cup of watered-down wine. Foulques finished his breakfast and again walked past the long line of sergeants waiting their turn, although, in this case, they craned their necks and shuffled impatiently. It would seem that breaking their fast held more appeal to many of these men than devotion did. After them, any hired mercenaries would be allowed to eat, and finally, the monks and nuns of the Order. All other souls in the compound would gather for what was left.

Foulques hurried back to his room immediately after breakfast. The sun was out and it promised to be a hot, early fall day. He had volunteered for patrol duties this morning and had been assigned to a small group of knights and sergeants, who were to be led by his good friend Alain. He did not know their destination, or their purpose, but that did not matter. It was enough to know he was once again doing God's work.

He mentally planned his wardrobe as he walked, so when he reached his room a few minutes later, he was able to remove his robe and begin to dress for the road.

First, he donned a clean pair of bries to cover his nakedness. He pulled their drawstring about his waist and then strapped quilted chausses to his legs. Next, he put on his quilted gambeson to both protect his upper body and to provide some padding between his mail and bare skin.

Then came the steel. He set his mail on the table to arrange it, thrust his hands into the arm holes, and lifted the entire suit above his head. It fell over his shoulders and he wiggled it down his body with ease. Foulques had worn this particular hauberk for years and the small metal rings allowed the steel shirt to mold tightly around his frame. It extended down to just above his knees, so to relieve his shoulders of some of the armor's weight, for the mail itself weighed close to thirty pounds, he strapped a wide belt around his waist and pulled a bit of the mail up over its top. Immediately, the weight of the armor was gone.

He swung his arms and twisted his hips a few times to make sure he had complete freedom of movement. Satisfied, he shrugged into a loose, black surcoat with the large white cross of the Order emblazoned in the middle of his chest. If he did not cover his mail, the sun would soon have it radiating an unbearable amount of heat. But covered, the cold metal of the mail would actually pull the heat of his body through his gambeson and keep him relatively comfortable.

He put on his sword belt next and slipped his rondel dagger onto it, pulling and testing the blade's sharp, diamond-profiled point before committing it to the ensemble. Finally, he placed a padded arming cap on his head and pulled up the hood of his mail. To keep both himself and the metal of his hood from overheating, he wrapped his head in a close-fitting, white turban. Many preferred to use a hat with a cloth attached under it that draped down to their shoulders, but Foulques had always preferred the turban, as it tended to stay on better when riding or fighting.

Again, he tested his movements in every direction. He

drew each weapon a number of times and made small adjustments to his sword belt. When he was ready, he marched out into the scorching sun of the Holy Lands, the contented smile on his face more than a match for its light.

When he arrived at the stable, a handful of brother-sergeants were already milling about polishing tack and saddling mounts. To his surprise, Kenneth already had Donovan out of his stall and saddled. This was strange, as Kenneth knew Foulques preferred to saddle his destrier himself.

"Good morning, Kenneth," Foulques said as he approached. The groom tied Donovan's lead line to a hitching post and returned the knight's greeting, but his face cringed. It was then that Foulques noticed it was not his own saddle that sat on Donovan's back.

"Whose tack is that?" Foulques asked.

"That would be mine," an approaching voice said. Foulques turned to see Everet de Blois, a heavy, well-built knight from one of the most powerful families in Auvergne approach. "Welcome home, Brother Foulques."

Foulques gave a curt bow of his head. "Brother Everet. I am told it is you I should thank for keeping Donovan in such fine shape."

Everet walked past Foulques straight to Donovan and ran his hand along his shoulder, then patted his neck a couple of times before turning back to Foulques. "He is a splendid animal. I have never ridden a more responsive beast."

"Again, I thank you," Foulques said. He nodded to Everet's saddle. "Where would you like Kenneth to put your saddle?"

"Oh," Everet said, "This is quite awkward. Did he not tell you? I will be riding Donovan from now on. I am told the Grande Cross has officially removed your rank so you no longer get to choose your mount. I, on the other hand, do. And a beast like Donovan deserves to carry the best man." He smiled and cocked his head to the side. "Kenneth, pick out Brother Foulques a nice mare for his first outing back."

Technically, Everet was right. He was a Knight Justice and now outranked Foulques. Wordlessly, Foulques nodded. He turned his back and took a few steps away from Everet and Kenneth, who visibly squirmed in discomfort. With his back to the men, Foulques slowly drew his sword. He turned back and rested the point lightly on the ground, folding his hands atop one another casually on its pommel.

"You are right, Brother Everet. Donovan does deserve to carry the best man and there is only one way to find out which one of us that is. So, to first blood then. Where do we do this? Here, in the stables, or outside, where all may watch?"

Everet paled. His eyes dropped to Foulques's sword and then came up again. "You would fight me? Over a horse?"

"I can think of no better reason," Foulques said. "But do not think I do it for myself. I do it for Donovan's sake."

Everet's face went from pale to red in the beat of a second. He raised a finger and pointed it at Foulques. "Do not think this is over. The Turocopolier will hear of this."

"Like you, I am sure the Horse Master will only want

what is best for his destrier. Although, I imagine he will suggest we tilt lances at one another, instead of swords."

"We will see," Everet said, spitting out the words. His neck and jaw quivered but his eyes could not find the courage to meet with Foulques's own. He spun on his heel and was gone before Foulques could respond. A few seconds later, Kenneth was bent over in laughter. Even Foulques could not keep the smile off his face as he removed Everet's saddle and began brushing Donovan down.

"Tell Brother Alain that I will meet him outside the city gates. I would like to take Donovan for a short ride to warm him up for today's patrol," Foulques said. After walking all the way back from the end of the world, he could not wait another moment to climb into his destrier's saddle.

Kenneth promised he would give Alain his message and long minutes later, Foulques was mounted and trotting through the gatehouse of the Hospitaller compound into the city of Acre. With his lance's sharp tip pointing toward Heaven and its butt end resting on his right boot, Foulques urged Donovan into a trot. He savored the clip-clopping of his horse's hooves as the sound echoed off the stone buildings pressed up tight along the narrow road leading up to the Gate of Saint Anthony. The city watch's guards stepped aside and saluted as the Hospitaller knight passed through the first wall. At the second, thicker wall, a group of merchants were lined up waiting to be admitted. The guards pushed them and their beasts of burden to the side of the path and motioned Foulques on. He passed into the cool darkness under the archway of the twenty-foot-thick main gate and, seconds later, emerged into the wide open expanse of red rock and soil that marked the outer boundaries of the city of Acre.

The sun hit him face-on and the scents of humanity fled back into the city behind him. Unable to resist the call of the hard-packed road ahead, Foulques spurred Donovan into a gallop. Once past the featureless killing grounds in front of the city walls, he veered off the main road onto a narrow, softer path that weaved between fields of lentils and other crops he could not recognize in their unprepared form. He knew little of the magic that allowed these fields to flourish in such a seemingly hostile environment. He recalled someone saying the plants drew their life in part from an underground spring, the same one that provided the city with its stable water supply. The truth of the matter was, he did not care. He was no farmer; he was a knight.

With a flick of his boot, he brought his lance up and leveled it parallel with the ground. He hunched forward, urging Donovan on, and couched the wooden shaft tightly under his arm. He felt Donovan respond beneath him, picking up speed until he was at full gallop. Foulques had no target, but it did not matter. The wind blurred his vision and water leaked from the corners of his eyes, but he could not be happier. This was where he belonged, not on a pot-bellied merchant ship bobbing over the waters of the Mid-Earth Sea.

He was a knight of the Kingdom of Jerusalem, put on this earth to protect its citizens from any that would do them harm. He may not be a Knight Justice any longer, but that meant little to Foulques. He had never asked for the title in the first place and was quite sure he would not miss it now that it was gone. Titles were given by men, but true callings were handed out only by God.

He raised his lance and reined in Donovan at the same time. With his knees, he commanded his destrier to raise up on his hind legs and lash out with his iron-shod fronts. Then he brought him down on all fours and made him kick to the rear. Donovan grew more energized with each move, so Foulques put him through a few more. Then he turned him back toward the walls and put him into a gallop once again. He gave him full rein, however, and let Donovan dictate the pace all the way back to the Hospitallers' usual muster point. Alain would be along shortly, and Foulques—and it seemed Donovan as well—was eager to get on with the day's mission.

CHAPTER SEVENTEEN

FOULQUES SAT ATOP Donovan at the muster point just outside the walls of Acre. The ground here was worn flatter and harder than anywhere else in the vicinity, but the real reason that it had become the chosen spot to gather, was the low-lying rocky ridge in the near distance. It was high enough to block out the morning sun and provide shade for a force of virtually any size, from a few merchants to an army, thousands strong. Over the past two hundred years, it had served both purposes many times over.

A force of a dozen knights under the direction of Everet de Blois was the first to exit Acre. He made a point of ignoring both Foulques and Donovan as he passed, but the dust cloud that followed him did not. Foulques coughed a couple of times and he reached for the blood cloth tucked into his belt to hold up in front of his nose and mouth, but he did not mind. Debris kicked up by horses' hooves was just one more welcome reminder that he was a long way from being on a ship at sea. If he could have his way, he would choose to never be more than a day or two's ride, not sail, from Acre ever again.

A few minutes later, Alain appeared at the head of a small cluster of men made up of only three sergeants of the Order. Foulques's heart sank a little at the unimpressive force, but he reminded himself to be thankful that he was once again going out on patrol.

As Alain approached, Foulques saw a grim look on his face, which was uncharacteristic of the peace-loving knight who had almost become a priest. Foulques assumed he felt awkward leading a force where his former commanding officer was now just one of the men, but when he pulled his horse up alongside Foulques and commanded the sergeants to go on ahead, Foulques knew there was something more.

"What is it?" Foulques asked.

"You do not know where we are headed, do you?"

"Does it matter? We are finally home. With all the roads of the Kingdom calling our names, I do not care which one we take first."

"Foulques. Our destination is Dunhal."

Dunhal. It was a name Foulques had not heard for many years. Mostly because people avoided using it in his presence. At least those who knew him from the days of his childhood, or who were old enough to remember his mother and father.

"If you left now, you could easily catch up with Brother Everet's patrol..." Alain said, looking down at the ground.

Foulques decided the best course of action was to not give himself time to ponder the past. "No. I have avoided Dunhal for enough years. Today is as good as any to remedy that. What is our cause?"

Alain looked at him questioningly, but for only a moment. He must have sensed Foulques's determination. He knew Foulques better than anyone, and Foulques found himself thankful that Alain did not press him further, nor did he hold back the details of their mission. "Bodies have been found on the road," Alain said.

"Near the oasis?"

Alain nodded, and he let out a breath as he leaned one arm over the hump on the front of his saddle.

"We are to investigate and report back. Nothing more. It is most likely the result of an argument gone wrong among merchants."

Dunhal was a small, walled village on the eastern edge of the Frankish controlled Kingdom of Jerusalem. The border had once extended far past the village, but as the Christian territory contracted and the Frankish armies grew smaller, the desert dwellers had moved back into the area. The village was built near an oasis that the local Bedouin tribe had claimed ownership over, but while the Christian presence was strong in the area, they had all but disappeared. Twenty-some years ago, however, they returned, swooping in from the Syrian sands on their white desert steeds. They laid claim, once again, to the nearby water source and proceeded to terrorize the inhabitants of Dunhal, laying waste to much of the town, killing many of its inhabitants, defiling its church, and crucifying its priest. The same priest that had almost baptized Foulques. The church had never been rebuilt.

"Are you sure?" Alain asked. "No one will ask a single

question if you return to the compound."

Foulques gave his friend a direct stare. He responded by reining Donovan around to point toward the sergeants receding into the distance, then whipped his horse across either side of his neck with the reins. Donovan sprang ahead into a full gallop, leaving Alain behind in a cloud of dust and pebbles.

They took their time on the road, for the horses' sake, in case their strength was needed. They were headed inland and the further they went away from the fertile fields along the coast, the more powerful the sun felt. As the morning wore into early afternoon, the desolate pre-desert landscape suddenly gave way to a low cluster of trees in the distance.

At the first sight of the oasis, Foulques felt the palms of his hands begin to sweat. It became so bad he had to pull off his gloves.

"Keep your eyes open, everyone," Alain said. Without being told, Foulques and the three sergeants pulled their horses up in line with Alain's. The road itself was narrow and there were rolling hills on either side beginning twenty yards away, but the immediate ground was flat and hard with enough room for all of them to ride side by side.

"I do not see any carrion eaters," Foulques said, squinting and looking up at the cloudless sky.

"That is because they have landed," Jean, one of the sergeants said. "Look," he pointed to the left side of the road ahead. Something moved, a shimmer, that at first Foulques took to be a trick of the heat. Then the vulture spread its wings and others moved nearby.

"Stay together," Alain said, just as Foulques was about to spur his mount ahead. It was all he could do to keep from heeling his horse into action. Donovan sensed it as well, for he stutter stepped to the side and Foulques had to rein him back into formation.

The horses would not get close to the bodies, so Foulques and Alain dismounted and told the sergeants to keep guard. The stench watered Foulques's eyes and once again he reached for his blood cloth. There were three bodies: an older man, and two younger ones. They were Arabs, and by their turbans and mode of dress, Foulques suspected Alain may have been right after all—they had the look of merchants. He could tell very little else about them for they had been cut up so badly, the vultures were having an easy time feeding on their entrails. He kicked at one of the birds and sent it squawking.

"There may be more at the oasis," Alain said.

Foulques suddenly was no longer bothered by the heat. He nodded and returned to his horse. They rode slowly, their eyes constantly roaming the low, nearby hills. Foulques saw a smear of blood on the road from one of the men. He had run from his attackers, fallen on the road, managed to get to his feet again but had been cut down with the other two shortly after.

Is that how it had happened with his father? No one ever talked about him. The stories were always about his mother's bravery. Her sacrifice.

They rode into the coolness of the oasis, where several fig trees and a few palms provided shade. The pool itself was little more than a watering hole five feet in diameter, but out here, on the edge of the desert, it was the difference between life and death.

There were several more bodies, hacked into pieces and piled on top of one another in such a haphazard fashion it was hard to tell where one began and another ended, or which arm belonged to which torso. The men stared in silence for a time. Alain mouthed a prayer and crossed himself several times.

"This was no merchant quarrel," Alain said. "They dragged the bodies well back from the water to preserve its purity."

Foulques was not listening. He stared at the pile of body parts. He thought he could make out two women in the mix. Alain said something to the sergeants about burying the bodies.

"Bury them?" Jean said. "They are all Mohammedans. I will not waste my sweat on sinners!"

"They are people," Foulques said, snapping out of his trance. He nudged Donovan to bring him up against Jean's mount. "People, who wanted nothing more than a drink of water. No god would call that a sin."

The other two sergeants cast nervous glances at Foulques, then Alain appeared at Foulques's side and put a hand on his shoulder. "We will bury them, Foulques. You go back to the road and keep a lookout." When Foulques continued to stare at Jean, Alain repeated himself with a little more authority in his voice. Foulques backed Donovan up a few steps and then wheeled him around toward the road, away from the pile of rotting body parts. He fought the impulse to look back.

Foulques stopped his horse near the blood trail of the man who had tried to flee. He had been told a similar trail over rock and sand had led to the discovery of his mother's body. Foulques looked back toward the oasis and wondered which tree was hers. She had been found beneath one of the figs, her body draped protectively over a silent, but still very much alive, baby less than four months old. His mother had been mortally wounded near the water. Presumably, after her attackers had left the area, she crawled to the tree where she had hidden Foulques from the raiders. According to his Uncle Guillaume, she had nursed her infant son one last time before dying, and it was that nourishment, and God's good grace, that sustained Foulques until his uncle found him much later.

Guillaume's brother had fallen in love with the daughter of a maid and a house slave. When she became pregnant they tried to marry, but, of course, the Villaret family had informed all the churches that such a union would not be condoned by the head of the Villaret household. Without the noble family's blessing, the young couple had no hope of ever being wed. At least, not by any church in Acre.

Foulques found himself coughing as dust settled around him. He reached for the cloth at his belt and simultaneously looked to the sky. His hand froze in place. There were no clouds and no wind, at least nothing capable of stirring up plumes of sand.

Behind the hills on either side of the road, dust billowed

up and the fine grains of sand kicked into the air glittered like shavings of gold. By the time the first black turban appeared, Foulques was already galloping toward the oasis. He did not bother to shout or sound his horn, for he had no doubt the thundering of Donovan's massive hooves over the hard ground would alert the others. He kept his eyes on his destination but his peripheral vision saw man after man crest the hilltops all around him. By the time he made it near the oasis, Alain and the sergeants were well aware of the danger and had already formed a shield square amongst the trees. Foulques pulled up just shy of the Hospitallers' location, debated joining them for a moment, and then decided against it. Once on the ground, he knew his options would be limited. Instead, he directed Donovan to face so he could watch both hillsides at once. He balanced the bottom of his lance on his boot and waited.

The desert dwellers, too, seemed content to wait. Dressed all in black, they remained on the high ground atop their lithe, white Arabians. Foulques estimated their number to be at least fifty. Perhaps more, but at that count it did not matter.

"Hold this position," Alain called out. "They cannot charge us in the trees. And if they come at us on foot, God help us, they will pay dearly."

Foulques slowly turned Donovan in a complete circle, trying to identify their leader, but it was an impossible task for their faces were covered and their dust-ridden desert cloaks were all faded to the same degree. A high-pitched trilling sound began in the throat of one man far down the line, and one by one, the others picked up the cry, sending a deafening wave across the hilltops.

"Foulques! Dismount and join us here," Alain shouted, his voice barely audible above those of the desert dwellers.

Foulques scanned the enemy, wondering which one would break toward them first. Their cries grew louder and they began drawing scimitars and hefting spears high into the air. And then, from amongst the middle of the line, one warrior detached himself from the main host and began bounding down the hillside. He held a long spear in his right hand and gripped the reins of his white horse with his left. Foulques did not think it possible, but the cries almost doubled in volume as the rider forced his mount down the hillside at breakneck speed, his front hooves sinking deep into the sand with every leap. Foulques could not help but admire the beautiful display of horsemanship as horse and rider fought their way down the slope together. They hit level ground with a landslide of rocks and sand nipping at their heels and, without a moment of hesitation, the raider couched his spear under his arm and pointed his mount toward the small band of Hospitallers.

"Do not do it, Foulques!"

Alain's voice was a distant murmur in Foulques's ears as he flipped his lance into position and kicked Donovan into action. The raider was an exceptional horseman, as Foulques had already seen, but he was no master of the lance. His spear jostled erratically as his horse pounded across the open ground. Foulques's own lance bounced three times, until he had its iron point centered over the raider's heart, and then it did not move again. At some point, the raider realized this was no ordinary opponent he faced and he lost his nerve. He leaned over to his horse's left side in an attempt to evade the unerring lance flying toward him. Foulques saw him move and he made a minute correction with his body to lower his target. His lance caught the raider on his right hip, with Foulques hanging on just long enough to hit the man with Donovan's full weight behind the thrust. The lance shattered into a thousand pieces, but before it gave in, it ripped both saddle and rider from the Arabian's back. The raider was stretched parallel to the ground and spun in place like a floating stick caught in the white waters of a raging river. His horse flew past beneath him and veered away into the desert beyond. Foulques struggled to bring Donovan to a halt, and when he had him under control he drew his sword. He saw the broken and bloodied body of the raider lying twisted amongst the rocks and knew he was dead.

He turned back toward the larger group of raiders, determined to stand his place and wait for whatever was to come. The desert dwellers remained on top of the hills, still making their high-pitched calls, though the intensity had died off since Foulques had unhorsed one of them.

A hand raised at the far end of the hill and the desert went silent. Foulques now realized he had his answer as to who was the leader. The Bedouin coaxed his horse down the hill in a much more sedate version of the man Foulques had just battled, and one by one, all of the desert dwellers fell in line behind him. The leader led the procession in a slow trot to within twenty paces of Foulques and then carried right on by, contemptuously showing his back to the Hospitaller. As each man followed suit, he locked hard eyes on Foulques. Some made foul gestures at the knight, some swung their scimitars in threatening arcs, but no one strayed from their line. Minutes later, the entire raiding party of Bedouin disappeared behind the dunes.

Foulques's heart was still hammering when he arrived back at Alain's location. Jean and the other sergeants hooted and welcomed him back.

"Well done!" Jean said. "The pagans will think twice before they come back here."

Foulques dismounted to congratulatory slaps on the back, which he shrugged off. The sergeants gave him some room, assuming he was still in the same foul mood as before. Alain, however, shared none of the enthusiasm of the sergeants. Foulques caught his eye. Both men knew they had won nothing here today. In fact, Foulques was sure the Kingdom of Jerusalem had just become a bit smaller. The desert dwellers would be back and they wanted the Franks to know that. Foulques had read it in their eyes. Why else had they let them all live?

The village of Dunhal, and its oasis, had been reclaimed by the desert. Foulques suspected neither he, nor any other Christian, would ever return here again.

CHAPTER EIGHTEEN

EARLY MORNING WAS the best time for martial training, as the sun had not yet risen over the city and the stone walls of the Hospitaller compound still held in the coolness of the night before. Foulques had joined a motley group of brother sergeants for their exercises after morning service. Many of the ordained Black Knights avoided practicing with their brown-robed brethren. The most common excuse was they lacked the classical training of the noble-born knights and if you sparred with them too often you would pick up poor habits. Foulques, on the other hand, relished his sessions with the sergeants. He saw it as a chance to pit his years of training against an assortment of unorthodox, and often unpredictable, fighting styles.

The sergeants were a rough lot. Many of them had been professional soldiers before their calling, others had fled into the Order from a life of crime. The Hospitallers did not judge a man's past life if he was willing to take the vows, but discipline was harsh, and any man that did not fulfill his new duties would take his turn bound to the whipping post in the square, or worse, the gallows. Although, the latter was infrequent, as it was a better use of resources to simply post the troublemaker to a hostile area that saw frequent clashes with the enemy and let God be the ultimate judge. In return for pledging their lives to the Order, new brothers and sisters were granted absolution for their past sins, a fresh start for their soul. That was the great attraction for most. For others, a safe place to sleep and two good meals a day, which frequently included meat, was enough.

Foulques knew most of the sergeants well, and they him. A few of the older sergeants had been sparring with Foulques for almost twenty years. His Uncle Guillaume had entrusted much of his upbringing to these men. Foulques did not know whether that was because he saw value in it, or simply because he was too busy to raise his brother's orphan on his own.

Foulques held a shield in one hand and his double-edged, hand-and-a-half blade in the other. It was light enough to be wielded in one hand, yet the hilt was of a length that one could get a second hand on the pommel to deliver devastating two-armed attacks if needed. A gift from his uncle on the day Foulques was knighted, the sword had been in the Villaret family for eighty years, yet it still gleamed like it was fresh from the master swordsmith's final polish.

The sergeant he faced, an Englishman named Roderic, stood across from him similarly armed, except he used a practice sword rather than risk his own weapon. Perhaps Foulques should have been using a practice blade as well, but he preferred to train with the weapon he would use in the field. And his sword was so well crafted that, other than the odd nick to whetstone out, Foulques was not worried about damaging it.

Rod had been a member of Longshanks's palace guards. Serving in the English king's own household was a coveted position. No one knew why Rod had given it all up to join the Hospitallers three years ago. As with many of the men, it was a personal choice that few chose to talk about.

The men circled each other warily, launching cautious attacks against one another. Around them, other sergeants did the same. Each pair fought until a killing blow was delivered and then they would change partners. The loser of each contest would sit on the ground, gradually forming a large circle around the remaining combatants. Eventually, only two would remain and the rest of the men would cheer them on.

Rod was a decent swordsman, but his arms had grown heavy. Foulques swung at his head to see how fast he could lift his shield. He blocked the blow easily but his shield came up slower than the last time. He was conserving energy.

Foulques began to see openings during each exchange. He could have ended it on several occasions, but then Rod would have to sit down and Foulques's own training would be finished until a new opponent was ready for him. Since that would have been a wasted opportunity for improvement, Foulques continued to work his partner relentlessly, until, from the corner of his eye, he could see a man waiting for a challenger. Foulques feinted a slash to Rod's knee and then finished him with a downward cut to the side of his neck, halting his blade just as it came to rest on Rod's mail hauberk.

Rod's hair was slicked back with sweat as he bowed to Foulques and then plopped himself down on the ground. With his legs stretched out in front, he propped himself up by leaning back on his hands and sucked in great mouthfuls of air.

Foulques's next opponent was a wiry, high strung, young man from Pisa, a baker's son. His name escaped Foulques and he did not have a moment to think about it, for the man charged him with a flurry of thrusts and slashes. Foulques was a little winded himself from his last bout. Instead of dragging this one out, he swatted one of the Pisan brother's thrusts aside and ran his own blade down the man's sword until it poked him in the center of his chest. Even though he wore mail, Foulques had to pull his sword back quickly so the man's unchecked forward momentum did not have him impaled on Foulques's keen blade.

Foulques fought three more times. For the final match, the man he looked across the circle at, to his surprise, was a man he knew only too well. A countryman of Rod's, Horace James Godhyr, was a builder by trade, a master craftsman from Huntingdonshire. As broad at the shoulders as some men were long, he possessed amazing strength in his upper body and hands. He was known by more names than the Sultan of Egypt. 'Jimmy the Neckless' was the first one that came to Foulques as he looked at him. 'Jimmy the Mouth' followed shortly after.

Jimmy was, perhaps, the poorest natural swordsman

Foulques had ever seen. He personally knew a blind leper with missing fingers who was twice as skilled with a blade. As cliché as it was, however, Jimmy was a fair hand with a hammer. Although, his skill with that weapon paled in comparison to the strength of his tongue.

"Ah, Brother Flukes. We meet again," Jimmy said, in his gruff, seemingly quiet voice that somehow managed to carry over all others. He poured half a water skin over his head already drenched in sweat, and shook like a rabid dog. The circle of onlookers got a little wider.

"Brother Jimmy," Foulques said, giving him a nod. "I would like to say I am not surprised to see you still standing. But I try my best to live an honest life."

Jimmy grabbed another skin, this one filled with wine, and squeezed a lengthy squirt into his mouth. Red dribbled off his chin and ran down his beard still streaming with water. "Looking at you brings back some beautiful moments in my life. Seems like just yesterday I was walkin' through the French countryside banging my hammer over the heads of fancy *chevalier* like you." He twisted his mouth around the foreign French word giving his face a poisoned-to-death look. A couple of the sergeants hooted and laughed. Foulques tried to keep a straight face while Jimmy nodded in appreciation of his own linguistic ability.

"I suspect that was the only French word you had time to learn before you were chased from our lands. My English friends tell me you were always a good runner," Foulques said.

"Now that, *Bother* Foulques," Jimmy pinched the very

end of his war hammer's handle and, in an impressive display of muscle control, held it straight out to point the spike on top straight at Foulques, "was uncalled for."

Jimmy was born the son of a peasant carpenter, a trade which he eventually took up. Like everyone, he had no surname until King Edward started taxing the local populace man by man. To keep track of his taxpayers, the King decreed that any man that did not have a surname would be given one. Thus, Jimmy was dubbed James Builder by the shire clerk.

Jimmy had a fit. If he was going to get a new name he was damn well going to pick it himself. After a few days of careful deliberation, he barged into the clerk's office and forced him at knife-point to change the *Poll*, as the list was known. He heard a priest once talk about a Roman Emperor named Horace. He liked the sound of that one. But he got it in his head that a man such as himself should have at least three names. Jimmy had already begun to collect nicknames by that point in his life, and one that had stuck was 'Goodyear'. If asked where it came from, he would say it arose because of his optimistic view of the future. Those who knew him, however, said it was because he was always borrowing money, which he would be 'good for next year'. Wherever it came from, 'Goodyear Jimmy' officially became 'Horace James Godhyr Builder'. It is unclear whether the clerk misspelled Goodyear on purpose, or slipped with the quill out of fear for his life.

Apparently, the whole purpose of having a registered name escaped Jimmy, for he never once paid his Poll taxes.

Eventually, he was declared wolfs-head and forced to take to the road, and he was smart enough not to stop when he reached the ocean. When Goodyear Jimmy ran, not even old King Longshanks could catch him.

Foulques took a drink of water offered by a sergeant, rolled his shoulders a few times, and then set his blade across the top of his forearm to check for nicks.

"Come on now, Brother Flukes. Quit stalling. Time to meet your headache," Jimmy said, tapping the head of his hammer into his hand. The hammer was of the double-spiked variety, having six-inch diamond-shaped spikes on both the back side of the hammer head as well as on the top.

The two men saluted each other with an overly grand display of formality and Jimmy charged before Foulques had time to take his sword away from his forehead. He closed the distance much faster than a man his size should have been capable of, thrusting with his hammer like a spear. Foulques backpedaled a few steps, parrying one-handed with his blade, for his shield was still down at his side. At the edge of the circle, he moved around to his right side and brought up his shield as Jimmy swung a hard two-handed strike. With the sound of splitting wood, the spike on the back of the hammer penetrated the shield and popped out the underside mere inches away from Foulques's hand. Then, with a vicious jerk, Jimmy yanked on his hammer, pulling the shield from Foulques's grip. Foulques did not have his shield strap fastened about his forearm and when he felt it fly from his grip, he was thankful that he did not.

Knowing Jimmy would be vulnerable now with the

shield stuck on the end of his weapon, Foulques stepped forward to finish him off. But Jimmy, too, pushed forward trying to skewer Foulques with the spike sticking through the shield. Foulques was forced to parry and step aside to avoid a head-on encounter with a man much stronger than he was.

"Who is running now?" Jimmy said. He took the opportunity to put a foot on the shield and yank his hammer out. He twirled the weapon once and took up a high guard. He feinted, then began moving around to Foulques's left side.

"Speaking of running," Jimmy said, "I heard you had to do some of it yourself the other day. Seems like them slavers caught you with your breeches down around your ankles though, huh?"

Foulques knew Jimmy the Mouth was just trying to rile him, but he had come to this training session with the intention of forgetting about his failures for a time. Now he found part of his head back in that slavers' canyon. He tried to put the thoughts from his mind. He assumed a relaxed low guard and began to stalk his opponent. "Are you here to fight or talk?"

"Unlike some, I can do both," Jimmy said.

To prove his point, he slid forward with a straight thrust and then circled his hammer around to the side of Foulques's head. Foulques flicked his sword up and easily turned the thrust aside, but he had to step away from the powerful follow-up swing. Grunting hard, Jimmy pressed the attack with another swing-thrust combination, forcing Foulques to dance away.

"And then I heard," Jimmy began again, as if the two of them were sitting at a table sharing a pitcher of ale, "that our Brother Knight Justice is now just a Knight. How did that come about, Brother?"

How had he heard already? Foulques wondered. Did everyone know? Idly, Foulques wondered how long it would be before word reached his uncle in England. Jimmy attacked again and even as distracted as he was, Foulques turned Jimmy's hammer aside and almost caught him with a thrust under the arm, but the big man weaved at the last moment and avoided it. The exchange left Jimmy breathless, but he still had enough air to force out a few words.

"You keep messing up, it will not be long before they take that knighthood away from you, too. Then you will just be a miserable sergeant, like the rest of us. Truth be told, cannot wait to see you in one of these itchy, shit-colored sacks they make us wear."

Foulques was growing weary of Jimmy the Mouth's tongue. It was time to end this contest. He began to time Jimmy's heavy breathing as they moved around the circle, then he stepped forward with a straight thrust to set him up for the kill. Jimmy stumbled under the attack and Foulques brought his sword around in a deadly arc toward Jimmy's neck. But the big man suddenly crouched under the swing and exploded forward at Foulques's legs. Too late, Foulques realized Jimmy was not tired at all. Jimmy hooked Foulques behind his thighs, lifted him into the air, and both men went crashing to the ground.

Foulques let his sword fly out of his hand, knowing it

was not the weapon of choice now. In a frantic scramble, Foulques managed to claw his rondel dagger out of his belt scabbard. Jimmy still clutched his hammer and he tried to sit up on top of Foulques so he could bring it to bear, but Foulques hooked one hand behind his neck to keep him close. He brought his dagger up and pressed it to the hollow in Jimmy's throat.

The two of them stopped moving, save for the heaving of their chests. Jimmy was no longer only pretending to be tired. There was some clapping and hollering from the other sergeants as they realized the fight was over.

"You know, Brother," Jimmy said, as the two of them disentangled themselves on the ground. "Seeing you up close like this makes me realize you really are a pretty thing. I bet if you scraped that bit of hair off your face and went to see 'ol man Villiers in the dead of night, you could persuade him to set you back up with that fancy title."

"Sergeants! Marshal on site!" Rod's voice cut through the air. He had spotted Marshal Clermont standing nearby, apparently watching the fight.

There was a sudden flurry of movement as everyone scrambled to their feet. Foulques stood and straightened his robe. How long had Clermont been standing there?

The Marshal remained in the area for a moment to acknowledge the sergeants standing at attention. He caught Foulques's eye. Foulques wanted to look away, but he forced himself to endure the Marshal's pitying stare.

"Good fight, Brother Goodyear," the Marshal said. He shook his head at Foulques and walked away.

When he was gone, Jimmy elbowed Foulques and winked at him. "It does not get any better than this, eh Brother?"

CHAPTER NINETEEN

FOULQUES LEANED AGAINST the keep wall and stared out over the children in the courtyard as they went about their exercises. There were almost three hundred of them, but they looked so small, so few, so helpless. What had his uncle been thinking when he suggested the idea of purchasing them? In time, Foulques had no doubt they would be a welcome addition to the ranks of the Hospitaller forces. In time. The question was, how much time did they really have? Qalawun's truce had been broken, and it was the Hospitallers themselves who were to blame for that. Perhaps his uncle had been away from the Levant for so long he had simply lost touch with how desperate their situation had become.

The road had been long and hard in getting the children here. *Good men died for you*, he heard Marshal Mathieu de Clermont's voice say. As much as it pained him to admit it, the Marshal was right. Foulques had failed them all.

A hand on his shoulder made him jump.

"You are alive, Foulques, though you do not look it."

The words were English but rang with the accent of the

Scotch. Weapons Master Glynn gave his shoulder a squeeze and tapped the center of Foulques's chest with his fist. "Heard you were dead, but you feel solid enough to me."

"Hello Glynn," Foulques said, speaking in English.

Glynn had been a sergeant-at-arms with the Hospitallers for twenty years, Weapons Master in charge of infantry training for the last seven, yet he spoke not a word of French. The Brothers from the English Langue said he spoke not a word of English either. But when teaching a man how to swing a sword, or fight from a shield wall, it was surprising how few words were really needed.

"So, you are the bastard responsible for all this, are you?" Glynn said, waving his arm over the courtyard filled with children.

Foulques nodded. "Do not pretend you are not pleased. You have hundreds of new bodies to torment."

"I, for one, would prefer them not so young," Glynn said. "Their bones are too soft at this age. But the cavalry master swears it is impossible to make a true horseman out of anyone unless his training begins before he has hair on his balls."

Foulques nodded. That was the general consensus. Foulques himself had been six the first time he sat alone on a horse and walked him around the paddock. He remembered his uncle lifting him up into the saddle and pushing the reins into his hands. He took them from his uncle's dry, calloused hands, and with the smell of sun-scorched leather creaking beneath him, stared out over the horse's ears into a whole new world. "Do not worry," his Uncle Guillaume said, "give the stallion some slack and he will look after you."

Glynn's voice brought Foulques back from the past. "Well, if you are going to help me train them, we will have to get you in shape first. You look pudgy."

Everyone looked pudgy compared to Glynn. He was a lean mass of corded muscle and seemed to get harder with every year. It had always been a joke between Foulques and his training partners that the only reason Master Glynn wore mail when he was sparring was so his bare torso would not damage his opponents' weapons.

"You have the wrong man, Glynn. My task was to get them here, and that was harder than I care to admit."

Glynn nodded. "So I heard. You have my sympathies for those the thieving slavers got. Cowards they are, the lot of them. Still, I hear you and Alain saved a great many of them. You did well, lad. Do not let anyone tell you different."

Had he, really? Foulques looked out over the crowd of children again. For these few, perhaps, he *had* made a difference.

He saw faces this time when he looked at them. Not just one seething mass of children from a foreign land whose language he could barely understand. They were individuals, each one filled with the unique dreams and hopes of youth. He had been so entirely preoccupied with remorse over his fellow Hospitallers killed on the road to Acre and what his uncle would think of his recent demotion, that he had given very little thought to the young souls stolen from his care. He told himself it was a miracle any of them had made it. It was unrealistic to expect better.

He remembered the peasant woman's face as she pulled her hand away from the gold. For the first time, he questioned how they could have done what they did. How desperate had those mountain villagers been to sell their own children into a life of slavery? For what else could you call a life forced onto children so young?

You have chosen wisely in putting your faith in my order.

It was his voice that had said those words. But exactly what benefit had those mountain people derived, save for a few coins that by now were already spent? Of what future had they been robbed?

He had said the words without thought, without listening to his own heart. He did not want to leave his home to journey to the Alps in the first place and, once there, he wanted nothing more than to get back. Perhaps it had been Christ speaking to him, telling him his mission was not a righteous one, and that was why Foulques had been so eager to be gone from those lands.

He turned his eyes again on the large mass of children and attempted to imagine what the courtyard would look like with an additional two hundred souls. He squinted, then closed his eyes completely. But no matter how hard he tried, he knew his imagination could never replace those who had been taken.

CHAPTER TWENTY

A SINGLE LANTERN, burning at half-wick, hung from the open rafters of the small, windowless room. As cramped as it was, it seemed even more so because almost two hundred children had squeezed themselves into only half its total available space. One might think they did this out of fear, or perhaps as a way to provide comfort to one another in the damp confines of their prison, but the truth was much less complicated. Along the length of the far wall, several urns stood in the gloom, and the odor they gave off was strong enough to burn one's throat.

The boy sitting next to Hermann groaned. He pushed himself first onto his hands and knees, and from there, raised up on shaky legs. He lurched across the room and hung his head over one of the urns, just in time to empty the contents of his stomach. Hermann turned his head away. He felt fortunate that his own stomach had remained intact. The floating floor they all sat upon had wrought havoc on many of the boys. Hermann did not understand why he should be spared their misery, but he was thankful all the same.

He took advantage of the sudden space at either side of

his elbows, and pressed his back up hard against the wall to straighten it, relieving the discomfort that crept up the muscles along the sides of his spine. They had been herded from the ship like goats, prodded and poked by their nauseatingly sweet-smelling captors, who scared them all with guttural words no one could understand. All the children, not only the sick ones, were looking forward to setting foot on solid land once again, but their hopes were crushed when they were pushed into a small house attached to the end of the dock only a short walk from the ship. Hermann did not know how many days they had been locked in the room. It had been night both times he had been taken from the floating house, but he was not sure if those excursions had occurred during the same night, or two different ones. Hermann's memory had lost focus. Ever since his father had left him in Schwyz, time had begun melding moments together for no apparent reason.

Hermann was one of the older boys in the group, though he was small for his age. He had always been small. His father had told him he would be bigger than everyone one day, but Hermann no longer believed that. His father had also told him that he would have to leave his brother and mother for a time, but once he had traveled the world and seen all kinds of unimaginable things, he could return. Hermann was old enough, now, to realize that also was not true. He had come to realize his life was nothing more than a string of lies held together with moments of suffering.

The door creaked open and two boys who had been leaning against it spilled out into the fresh air. Men there shouted and kicked, and the boys tumbled over one another back into the room, rolling to a stop in a tangle of arms and legs with those children who had been in their path. Three men waded into the room, the children scooting away from their feet like minnows fleeing from a hand submerged in a still pool of water. The men moved through the crowd, here and there grabbing a boy and propelling him toward the open door.

Hermann recognized one of the men. He closed his eyes and shrunk against the wall, but he could still see the bearded man with the glistening teeth, could still smell the mutton on his breath. He wished his sick companion was still beside him, so he could more easily hide.

"Hermann…" he heard the man call out softly. "Hermann, where are you?" The man's German was terrible, but there was no mistaking his own name, and the boy clenched his eyes shut with the strength of a fist when he heard it called over and over.

"Hermann! Come!" The voice was closer now, and beginning to lose patience.

Hermann was old enough to know what a coward was, and as he slouched and wrapped his arms around his trembling knees pressed up to his chest, he suspected he had become one.

"Ah!"

He felt a rough hand grab him by the shirt and pull him to his feet. Afraid to open his eyes, he allowed himself to cry, for he was a coward after all, and that is what cowards did. His legs went numb and he fell from the man's grasp onto the floor. For a moment, he thought the men would leave him behind this time. Perhaps they had tired of him, which they should have, for he was nothing special.

The stench of rotting meat wafted his way and, even though he knew what he would see, he could not help but force open his eyes. A pair of dark ones, their whites criss-crossed with jagged blood lines, stared back at him from inches away.

"Ah, Hermann…"

And then the teeth appeared as the man's beard split apart to allow a smile.

Hermann wanted to move, to run, but he could not. His body was frozen, his muscles no longer listened to his mind.

But that was to be expected. He was a coward, after all.

✳

BADRU SAT ON the floor of his room in the Gibelet manor, his legs stretched straight out before him. Every night before turning in, he liked to perform a series of simple stretching exercises to help him sleep. He laced his fingers together and bent forward slowly at the waist, reaching with his hands until he could hook them over the soles of his feet. He remained there for half a minute or so, until he felt the muscles of his legs and the small of his back lengthen and relax. He breathed in through his nose, out through his mouth, and with every exhalation pulled his chest further down toward his knees. When it touched and he could go no further, he raised his eyes to look at his feet and settled into a deep breathing cycle to fully stretch out his protesting ligaments and tendons.

Veronique always rented the same house whenever they had business in Gibelet. Years ago it had belonged to the Governor of the city, but had changed hands several times since. Most recently, it was the property of a Venetian merchant who never used it, probably because he was too afraid of the Muslim presence in Gibelet. There was still the odd Venetian who frequented the city, and more than a few Genoans, for they were everywhere, but this particular Venetian was already rich. He had no need to travel to undesirable locations in the pursuit of business. Especially when he could just rent out the property for a pretty sum.

A knock on the door pulled Badru out of his trance and the large muscles at the backs of his thighs protested as he lost his concentration. He exhaled and allowed himself to ease upright until the pain dissipated.

"Enter," Badru said.

The door swung open and Safir, a tall, solidly built Mamluk, who was one of Badru's more experienced warriors, stood in the doorway. He stood at attention, and stared straight ahead, not in the least bit surprised to see Badru sitting on the floor doing his exercises.

"Forgive the intrusion, Emir," Safir said.

Badru waited for the man to continue. He opened his mouth to begin but the words did not come easily.

"What is it?" Badru finally asked, knowing it would be important if Safir felt the need to come to him at this late hour.

Safir cleared his throat. "It is the mercenaries, Emir.

They have been taking liberties with some of the children."

Badru pulled his knees in and massaged his legs to life. "I dismissed them from service. How many of them are still here in the city?"

"Only the captain and five of his men. I put them under guard the moment I learned what they were doing."

"Have they damaged any of the Mistress's slaves?"

"I do not believe so. At least nothing I have noticed."

Badru shook his head. Hiring mercenaries was always more expensive than the simple fees agreed upon. But still, it could be worse. It was good his Mamluks had caught the men before the Mistress arrived.

"Cast the captain and his men from the city immediately," Badru said. Then, a troubling thought found its way into his mind. He looked up at Safir. "How exactly did they gain access to the slaves?" As far as he knew, the warehouse had been under constant guard by his own Mamluk warriors.

Safir averted his gaze. "It was one of our own, my Emir. While standing guard, he allowed the mercenaries to take a few of the boys to the stables."

Badru felt the blood rush into his head. He flipped his feet beneath him and stood up.

"Who was it?"

Safir stared straight ahead at Badru's chest. "Andor."

"How many times did he permit this?"

Safir shrugged. "More than once, my Emir."

The veins at Badru's temples pulsated. "Assemble the men. Put the mercenaries, and Andor, on their knees until I arrive. And do it on the road away from the Mistress's house. I would not have her walk through blood."

"Of course, my Emir." Safir hurried from the room, eager to be gone.

✠

THE ASSEMBLED MAMLUK warriors formed a horseshoe formation with six men on their knees, hands behind their heads, at its open end. They had been there only the better part of an hour, but the cobble-stoned street was unforgiving. The mercenaries grunted and squirmed from one uncomfortable position to the next, the only sound around them was the spitting and hissing of torches held by the Mamluks standing at attention nearby.

When Badru finally emerged from the darkness, the captain of the mercenaries wasted no time in pleading his case.

"Badru, come now. It was a little innocent fun. What was the harm?"

He made the mistake of removing his hands from the top of his turban to gesture with. The nearest Mamluk stepped forward and struck him in the upper abdomen with the butt end of his spear. The mercenary collapsed forward onto his hands and knees and the Mamluk struck him again near one of his kidneys.

"Knees!" He rapped him again on the other side of his back. "Knees!"

The mercenary made a begging squeal and pushed himself back up. His face was purple and he held his hands stretched out in front of him as he tried to catch his wind.

The Mamluk nodded at his hands and pulled back his spear like he meant to strike him again. The mercenary's hands flew together on top of his turban. He closed his eyes as he continued to suck in chestfuls of air.

All the mercenaries tried to straighten up, grimacing in pain as they struggled to keep their hands on their heads. Andor, the Mamluk warrior, was the only one who had remained ramrod straight the entire time. Badru knew his knees would be throbbing in agony by now, but one would never know by looking at him. All men felt pain. Whether or not a man showed it was up to the individual.

Badru walked slowly by each squirming mercenary, refusing to look at any of them. He stopped in front of Andor and turned to face him straight on.

"Which code have you broken?" Badru said, quietly.

Andor stared straight ahead, his fingers still laced together behind his head. "I took coin for turning the other way, Emir. I have failed 'to despise pecuniary rewards'."

"Any others?"

Andor looked up at Badru with a questioning look on his face. "I… have failed my duties in the eyes of Allah."

Badru struck Andor with an open-handed slap across the face before the final syllable left his lips. When a wide-eyed Andor turned back to Badru, the Emir could see the red outline of his hand covering the entire left side of Andor's face. Blood trickled from the corner of his mouth.

"It is not to Allah that you owe your allegiance. It is your master's slaves who are your lords."

Andor's brows furrowed. "Forgive me, Emir. They are

slaves and I did not—"

"They are your master's slaves, as are you. The code demands that you 'protect the weak and defenseless'. Did you do this?"

Andor directed his gaze at the ground. "I did not, Emir."

Badru nodded. "No, you did not." He spun and directed his next words at the mercenary leader. "Andor failed his master. If he were your man, how would you punish him?"

The mercenary leader shifted uncomfortably from being singled out. "I would whip him," he said.

"We do things differently," Badru said. "A Mamluk warrior must weigh the consequences of his actions and offer an apology." He turned back to Andor, clasped his hands behind his back, and waited.

Andor's eyes twitched as he studied his Emir's face and beads of perspiration began to collect on his forehead. He seemed to come to a decision and his face almost relaxed. He drew his belt knife with his left hand and placed his right stretched before him on the ground. He set the knife gently on the crease of his right wrist and took a deep breath as he adjusted his weight.

"Andor," Badru said, gently.

The Mamluk looked up, confused, but with the light of hope deep in his eyes.

"You are a warrior. Take your left."

The hope vanished. "Yes, my Emir."

In one deft motion, he tossed the knife into his right hand and levered it up and down onto his left wrist. He finished the job before the pain took over and the first scream escaped his lungs.

Badru turned his back on Andor as he curled himself into a ball, groaning and bucking on the cobble stones. Badru walked past the mercenaries. Almost as an after-thought, he shushed them away with the back of his hand.

"You are free to go," he said.

CHAPTER TWENTY-ONE

NAJYA HAD ASKED everyone she could think of about the Northman, but after five days she felt like she knew even less about him than when she started. He was a Mamluk of Turkish and Norse blood. That much everyone, who had heard of him, agreed upon. Najya had already known this, though she could not remember how she had learned it. She was becoming frustrated. She could think of one last person to ask.

Kemal was a Turkish pastry maker and a regular honey customer of Najya's. He had strong ties to the Turkish community and she hoped he may be able to tell her something useful about the Northman. She had hesitated to seek him out, however, because she only knew him as a customer. But she had exhausted all other potential sources and she did not want to let Foulques and his children down.

Kemal's shop was not far from her home in Montmusart, the northern district of the city. Najya set out first thing in the morning carrying a clay jar of honey by a thin rope wrapped several times around its neck. She weaved her way through the narrow streets until she stopped in front of a squat, white-washed house, its corners rounded with age. Attached to the front of the house was a small, open area half covered with an awning. The other half had a brick oven with a tall chimney extending just above the house's roof line. Kemal stood in front of his oven, head turned upwards, eying the plume of smoke pouring from the chimney, when Najya approached. Judging by the thick, gray clouds, he had just lit the fire for the day.

"Good day, Kemal," she called out.

Kemal turned at the sound of her voice. "Najya? What good deed have I done to have you visit me in my humble shop?" He was a small man with the smile of a giant, but Najya could tell he was surprised to see her here.

"I brought you some honey," she said, dangling the jar of honey in front of him.

Kemal's eyes lit up, but the curiosity in them did not fade. "Wonderful," he said. He opened the low stick gate blocking off his patio and ushered her inside. "Come. I will make some tea and if you do not mind eating yesterday's fare, I am sure I can round up some cake."

They sat at a tiny stone table right there in front of the oven's crackling fire. The stones absorbed all the heat of the flames so it was not uncomfortable. After exchanging the necessary pleasantries of host and guest, Kemal asked if there was something he could help her with.

"There is a person I would like to know more about. If you could tell me anything at all about him I would be in your debt."

Grinning, Kemal refilled her teacup. "You have come to

the right place. A man with the right pastry at the right time can learn more secrets than you would imagine." He laughed and sat back in his chair, giving her his full attention. "What is the name of the fortunate person who has captured your curiosity?" He raised his teacup to his lips.

"That is just it. I do not know his name. Only that he is called 'The Northman' by those who know him."

Kemal's tea cup stopped shy of his lips. Najya was sure she saw a tremor take hold of his hand before he lowered the cup back to the table without drinking. It took some time before he spoke.

"Najya. Why would you want to learn anything about this man?"

"It is a favor for a friend. He seeks the Northman and I have promised to help him however I can."

"This must be a very good friend." Someone walked by on the path behind Najya, and Kemal's eyes followed whoever it was.

Najya nodded, but she was not sure Kemal saw as he seemed to be avoiding eye contact. He knew something but it was not going to come out easily. "Please, Kemal. Anything would be helpful."

Kemal took a sip of his tea and set the cup down slowly. "He is a slaver. One of the best, they say. His blood is that of a plains Turk mixed with a witch—"

"From the Norse countries. I know that," Najya said. She had tired of this particular story. "It is all people have been able to tell me. Or all they want to tell."

Kemal started at her sudden frustration. "Why does your

friend want to find a man so few wish to speak about?"

"The Northman stole something from him. Something of immense value, and my friend would have it back."

Kemal shook his head. "Nothing can hold a value so high. What if you tell your friend to reconsider?"

"He is a very stubborn man," Najya said. "And honorable. He cannot reconsider."

Kemal refilled their cups once again. He did not speak and it was Najya who had to break the silence. "Will you help me, Kemal? Please, I will not breathe a word to anyone that it came from you."

Eventually, with the corners of his mouth turned down in a tight-lipped grimace, he nodded once. "I will help your friend. Come with me."

He stood and, wordlessly, Najya followed him out the stick gate, leaving their full tea cups behind. Kemal led her down side street after side street. Amongst the press of the buildings she lost sight of the sun and was no longer sure of Mecca's direction. Eventually, they came to the end of a long alley choked with tiny ramshackle houses split into even tinier apartments, their dividing walls built with nothing more than carpets. Kemal ducked his head behind one carpet, then another, and finally on the third one he beckoned Najya to come closer. He stepped into the space beyond the dusty, threadbare wall and Najya followed.

A man, or at least Najya believed him to be a man, lay on his side on a stack of carpets in even worse condition than those that made up the walls of his home. Kemal walked forward and knelt in front of the man's face. He unwrapped a piece of yesterday's cake from a bit of cloth, and set both the cloth and cake on the ground. The man stirred. It was then that Najya realized he had no arms.

Kemal helped him up to a sitting position, then he held the cake and let the man eat it from his hand like one would feed a horse. Once the cake was gone, he licked at Kemal's palm until every last sweet crumb was gone. He looked at Kemal and a croaking sound came from his throat.

Kemal held up both hands. "All gone. I will bring you more soon."

The man's face clouded over and then silent sobs scrunched up his face. He lowered himself back onto his carpets and rocked back and forth on his side, crying the whole time. As Kemal rested a hand above his stumped shoulder, the man quivered at his touch. The crying increased to a violent intensity. Kemal waited until the quiet sobs lessened, then stood and returned to where Najya waited.

"Who is he?" She asked.

"Basir used to work for me," Kemal said. "I took him on as an apprentice at the request of his father. But the boy soon grew bored with the work and he ran off to join a galley crew."

"What happened?"

"The Northman," Kemal said, shrugging. "We do not know if Basir's crew accidentally attacked the Northman's ship, or if it was the Northman who attacked Basir's ship." He shrugged again. "It does not matter. The result was the same. Basir was the only survivor."

Najya shook her head. "How could he have lived through those wounds?"

"It was no accident. His arms had been tied off and burnt to stem the flow of blood."

Najya could not take her eyes off Basir as Kemal talked. She could see now that he was a young man. He may even have been handsome at one time. "How could anyone do such a thing? And why would they bother keeping him alive?"

"The Northman always leaves one alive to tell others what happens if you cross him. But his strategy did not work so well in this case. Basir has not spoken a coherent word since he was found floating on the ship of corpses, his arms hacked off like a slaughtered animal."

"His words are not needed," Najya said. Tears had found their way into her own eyes. "Basir is evidence enough of the Northman's cruelty."

Kemal closed his eyes. "No, Najya. There were those who suffered fates far worse than his on that ship. And I think poor Basir relives it all everyday."

Kemal suddenly turned and grabbed Najya by the shoulders. "Look at him. This is the best your friend can hope for if he continues down the path he is walking. Is this what you want?"

Najya turned her head slowly in Basir's direction. He had stopped crying, but every now and then a shudder ran through his body. He stared at Kemal's piece of cloth on the ground that had once held the piece of cake, but his dead, empty eyes saw something else entirely.

CHAPTER TWENTY-TWO

FOULQUES ROSE BEFORE dawn and, after morning service and breakfast, attended martial training with his fellow knights. They drilled formations with sword and shield, broke for the third hour prayers of Trece, and then resumed their training until the noon service. After leaving the church, instead of sitting down to the midday meal with the other knights, Foulques detoured through the kitchens to pick up a half-loaf of bread and a small sack of almonds. Eating as he walked, he headed for the compound's gates, intending to use what little free time he had to find Najya, and ask her if she had been able to discover anything about the Northman. He had only a few hours before the next service, and then he was scheduled for his weekly duty at the infirmorum from None to Vespers.

Many of the knights did not enjoy the hours they were required to put in changing sheets and caring for the sick and wounded, but Foulques had been doing it since he was a child, so it was neither a task he despised, nor one he relished. It was simply the required duty of a devout Hospitaller, and as his uncle always said, one he should be proud to have the privilege of performing.

A crowd had gathered at the gates, on the city's side. Foulques groaned as he remembered today was Meat Day, the day when the Hospitallers gave out free cooked meat to the city's needy. It would take long minutes he did not have to fight through the rush of eager men, women, and children.

The densest part of the crowd was near the covered wagon, which carried several haunches of pork and beef. A half dozen monks sliced slabs off the roasted meat and distributed it as fairly as possible, blessing each recipient with a quick wave of their hands. A couple of fully armed sergeants assisted the monks, but their main function was to ensure the crowd did not get out of control. To Foulques's surprise, one of the sergeants assisting today was Goodyear Jimmy. Because of his background as a master builder, Brother Jimmy was usually put to work on projects more fitted to his expertise. Perhaps he had volunteered with his free time, Foulques thought, and did not dwell on it any further.

Foulques stuck to the outskirts of the mob and pushed his way through, trying to avoid being dragged into the middle. A woman holding an infant in one arm, clutched at Foulques's black mantle, perhaps thinking he had meat to distribute.

"Please, m'lord…"

Foulques shook his head and gently removed her hand. "I am no lord," he said, then pointed her toward the wagon. She bowed her head, clutched her baby to her chest, and launched herself into the throng of people. Foulques watched until she disappeared. He knew the wagon would be empty long before she reached it.

Meat Day had not always been like this. He had worked the wagon with his uncle many times as a child, and in those days, people lined up peacefully to accept the charity of the Knights of Saint John. There was not the sense of desperation that Foulques now felt all around him. Acre had been the main hub connecting all the cities of the Kingdom of Jerusalem together, and work was available for anyone who wanted it. But as those other cities fell to Islamic forces, the spokes connecting Acre to the rest of the Levant broke away, leaving the city spinning away on its own. Trade fell, tax revenues dried up, and suddenly, it was not just the very poor that relied on the charity of the Orders and the Church. Merchants and members of the middle class joined the Hospitallers' meat line and the Church's bread days. These events, which had once been calm and orderly celebrations of God's good grace and generosity, now required the presence of armed guards.

Foulques pushed on, and eventually broke through one side of the eager gatherers. He took the first alleyway on his right, even though he knew it would lead south toward the water, which was not the direction he wished to go. With the murmurs of the crowd fading behind him, Foulques walked quickly down the alley. A few minutes later, he reached Patriarch's Way, the wide street that ran in front of the Patriarchate, the gated residence and offices of the Archbishop of Acre and the Kingdom of Jerusalem. He headed east until he could see the gardens of the Patriarchate, and then he turned north. He wound his way through a series of alleys and streets until he came to the east-west wall that effectively cut the city in two. Passing through the unguarded gatehouse, Foulques stepped into the northern district of Acre, the part of the city known as Montmusart.

The squat, white and sand-colored buildings here gave the impression of a much older, and more established, city, even though it was not as ancient as the southern section. The inhabitants of Montmusart were not any richer, or poorer, than their southern neighbors, but the difference between the two districts was palpable. Foulques suspected it was because this part of the city had not suffered as much in the clashes of the Holy Wars. Acre had been under Christian control for the better part of a hundred years, now, but it had exchanged rulers more than once before that, with each new king ordering a swathe of destruction down upon the city and its inhabitants.

Najya's workshop was easy to spot. Unlike the other nearby buildings, which were built next to one another so they could share a common wall, her one-story, stone hut was set off on its own. Like sentries, two bee hives flanked the front door and Foulques could hear the buzzing of its inhabitants as he approached. He was about to walk around to the back of the house, for that was where the entrance to her living quarters was, when the front door of her workshop squealed open and Najya stood in the sunlight, her eyes blinking at either its brightness or because she was surprised to see Foulques standing in front of her.

"Foulques? What are you doing here?" Her voice did not sound happy to see him. In fact, Foulques was left with the impression that he was somehow intruding.

"I brought you these," he said, holding out his bag of almonds. "And I was hoping to have a word, or two. That is, if you have time," Foulques said, wondering if he had made a mistake coming here. "If that is all right…"

"Yes, yes, of course," Najya said, accepting the almonds from him and seeming to collect herself. "I will make us some tea. But come inside before my neighbors begin to wonder what a black knight is doing on my threshold."

Foulques followed her inside, ducking beneath the stone lintel above the doorway. It took a moment for his eyes to adjust to the dim interior. A wave of heat hit him from a small fireplace in one corner of the workshop. A tripod with metal legs held a small cauldron hung suspended over the low flames. Above the rim of the blackened pot, jagged sticks of wax poked out waiting to be melted down. She motioned for Foulques to wait, while she raised the pot a few links higher on its chain, and then hung a kettle of water below it. They weaved their way between shelves jammed with clay jars and rolls of wick material. Najya slid open a thick curtain and they stepped into her living quarters.

Foulques took a deep breath, thankful for the relative coolness of the room. A sleeping pallet took up a third of the small space. The rest of the area was split between a closet and a small table with two chairs. Fresh flowers poked out of a re-purposed honey flask on the table and colorful carpets covered the floor. A single window with real glass, albeit cloudy and impossible to see through, was set in the wall near the door leading out to the alley.

Najya motioned for him to sit, and before he was completely settled, she asked Foulques what was bothering him. They knew each other too well for the customs of host and guest to come between them.

"I came to ask if you have had any fortune with your inquiries about the Northman," Foulques said.

Najya eased herself onto the other small chair. "I am sorry, Foulques. I asked everyone I could trust. The Northman has taken them underground and no one is talking," Najya said.

"Nothing at all? Someone must know something about him. A rumor even?" Foulques knew it had been a long shot, but he was surprised Najya had turned up so little. She knew more people than anyone in Acre.

Najya shook her head. "As soon as anyone heard it was the Northman's slaves I was looking for, they closed right up. From the stories I have heard about him, I cannot say I blame them. Perhaps, it is for the best. You should not go searching for such a man."

Foulques could hear a tremor in her voice. It was not like Najya to fear anything.

"Najya, are you all right? Did something happen?"

She shook her head. "No. No, I am disappointed is all. I will keep my ears open, but, sadly, that is all I can do for you now." She avoided his eyes, and pushed off the table with her hands to stand. "I think I hear the water." She disappeared through the curtain into the other room.

Foulques stared after her. Even the Fires of Hell, themselves, could not boil a kettle so quickly.

✠

FOULQUES LEFT NAJYA'S home and headed back toward the Hospitaller compound. He walked quickly, hoping to have some time to relax in his apartment before his shift in the Hospital. The monks were still at the gates with their meat wagon but the crowd had mostly dispersed. The woman Foulques had seen earlier was still there, however, sitting on the ground rocking her infant in her arms. As Foulques had suspected, the dejected look on her face told him she had not managed to get any meat.

As the monks readied their empty wagon to return to the compound, Jimmy Goodyear held up his hand to the monks in a farewell gesture and began walking away. Any normal observer would not have noticed anything odd, but Foulques had trained with Jimmy too many times. He knew the big man's strengths and weaknesses equally well, and his eyes told him something about Jimmy the Mouth's movement was off. He almost looked like he had a limp. Perhaps he had been injured in training? Possibly, Foulques thought. But it was more likely that Jimmy had fallen prey to a different kind of weakness. He jogged a few steps and intercepted Jimmy before he could reach the Hospitaller gates.

Jimmy blinked and his eyes went wide when Foulques suddenly appeared in front of him.

"Good day, Jimmy. Nice of you to help out the monks today," Foulques said.

"Just doing my duty, Brother Foulques." He shrugged, and gave off a beatific smile worthy of any saint. His brow, however, began to glisten with sweat.

"And a fine job you have done, Brother Jimmy," Foulques said, "but there seems to be one more waiting upon your charity." Foulques pointed at the woman sitting on the side of the street.

Jimmy pursed his lips as he turned his head and looked at the woman and child. "Sadly, the wagon is empty for the day," Jimmy said.

"Yes. Yes, it is, Brother Jimmy."

Jimmy the Neckless forced himself to meet Foulques's gaze and they stared at each other for a full three seconds before the innocence in Jimmy's eyes died away and he threw up his hands. He muttered something and limped his way over until he stood front of the mother. She looked at him suspiciously, and then clutched her baby to her chest, and recoiled in horror, when Jimmy hiked his robe up over his hips. He pulled at a knotted string tied around his leg and a full haunch of lamb fell to the ground in front of the woman.

"Well, do not just gawk at it woman. Take it, feed your family, and give thanks tonight in your prayers for the men of the Hospital!"

The woman snatched up the meat and thanked Jimmy over and over for his generosity. She was still kissing the hem of Jimmy's robe when Foulques continued on his way.

He rounded the main keep and approached the two-level building which was reserved for the personal quarters of the

Order's knights. Once inside, he took the side stairs to the second floor apartments. Normally, this floor was reserved for higher ranking brethren and official guests, but since Foulques's uncle was in England, Foulques had, with his uncle's blessing, taken over his apartment. He pushed open the heavy door and stepped inside. The sudden smell of fresh figs sent his hand flying to his sword hilt. He spun and saw an Arab stand up from the small eating table in the corner of the room.

"Peace be upon you, Brother Foulques." The man was dark, even for an Arab. He was thin as a whip, well into his middle years, and wore a neatly tied black turban. A curved dagger at his belt seemed to hang with a life all its own. Foulques had known the man since he was a child, but the innocence of youth had protected him from realizing what he truly was. Nowadays, Foulques saw the man in a whole new light.

"Peace be upon you, Monsieur Malouf," Foulques said.

Malouf seated himself once again. He held a fig in one hand and a tiny blade in the other that reflected the light from the windows like it was made from diamonds. There were two plates in front of him, each with several pieces of cut figs.

"Please," Malouf said. "Sit. I have prepared refreshment."

Foulques glanced around the room before easing his hand away from his sword hilt. He pulled over a second chair and took a seat opposite the older man, who then pushed one of the plates in front of Foulques.

"Eat," Malouf said, gesturing toward the figs in front of

Foulques with the tiny knife. It was so small it would sometimes disappear entirely in Malouf's hand depending on how he held it. "Go ahead. They are not poisoned." He did not laugh. He did not even smile.

Foulques picked up a quarter section of fig, the juices in its center red and dripping.

"Wait," Malouf said. He reached inside his robe and pulled out a small ceramic jar. He popped out the cork and then tipped it over the plate in front of Foulques, drizzling the figs with honey. "This makes them much nicer." He added some of the honey to his own figs and popped one into his mouth.

"Monsieur Malouf, I—" Foulques began, but Malouf cut him off with a wave of the knife that had once again reappeared in his hand.

"Eat, Brother Foulques. Eat."

Foulques exchanged the fig he had been holding with one covered in honey and slowly put it in his mouth. He was sure it was delicious, but his sense of taste failed him for the moment.

"I have a daughter that makes honey," Malouf said, suddenly, "but, of course, you know this."

Foulques was still chewing. He coughed once but managed to get the sweet fruit down.

"People tell me she makes delicious honey, perhaps the best some even say. But I cannot know this. Maybe these men lie to me because of who I am. Who I work for. And I cannot taste it to see for myself because my daughter will not talk to me. Life is full of problems, is it not, Brother

Foulques?"

Foulques nodded. "Many problems," he said.

"Some small, some large. The Northman, he is a problem," Malouf said. "And I hear my daughter has been asking about him." He looked at Foulques and pointed again with the knife. "That is a large problem. If the wrong people were to hear of this, it could make her life… difficult."

"I am sorry. I did not mean to get Najya into any trouble," Foulques said.

"She is not in any trouble. She is a good girl. But you may be, if you keep looking for this Northman. For you may find him, then what will you do?"

Foulques shrugged. "Your daughter thinks I will go after the Alpiner children. She thinks I have the resources to mount a rescue. But I am not so sure. It sounds like the wise thing would be to step away and forget I had ever heard of this Mamluk."

"That would be the wise thing to do," Malouf said. He then stared at Foulques for a long moment, measuring him in some way Foulques could not quite fathom. He was a man who sought the truth and he would stop at nothing until he had it. Even if that meant dragging it out of a man by questionable methods.

"I have never been counted amongst the wise," Foulques said, finally.

Abruptly, Malouf picked up another fig and began carving it into sections. As he worked, he spoke. "An encounter with The Northman could change your life. Or, perhaps end it. Are you ready to accept that?"

"I have already seen his work firsthand. He is an abomination in my eyes, and I suspect God's as well. If I have the opportunity to rid the world of him, no force will stay my sword."

Malouf looked up from his fig. "The Northman is, himself, a force."

Foulques was growing tired of Malouf's evasiveness. "Tell me what you know, Monsieur Malouf."

Malouf shrugged. "I know more than most. His name is Badru Hashim, an Emir of thirty Mamluk, and he is owned by Veronique Boulet, one of the most affluent slave traders in Marseilles. He was trained in Cairo at the Sultan's own tabaqa. Do you know what that means, Brother Foulques?"

Foulques leaned back in his chair. "He was a talented soldier. One of the Sultan's personal bodyguards."

Malouf nodded. "Yes, but ask yourself this: how often does the Sultan simply sell off members of his own guard?"

"I know nothing of how the Mamluk Sultanate conducts its business, but Mamluks are bought and sold all the time."

"The correct answer, Brother Foulques, is *never*."

Monsieur Malouf was trying to tell him something, but Foulques had no inkling of what that was. Malouf, apparently, could read the confusion on his face. "The Sultan," Malouf began, "spends more on the training and upkeep of one Mamluk of the Royal Guard than many Frankish Kings spend on entire armies. Do you think the Sultan can then simply sell off a man like Badru Hashim for a profit? Who could pay that much? Surely not a slave trader from Marseilles."

"Why sell him at all, then?" Foulques asked, narrowing his eyes at the thought. "Unless he wanted to be rid of him."

Malouf smiled, his white teeth sparkling against the darkness of his beard. "Precisely. My sources say he was afraid of Badru Hashim."

"Afraid?"

"Imagine that," Malouf said. "The Sultan of Egypt, arguably the most powerful man in today's world, afraid of one man." He tossed half a section of fig into the air and caught it in his mouth.

"And why would that be?" Foulques asked.

Malouf held up his hands. "That I cannot tell you."

"Cannot, or will not?"

"Does it matter? Either way I will not say any more on the subject. I only mention this as something you should consider before chasing after this man."

"Does this mean you know where the children are being held?"

"I do not know where your children are now, but Veronique Boulet is intimately involved in her business."

"You speak of this woman with some familiarity," Foulques said.

"The slave markets of Marseilles are well known. As are the main players in its lucrative flesh trade. I know this woman well enough to say she will not be able to resist seeing the children in person before they are sold. My sources tell me she took ship three days ago, and her destination is the ancient port of Gibelet. Do you know it?"

Foulques nodded. "The Greeks called it Byblos. It is only

a few hours up the north coast and was taken by Baybairs several years ago. Last I heard the city was destroyed and its harbor filled with stone."

"That is only what others would have you know. The harbor thrives these days, and the city, too, has reawakened to the sounds of rattling chains. I suspect there you will find your children."

Foulques could feel his heart hammering faster with every detail Malouf filled in. His excitement, however, was curbed immediately when he remembered who he was dealing with. "Why are you telling me all of this?"

"I help you for two reasons. One: your uncle was always good to us, to Najya, especially. Two: you will do something for me."

Foulques let out a breath. This is what he feared. Malouf was not a man he could afford to be indebted to. "And what would that be?"

"Najya. She will not have me in her life. I can accept that, but she is still my daughter. And she is alone in a big city full of dangerous people. Yes, she has her brother. But in this city, a Christian can often see things a Muslim cannot. I want you to keep an eye out for her, Brother Foulques. Like a father would."

"You know I would," Foulques said. "You do not need to ask."

Malouf held up half a fig and inspected it closely. "I do know that. But me asking, and you accepting, makes it so much more... official."

Foulques could live with those terms. But Malouf had

shown he possessed a weakness when it came to his daughter. And if he were to attempt a rescue, he would need help.

"Very well," Foulques said. "On one condition."

Malouf's eyebrows arched. He poked at the figs on his plate with his knife. "You have a condition for me."

Foulques nodded, wondering if he had gone too far. "If I go after the Northman, I will need a ship and a captain."

"Do you have someone in mind?"

"I do. But the city has seemed to swallow him whole, and I have no idea where to begin looking. I think your son could help me with this."

"You wish only to find him?"

Foulques nodded.

"Then we have an agreement," Malouf said, staring at Foulques with his dark eyes. He squished a half-fig into his mouth and chewed slowly, moving it around, and around, until a tiny stream of its dark juices leaked from one corner of his lips. He bent forward to wipe his mouth on the edge of the white table cloth, and then stood.

Malouf brought his hands together in front of his face. "Peace be upon you, Brother Foulques."

He closed the door silently behind him, leaving Foulques alone with two plates—one empty, one still filled with cut figs—and a tablecloth with a dark red smear running along one edge.

CHAPTER TWENTY-THREE

"COME IN, BROTHER Foulques," Grandmaster Villiers said, looking up from a stack of parchment with quill in hand.

Foulques stepped into the Grandmaster's office, half expecting to see Marshal Clermont lurking in one of its corners, but the Grandmaster was alone. He sat behind his large oak desk, the two flags of the Order hanging behind him on stands; one black and white, the other red and white. He set the quill in a holder nearby, pushed the parchment aside, and interlaced his fingers. His gray and black speckled beard almost touched the desk.

He gave Foulques an approving nod. "You have been busy since your return, so I have heard. That is good. The more the council sees of you fulfilling your duties, the sooner they will reinstate you to Knight Justice. I want you to know, I voted against your demotion, Foulques." He pointed at a simple chair in front of him with a small hole in the shape of a cross carved into its high, straight back.

Foulques sat, automatically reaching down to lift his sword, but remembered he had been relieved of his weapons upon entering the main keep. "Thank you, I appreciate your support, but to be honest, I am not so concerned with regaining rank. In fact, I have found it quite freeing to have fewer responsibilities. This may prove best for everyone."

"Your uncle would be disappointed to hear you speak so, but I can see reason in your words. God has set a specific path for each one of us, but it is up to the individual to discover where that path begins. The surest way I know of to do that, is to take a few steps down many different ones. Eventually, one will feel right." His eyes twinkled and his eyebrows arched. "I was not born a Hospitaller, you know."

"I suspected as much," Foulques said. Grandmaster Villiers had an affable manner about him and Foulques frequently had to remind himself of the differences in their rank. In some ways, he found it easier to speak with the Grandmaster than he did his own uncle. His uncle Guillaume was a fair man, but he had an austere, serious side that was sometimes hard to get past for most people.

"I was married, once."

This caught Foulques off guard. For the briefest moment he thought the Grandmaster had made a jest.

"Well, in God's eyes, I suppose I still am, for we never had the marriage annulled."

Foulques was not sure why he was so surprised. It was not uncommon for a married man to join the Knights of Saint John. But in order to do so, he had to first get his wife's permission. A marriage was, after all, a holy union sanctioned by God. Only with the wife's blessing would the Hospitallers allow a married man to take the oaths of the

Order.

"Did you have any children?" Foulques asked.

The Grandmaster nodded. "A daughter and a son. They both still live and are married themselves now, I am told."

"Then, perhaps you have grandchildren," Foulques said. A vision came to him of Grandmaster Villiers in the French countryside yelling at children to not touch the fruit in the orchard until it was ripe.

The older man got a far off look in his face and one hand fidgeted with his beard. "That I cannot say. You know how news is from the other world. Rare. And it comes in such small bits and drabs, it is never near enough to slake one's thirst."

"Perhaps with the next ship," Foulques said.

The Grandmaster smiled. "Perhaps."

There was an uncomfortable moment of silence. Foulques was relieved when the Grandmaster spoke up. "What brings you here today, Brother Foulques?"

Foulques cleared his throat. "Thank you for seeing me, Master. Speaking of ships, have you received any word from my uncle?"

The Grandmaster shook his head. "Brother Guillaume has been rather silent of late. But so have all our priories in England. I pray they have not forgotten about us over here." He smiled at his joke, but it was one his eyes did not share.

"I see," Foulques said. He did not know why he had asked. There was no possibility that word could have traveled to England already about the disaster that had befallen Foulques's mission. Mind you, no one seemed to consider his mission a disaster any more. The two hundred stolen children had already been largely forgotten. By most.

"I will send word for you the moment I hear something," the Grandmaster said. His voice was kind. He had perhaps mistaken Foulques's silence as concern for his uncle. When Foulques did not reply, the Grandmaster waited for another few moments and then said, "If that will be all, Brother Foulques?"

"I want to go after them," Foulques said. Once he started speaking, the words rushed out. "I will ask for volunteers from the sergeants and mercenaries only, if you prefer. I will need no more than forty men and the funds to secure a ship."

"Tell me you do not speak of the lost children?"

"They are not lost," Foulques said. "They are in Gibelet, but not for long. We must act fast."

"Absolutely not."

Foulques kept talking as though the Grandmaster had said nothing. "I have complete faith in my source. And there is no need to risk a single knight's life, besides my own, of course—"

"Brother Foulques!" The Grandmaster slammed his open palm on the desk. "Stop talking and listen to me."

Foulques blinked. He eased himself back into his chair.

"First of all, I alone do not have the authority to send the Order's soldiers anywhere. Only the Marshal can do that, but I suspect you knew this. Even if I approved of your plan, we would have to have his blessing. I think you and I can both accurately predict how that conversation would go."

"Surely there must be something you can do."

"Short of assembling the Grand Cross and voting in a new Marshal?"

"You could do that?"

The Grandmaster snorted. "Of course I cannot do that! Nor would I want to. Mathieu de Clermont can be tiresome at times, I will give you that, but no one is better suited for his position. He is the finest military commander I have ever seen."

"I understand," Foulques said. In his heart he had known this would be a waste of time. Why did he not listen?

"And from a practical standpoint, it does not make sense. There are two hundred children, you say? How many will still be alive fifteen or twenty years from now when they have grown into actual fighting men? Half? And how many of those will not have the will or the physical aptitude to complete their training? Half again? You would risk forty seasoned campaigners today for a possible gain of fifty, some years in the future. That is extremely poor tactics."

Foulques slowly raised himself to his feet while the Grandmaster lectured him. "I cannot argue with your tactics. You are right, of course." He reached down, lifted his chair, and set it against the wall. The gray stone shone through the cross in the chair's back, contrasting against the dark, well-worn wood. "But there are two hundred souls out there, through no fault of their own, who are about to be plunged into a living hell for the rest of their lives. They think the world has forgotten them and, from how you speak, it would seem they are right."

Foulques was at the door when the Grandmaster called his name. "I said your plan was foolish and I could not give you men. I stand by those words." He pulled open a lower drawer in his desk and withdrew a large purse. "I said nothing about coin."

He tossed the bag at Foulques, who needed both his hands to juggle it to a rest.

"That is the half payment we withheld from Captain Vignoli. Perhaps you can use it to draw him into service once again."

The bag of coins weighed heavy in Foulques's hands. "Master, I do not—"

"God's speed in your travels, Brother Foulques. Both there, and back."

CHAPTER TWENTY-FOUR

V IGNOLO DEI VIGNOLI was careful to make no sudden movements when the two dark-robed, turbaned men slid into his booth. The woman sitting on his lap stopped grinding against him and cocked her head curiously at the newcomers. Vignolo knew she had no idea who they were but, unfortunately, he did, and that knowledge alone could very well cost him his life. It was times like this that he wished his information was not quite so good.

The short, stocky one held a coin out for the woman and told her with his dark eyes and a nod of his head that her services were no longer needed. She pouted, but snatched up the coin and drifted away.

"You are a hard man to find, Vignoli. Took us almost ten minutes once we put the word out," the stocky man said in a quiet voice laced with a thick Arab accent. He slid onto the bench beside Vignolo and the taller man sat directly across from the Genoan, fixing him with hard eyes. When Vignolo began pulling his hands off the table, the man shook his head and motioned with a nod for Vignolo to keep his hands where they were.

Vignolo took a sip from the clay mug in front of him and forced a smile. "Trust me. If I wanted to disappear, all the gold in Damascus would not find me. Even the Old Man of the Mountain might have a time of it."

Vignolo's words sounded braver than he felt. Who knew he was staying at this inn? He had been especially careful after his experience with Giacomo at the Frolicking Eunuch. To make matters worse, word had it that Stephanos, the Frolicking Eunuch himself, was also looking for Vignolo. He just wanted to *talk* with Vignolo, his source had said.

Vignolo did not feel like talking much, so he pulled a couple of favors and got a room under another name in a well-run establishment in Montmusart, the district north of the wall that cut Acre in half. It was as far away from the docks and the Genoan Quarter as one could get.

"So you know who we are," the talkative one said. "That is good, for it shows you are a man of means. But you have chosen not to hide very well, and that is, perhaps, not so good. It shows you think yourself a wiser man than those who look for you." He shrugged. "Come. We will take you to *him*, and then we will see if *he* believes you to be a wise man."

A list of his creditors flashed within Vignolo's mind with, of course, Francesca Provenzano taking first place. But there was no possible way these men were here at her bidding. She may have moved far up the social ladder in Venetian circles, but Vignolo knew she had no connections that would enable her to have a high ranking member of the Dark Brotherhood on her payroll. Or, perhaps by now she did. There was no denying that she had long ago left her modest beginnings behind. Climbing out of the streets of Milan to the courts of Venice was no small task. Ironic, Vignolo thought, how her story was the exact opposite of his own. Although he had once known a life of privilege, the memories of those days were now more than a little ragged around the edges.

The two men led Vignolo up the stairs of the tavern where several boarding rooms were built under the eaves. They stopped in front of the last door, which just happened to be Vignolo's room. The taller man worked the handle and pushed open the door. The fact that his door was unlocked was not lost on Vignolo. He knew he had locked it before going down to the common room.

They pushed Vignolo through the open door but remained outside, closing the door behind him. A single taper burned on the table in the corner, illuminating a lone figure sitting on a chair between it and Vignolo's straw-stuffed mattress on the bare wooden floor.

Vignolo's eyes adjusted and he let out a deep breath when he recognized the man in front of him. "Ah. I do not suppose you brought the rest of my payment with you?"

Foulques de Villaret leaned into the candlelight, his arms folded across his chest with one hand in his short beard. Gone were his Hospitaller robes. He was dressed in the local fashion: loose breeches and shirt under a lightweight layered robe, his head wrapped in a black turban. He fixed Vignolo in place with his blue eyes and said nothing.

"I swear, on my mother's memory, I knew nothing about

the slavers. How could I have? I was with you the whole time. How could I have arranged the attack? You are mad for even thinking it."

"I have made some inquiries," Foulques finally said. "Most say I am mad for dealing with you in the first place."

"Is that what this is about? Personal reputations? Well, there seems to be a fair bit of blackness in your past, my friend. Take, for example, those two hashashin standing out in the hall. You could have come to me yourself. No need to send those animals."

"Enough of the dramatics, Vignolo. They will not help me make up my mind as to whether or not you betrayed me. I am a careful man. I do not make rash decisions and that is why you are still alive. But, I also have a very long memory."

"I swear. I knew nothing of the attack. As I have said before, the Order has always been my best customer. Why would I jeopardize that?"

Foulques stood and walked up to Vignolo. "Then you will not object to proving your loyalty by performing a task."

Vignolo hesitated, trying to scry into the knight's mind. Here it comes, he thought. "Of course. If it is within my power."

"How quickly can you assemble a reliable crew?"

Vignolo thought for a moment. Vagelli was still in the city, he knew that. Along with more than a handful of his Rhodesian mates. It would be a simple matter to add more men if he needed. There were always capable sailors looking for work in Acre. "Tomorrow afternoon. For the right contract, of course. The crew is easy, it is the ship that may prove difficult."

Like sailors, there were plenty of ships for hire in Acre. But by now, word would have gotten out that Vignolo was short on funds. No shipmaster would risk his vessel without an upfront payment of some kind.

"I have already secured the ship," Foulques said. "But it has no slave rowers. You would have to supply men to work the oars."

Vignolo shrugged. "That is no problem. Providing I have a bit of coin to tempt them up front and the promise of more to follow." Vignolo actually preferred using paid rowers. Slaves were too unreliable, especially if they were not your own. One never knew what kind of shape their master kept them in.

Foulques reached inside a pouch at his belt and removed a small purse. He put it in Vignolo's hand. "This will be more than enough to get you started."

Vignolo hefted the small, leather bag. It felt good to the touch. Very good. He was beginning to see a way out of his recent string of bad luck. "So, where are we going?"

"You will assist me in taking back those children the slavers captured."

With those words, Foulques de Villaret banished the euphoria Vignolo had been about to bask in. "Take them back? What do you mean by that?"

"It is exactly as it sounds. This Northman took property belonging to the Order, and I would have it returned."

Vignolo closed his eyes and shook his head. "You are one mad monk. You lost what? Two hundred children? And you hope to just round them up from where exactly?"

"One hundred and eighty-three children are unaccounted for," Foulques said.

"Look Foulques, I would like to help you. I really would. My purse, also, would like to help you. But those children could be anywhere by now. And even if we did find out where they are, there is almost no chance they are still together."

"They are in Byblos."

"Byblos? You mean Gibelet? And how do you know this?"

"My source is reliable enough. But we have to act fast, for they could be moved any day."

Vignolo glanced toward the door and the two men waiting just beyond. The Hospitaller did have some pull with powerful people. It was possible he knew what he was talking about. But as he had already stated, what the Hospitaller suggested was pure madness.

"Let us say that they are in Gibelet. What do you intend to do? March in there with an army of Hospitallers and lay waste to the city looking for them? The Northman will see you coming. He will move his new slaves before you get within ten leagues of the place."

"That is why there will be no Hospitaller force. This has to be a subtle rescue. You, me, and your crew. That is it."

Vignolo could not believe his ears. "I used to think you just strange, Brother Foulques. Now I know you are beyond reason. That is fine, though. Some of my best friends have been touched by madness. Unfortunately for you, I do not wander around the seas attacking Mohammedan pirate bases with them."

"Fortunately for me, I am not your friend," Foulques said.

"Excuse me, while I pick up the shards of my heart."

Vignolo shook his head. A clandestine operation by the Knights of Saint John. That was definitely not their usual style. That realization took Vignolo on a whole new path of thought. "The Grandmaster does not want to have anything to do with this operation, does he? This is all your idea."

"And if it is?" Foulques said, crossing his arms again.

"Who would pay me?"

"I will see to it that you are paid handsomely."

"Define handsomely," Vignolo said.

"Before we leave, you will get the other half of the payment from our first voyage, plus that amount again when the mission is completed."

That got Vignolo's attention. But then he reined in his excitement. "I thought you were in the Grandmaster's bad books. Exactly how is a knight who has sworn himself to poverty going to come up with that kind of coin?"

"I have connections that extend beyond the Order," Foulques said. Although his eyes did not drift to the door and the two men standing on the other side of it, Vignolo was still keenly aware of their presence.

"And if I politely opt to decline your offer?"

"That is a question you do not want answered. The ship is in berth sixty-two. We leave tomorrow, one hour before dusk."

Vignolo laughed. When faced with impossible situations he always laughed. "Who is being dramatic now, my friend?" He pulled a flask from inside his shirt and tipped it back. Then he took a moment to run a hand through his hair, trying to give the impression he was thinking the deal through. He knew he had no choice in the matter. He could not run from Francesca forever and he did not doubt Foulques would be good for the payment. Vignolo suspected God had a good hold on this man's tongue.

"Well. Then, it appears I shall begin with the preparations." Vignolo gave a short bow and by the time he straightened, Foulques was already at the door. He turned with one hand on the iron ring handle.

"And Vignolo. Remember whose purse that is. Spend it only on what is necessary." He opened the door and walked out into the hallway, taking the two men there with him.

Vignolo went to the door and eased it shut. He barred it and stood with his ear pressed against the wood for long minutes after the sound of their footsteps faded away. Satisfied they were gone, Vignolo leaned his back against the door and undid the leather thong cinching the coin bag shut. He peered inside and a low whistle escaped his lips.

Spend it only on what is necessary.

Vignolo remembered the woman that had been sitting on his lap downstairs before the Hospitaller's friends had interrupted. At the time, he knew he could not afford her. He fished a couple of coins out of the bag. He was quite certain Brother Foulques would not approve of what Vignolo was about to deem *necessary*, but fortune was a fickle mistress. One never knew when she was going to visit, or if she would ever come again. So, the prudent thing to do, was to always let her in when she came calling.

CHAPTER TWENTY-FIVE

WHERE WAS VIGNOLO? Foulques stood on the dock in front of berth sixty-two. Vignolo's crew were all accounted for and on board. Dusk was retreating into night, and the flicker of lanterns had begun popping up in the darkness as far as Foulques could see. He began pacing back and forth in front of the sleek merchantman that he had procured for the short trip up the coast. It was of a Greek design similar to the ones many Arabic traders used. This was important, as even though Byblos, or Gibelet, was only a two-hour sail away, the waters around it, and the port itself, were known to be hostile to Frankish vessels. Sometimes they put up with Venetian and Genoese merchant ships, but Foulques did not want to make this mission any more impossible than it already was.

Vagelli ambled his way down the gangplank and joined Foulques on the dock. He said nothing, but crossed his arms and stared down the wooden dock with an intensity as if he was willing Vignolo to appear out of the darkness.

"Is he always late like this?" Foulques asked.

"Never," Vagelli said.

"Never?" That surprised Foulques.

The Rhodesian nodded. "The captain always inspects the ship himself before he takes her out. It is a ritual with him. If he is not here soon, he is not coming."

A stab of anger coursed through Foulques's veins. He wondered, and not for the first time, if Vignolo had betrayed him.

✣

VIGNOLO BELTED ON his sword, a thin, functional blade curved in the Persian manner. It was a soldier's weapon, nothing special to look at, but when it came to weapons, that was how Vignolo liked them. He picked up his sailing sack full of personal effects and opened the door to his room. He leaned out, looked both ways down the hall, and when he was satisfied no hashashin were waiting for him, he exited his room. He went down the stairs, but to avoid the common room he ducked into the kitchen. He greeted the cooks and kitchen boys as they glowered at him and told him to get out. He made his way through them to the back door and stepped out into the alley behind the inn.

The sun had already set and Vignolo realized that he was late. *If I am fortunate, perhaps they will leave without me.* But, for the hundredth time, he told himself he had no choice. He had to take this contract. As much as he liked skulking about, avoiding the world, it would be nice to pay off enough debt that he could walk into a tavern under his own name. Although being intimate with a woman while she cried out a stranger's name could be freeing, it soon became old. It was time he heard his own name upon some lips.

"Marco Polo." A shadow detached itself from the mouth of the alley. Another one followed from around the corner.

"Yes?" Vignolo answered.

"That is your name?" The man walked slowly toward Vignolo.

"Of course it is," Vignolo said. "Why would I have answered, otherwise? Since you know my name, I believe introductions may be in order for you and your friend."

The other man came up behind the first and then stepped forward to his left, effectively cutting off Vignolo's access to the alley and the streets behind them. They were both long and lean and, although they kept their hands away from the swords at their sides, the way they moved told Vignolo they could have those weapons in their hands in the wink of an eye.

"Marco Polo sounds like a made up name to me," the first man said.

"Not nice to make up names," the second man said. "That is something a dishonest man might do."

Made up name? It most definitely was not, thought Vignolo. At least not by him. He had shared drinks, many drinks in fact, with a man not too far back that had gone by that name. A likable fellow, who had no shortage of tall tales when he was in his cups.

"I was just on my way back inside. How about you join me and I buy you a mug?" Vignolo asked.

Vignolo held no illusions that these men were here for a

drink. As he spoke he turned away from them, being very careful to keep his hand away from his sword. If there had been only one, he would not have hesitated to draw his blade. But he knew he did not have a chance against the two of them if swords were drawn. Knives, on the other hand, were a different matter.

He took two quick steps back to the stairs leading into the inn's kitchen. He heard the men's boots scuff across the ground, moving to catch him before he entered. Vignolo put his right foot on the second step, like he meant to go up the stairs, but then he dipped slightly at the waist, pulled his boot knife and spun around just as one of the men was about to grab him by the shoulder. With a swift in and out, he stuck the man once in the midsection then slashed him across the muscle of his upper right arm, just in case the first stab was not fatal. The man grunted in surprise. Vignolo pushed him as hard as he could into the second man, who was now drawing his sword. But the man was even quicker than he looked and he stepped nimbly to the side as his companion flailed past him and landed on the ground. He clenched his eyes and clutched both hands to the wound in his abdomen.

Vignolo saw a clear path out of the alley and he took it. He darted past the man before he was able to clear steel from scabbard. The main street was just ahead. He bent forward and was almost at a full run when three more men appeared immediately in front, choking off his escape route. He scrambled to a full stop and drew his own sword. His eyes went left and right, searching for another option. He was trapped.

"Marco Polo is it? Strange how you are the spitting image of a man named Vignolo dei Vignoli."

Vignolo suspected he knew that voice. He scrutinized the speaker's face as he moved forward into the meager light. He had never wished to be so wrong.

"Hello, Giacomo," Vignolo said.

"So, it is you," Giacomo said. He was close enough for Vignolo to see his tight-lipped sneer. "I learned the hard way that you are part man and part rabbit, so I thought I would bring along a few friends this time. Put down your weapons and I will let you live. For a time."

Four against one with all avenues of escape cut off. Giacomo kept walking toward Vignolo with no hesitation. Knowing he had to decide on a course of action before Giacomo got within disemboweling range, Vignolo weighed his options. The scale was broken.

Vignolo threw his sword and knife to the ground and held up his hands. Giacomo looked sorely disappointed, and when he reached Vignolo he reversed the grip on his blade and drove its pommel into Vignolo's forehead. Vignolo's head snapped back and he crumpled to his knees. Two pairs of arms pulled Vignolo to his feet making his skull throb with the sudden height change.

"He cut open Lorenzo!"

Giacomo walked past Vignolo to where Lorenzo squirmed on the ground. "Pull your hands away. Show me."

Lorenzo, gritting his teeth, separated his hands to show his wound. Giacomo shook his head. "Bad news, friend." He pushed the tip of his sword into the center of Lorenzo's throat and kept up a slow, steady pressure until it came up against the hard alley floor. He withdrew it at the same leisurely pace. When Lorenzo no longer moved, Giacomo walked slowly over to where Vignolo was held by a man on each arm.

Giacomo held his red blade in front of Vignolo. "See what you have done?" He had a wild expression on his face. Vignolo had seen that look in men's eyes before and he suddenly regretted giving up his weapons.

"Take me to Francesca. I have news for her," Vignolo said.

Giacomo shook his head. "I am afraid I cannot do that. She has returned to Venice. But she asked me to take care of things here, and left me with very detailed instructions concerning yourself."

"Oh?"

"Two simple instructions, really. 'Collect what Vignolo owes by month-end' she said."

"I see," Vignolo said. "About—"

"And the second one was just as straight forward. 'If he does not have it, kill him. However, you see fit.'" Giacomo wiped Lorenzo's blood off his sword by sliding it diagonally across the front of Vignolo's chest. "It is the second part of that instruction that I love the sound of. However I see fit. Has a nice ring to it." He tapped the side of Vignolo's cheek with an open hand. "So, month-end was three days ago. Do you have the coin or not?"

"As I was about to say, I do have the money. But not

with me, of course."

Giacomo nodded, his lips compressed into a smile. "Not with you, you say. Good. That will do fine."

A ringing sound had begun in the back of Vignolo's head a few seconds ago. He had dismissed it as the aftereffects of Giacomo's blow, but he now heard it growing louder. As it became nearer and more discernible, he realized it was not so much a ringing as it was the sound of metal grating on metal. Finally, at the same time his four captors looked toward the mouth of the alley, Vignolo placed the ringing sound. It was the rustle of mail. The type only a knight could afford. It stopped ten feet behind Vignolo. The next sound he heard was Brother Foulques de Villaret's voice.

"I have need of the Genoan. Any who wish to live, may leave now. I will not offer this again."

The men holding Vignolo dropped his arms. The small alley was filled with the swish of steel clearing leather and wood. Vignolo turned and took a step back toward the inn. There was still one of the two original thugs behind him, standing over the dead body of his partner, but Vignolo paid him no heed. All he knew was he did not want to be between a fully armored Hospitaller knight and his quarry.

Foulques stood in the exact center of the narrow alley. He wore the black fighting mantle of the Hospitallers over his mail hauberk. Unlike a monk's relatively tight-fitting robe, the mantle was split open all the way down the center, allowing its wearer mobility and ease of movement. The white cross on his left breast seemed to create a light all its own in the semi-darkness of his surroundings. Foulques stood with one foot in front of the other, his hand resting on the pommel of his still-sheathed sword. A breeze found its way into the alley and stirred his wild hair, which was uncovered, as he had not bothered to pull up his mail coif.

Giacomo and the two men who had been holding Vignolo spread out to take up the width of the alley. There were no words, no idle threats. They knew they did not face a man who could be cowered. And being experienced men of violence, they knew their best chance was to take the knight together. Their grim faces made no attempt to hide their intentions as they stalked forward with their weapons held before them.

Instead of waiting for them to close the distance, Foulques strode forward to meet his attackers. With his steel still in its scabbard, he feinted by dipping his shoulder toward the middle man and then suddenly his blade was in his hand. He spun and brought his weapon down in a slanted arc that caught the man on his right, high on his shoulder. The Hospitaller yelled, following through with the blow. His sword carved through the thug's collar bone, the upper right of his ribcage, and exited somewhere near his hip. There was a moment of complete silence as everyone watched the man's shoulder and a good part of his guts spill away from his body before it collapsed. Foulques, however, never stopped moving. The point of his sword plunged through the sternum of the next man. Either the man had been moving forward, or perhaps Foulques's thrust had simply met less resistance than he had anticipated, but his sword sank all the way to its hilt, leaving most of the blade protruding out of the man's back on one side of his spine.

Giacomo eyes were wide with a mixture of rage and sheer terror as he stepped in to bring his blade down on the knight's exposed head. Vignolo watched the scene unfold and it seemed as though Foulques operated under a different set of natural laws than Giacomo. It was said that the true knights of the Orders, those men who had wholly given themselves over to Christ, not the pretenders that joined for personal gain or political agenda, were a force of God on the battlefield. They were God's weapons and through them He imposed His divine will. Vignolo had always thought that to be just another cartload of bull dung shoveled on the common populace by the Pope and the Church. That was before today.

Giacomo's sword jerked its way toward Foulques's head while his own blade was still hilt-deep in a man who was dead, but had not yet realized it. It seemed Foulques was allowed three or four movements to every one of Giacomo's. He saw the danger coming from behind, turned back to his blade, and with both hands pulled it out as he stepped back toward his attacker. The blade slid out of the man's chest and Foulques grabbed the blade of his weapon in his gloved hands, then he slammed the pommel into Giacomo's face. The henchman's blade completed its arc and found nothing but air and hard ground. Still gripping his sword by its blade, Foulques yelled again and brought it around club-like from the side. The crossguard of the hilt shattered the fragile bones at Giacomo's temple and lodged itself in his skull.

Giacomo's blade clattered to the ground a full second before his body. Foulques allowed Giacomo's body to drag his sword to the ground, and then gave it a sharp kick to dislodge its handle. He nuzzled his boot under the blade near the hilt and flicked it back into his hand. He turned on the last man.

He had his hands up in the air, his back pressed into the wall of a building to get as far from the murderous Hospitaller as possible. Vignolo noted a dark patch on the front of his breeches that had not been there in their earlier encounter. Foulques raised a finger and pointed at the sword the man still held in his hand. He turned his head, flinched in horror at the sight of the blade, and threw it to the ground.

If Foulques had taken one step toward the man, Vignolo was sure he would have slid down the wall and curled up into a ball. But Foulques pulled a blue cloth from his belt and began wiping down his sword. The man slid along the wall and when he had put enough distance between Foulques and himself, pushed off and ran from the alley like Cerberus the Hell hound was chomping at his heels.

"Get your things," Foulques said, as he continued wiping down his sword. "We are late."

Vignolo could not help noticing how the linen cloth had been neatly folded and appeared to be freshly laundered, however, it had several dark stains that no amount of cleaning could ever fully purge.

CHAPTER TWENTY-SIX

FOULQUES LEANED AGAINST the sleek merchantman's railing and peered into the darkness. Byblos, or rather, Gibelet, as it had been known for the last few hundred years, was a city so old no one knew for sure how many names it had. The Greeks called it Byblos, and because it was renowned for the production or trade of papyrus, they eventually used the city's name as the root word for 'book'. In time, that word, *biblio*, was then adopted for the sacred collection of Christian writings which the world would come to know as simply *The Bible*.

Foulques wondered at the irony that should bring him here. He could not help but think it was a sign that God was with him in this quest.

Vignolo's first mate, Vagelli, stood next to the Hospitaller. They had pulled into the harbor of Gibelet, a short sail up the north coast from Acre, in the darkness of early evening. Knowing they had a better need of speed than cargo carrying ability, Foulques had procured a better vessel for them this time. While the ship only had one bank of oars, manned by Vignolo's Rhodesian crew, not slaves, it was built low to the water and handled easily. It could not hope to outrun the Wyvern under oar power alone, but it had four sails rigged in the lateen fashion that would prove its match in speed on the open seas.

"Do you think Vignolo will find them?" Foulques asked. He was dressed in a dark tunic and breeches, over which he wore a non-descript brown cotton robe with a full hood. The cross of Saint John was nowhere to be seen.

"Oh, if they are here, he will find them," Vagelli said. "For good or for ill, Vignolo will find them. He has a talent for this sort of thing."

As if on cue, a dark figure emerged from the shadows and walked casually down the wharf toward their berth. Vagelli squinted and shielded his eyes from the lantern he held. "It seems he found something. Strangest looking children I have seen, if that is what they are."

Foulques followed Vagelli's lead and blocked the light from his eyes. He heard them before he saw them. Vignolo strutted down the dock, holding a rope in each hand. Attached to the ropes were four donkeys, walking two and two. The clip-clop of their hooves punctuated the night's silence with a lazy beat.

"Where did he get those?" Foulques asked. Vagelli just shrugged and went to lower the gangplank. Moments later, with donkeys in hand, Vignolo joined Foulques on the mid deck.

"We have them," Vignolo said.

"I hope you mean the children," Foulques said, but already he felt the tension in his shoulders that had been building over the last few days dissolve a little into the night.

"But they are heavily guarded."

"Of course they are," Foulques said. "Now tell me your plan and let us get on with it."

Vignolo grinned and his white, even teeth flashed in the dim lantern light. "How do you know I have one?"

Foulques looked at the donkeys and rolled his eyes. "You should have brought horses."

"I learned a long time ago to never steal a Saracen's horse. But donkeys? They are fair ground."

"You stole them?"

"Of course I did! You think this port is crowded with donkey merchants this time of night?"

Foulques crossed his arms. "The plan," he said.

Vignolo's grin got bigger. "We will need rope," he said. "A lot of rope, and more importantly, I hope you can swim."

✠

SOAKING WET AND shivering, Vignolo and Foulques crouched against the back wall of a small warehouse where Vignolo was sure the children were being held. Both men were bare from the waist up and wore only their breeches on their bottom halves. Foulques had his sword tied around his back and Vignolo had only a knife belted at his side.

The warehouse was a small building that stood on its own wharf. A wide walkway branched off from the main harbor dock and led up to its only set of doors. It was a merchant hut, available for rent from the harbor master, and was used for temporarily storing goods brought in from ships. Two armed Mamluk guards stood immediately in front of the warehouse doors.

Voices could be heard coming from further down the dock. Foulques shifted his feet carefully on the narrow lip running around the warehouse, and leaned his head around the corner. Another ten or twelve men were involved in a raucous game of hazard fifty yards away in front of another similar merchant hut. As Foulques watched the men throw their dice on a makeshift table they had constructed, he felt a tap on his shoulder. Vignolo motioned for Foulques to make his way around his side of the hut and he would go the other.

Hugging the building's wall, Foulques inched his way along the ledge. He had decided that he would take out his man first to give Vignolo the benefit of the distraction. He had never seen the Genoan fight and was not sure if he was up to the task. He took a deep breath and was about to step out when he heard a hiss of surprise come from his guard. He stepped around the corner and saw Vignolo with his hand clamped tightly over the furthest guard's mouth. Blood poured down the man's mail from a wide open slit across his throat.

The other guard had his sword half drawn by the time Foulques threw his arm over his head and clamped the guard's throat in the crook of his elbow. The guard was an experienced warrior. The moment he realized an attacker was on him from behind, he let go of his half-drawn sword and grasped for a knife at his belt. Foulques beat him to it. Leaving one arm wrapped around the Mamluk's throat, he swiftly drew out the man's knife and let it fall to the wharf. Then he slid his arm up behind the guard's head and leaned back with all his weight. He felt the man try to call out, but it was too late, as Foulques had cut off his air. Foulques used his head to nuzzle the flailing man's neck into the right position and brief seconds later, the Mamluk's struggles ceased. Foulques eased the body down into a sitting position.

Vignolo tugged the helmet off his dead guard and tossed it to Foulques. "Thought you had fallen in the water for a minute," he said.

As Foulques donned the helmet, he watched in surprise as Vignolo walked over to the guard Foulques had just rendered unconscious. The ship captain bent over and cleanly slit his throat. He wiped the knife on the guard's sleeve and when he caught Foulques looking at him said, "What? You think you are the only careful man around?"

Apparently, Vignolo was more than up to the task, Foulques thought.

Foulques drew the guard's scimitar from his sheath and took a few practice swipes to learn its balance. "How much time do you need?"

"As long as it takes," Vignolo said. He gave Foulques a quick wave and disappeared back around the side of the hut.

"As long as it takes," Foulques muttered to himself as he stood up beside the door. The plan was for him to pretend he was one of the guards. In the darkness, and this far away from the Mamluks gambling in the distance, that should be easy enough. So he leaned against the door, crossed his arms against his chest, and waited.

Through the door he could hear the occasional muted voice, a shuffle here and there. There were definitely people inside. He hoped Vignolo was right.

After about fifteen minutes, Foulques felt his hopes rising. He was sure Vignolo would be along at any moment. No sooner had the thought entered his mind, a voice called out in Arabic and a warrior detached himself from the main group of dice players. He began walking toward the hut and gave his head a disgusted shake, like he had just lost a month's salarium. He waved toward Foulques, obviously suggesting it was time they exchanged places. Foulques glanced around on all sides.

"Vignolo... now would be a good time," he said under his breath.

The Mamluk slowed at twenty paces. He sensed something was not right. A couple more steps and even in the low light he could tell Foulques wore no armor save the helmet. He turned and shouted at the group of warriors behind him. An alarmed murmur shot up in the night and the sound of steel being drawn whispered through the air. Standing there in bare feet, his cotton breeches still dripping from his recent swim, Foulques felt worse than naked. He tightened his grip on the scimitar in his left hand and drew his own sword from the sheath slung over his shoulder. Even in this impossible situation, seeing and feeling his perfectly honed blade in his hand calmed his heartbeat.

Foulques stepped out onto the walkway which joined the hut to the main dock. Only three or four paces wide, its edges lined with drooping railings made from thick rope,

Foulques thought with two swords he may be able to create a bottle neck and hold the Mamluk force back for a time. How long he did not know, for sure. Until he tired, he supposed, or one of them got in a lucky thrust. Even though he was bare chested and facing trained warriors in full armor, the thought never occurred to him that one of the warriors might simply be more skilled. All such thoughts had been banned from his mind years ago under the tutelage of Marshal Clermont. Confidence is what separates the dead from the living, the old sword master had always said.

Foulques took his spot in the middle of the walkway, swished his blades left and right to gauge their range and see how they worked together, then he mouthed a quick prayer. The first Mamluk came up slowly, a few others close behind. The rest took up defensive formations on the dock: one facing land, the other the sea. They were professional soldiers and assumed that Foulques was not alone.

The Mamluk stepped onto the walkway, his eyes took in the half naked man in front of him and then scanned left and right. He saw the bodies of his fellow Mamluks and that brought a growl to his throat. He stepped forward and swung his sword in a forty-five degree downward arc aiming for Foulques's left ear. It was a hard swing, but checked.

The advantage of fighting with two blades was that one could be used to parry or entangle an opponent's weapon, while the second could be brought in for the killing blow. Foulques knew this, but so did the Mamluk. Hence, the Mamluk's attack was balanced and under control. Once his blade made contact with Foulques's own, he would use the momentum of the block to bounce his blade away and immediately bring it back for another attack from any number of angles before Foulques could bring his second blade into the fray.

Foulques was determined to not let his opponent dictate the course of the fight. He brought his sword up like he was going to parry, but at the last moment he slid forward and twisted away to one side, keeping both his swords pressed in close to his body. The Mamluk's sword whistled through the air next to his head and down past his side. The Mamluk stumbled when Foulques did not block his attack, and for a split second, was off-balance. Foulques brought his scimitar around and used it to strike the man's arm and to pull him forward with his own momentum. The Mamluk's mail protected him from injury but he pitched forward, his blade striking the wood at his feet and, as he tottered in place to regain his balance, Foulques brought his other sword around in a deadly arc, striking the man in the back of his neck. The blade found little resistance there so Foulques allowed it to continue on its gory journey through tissue, artery, and bone. Foulques finished his follow-through, brought both blades down into a low guard, and watched the Mamluk's head slide off its rest. It hit the wood planking with a heavy thud, rolling to a stop on one ear in time to see its own body fold and collapse.

A half dozen warriors charged down the dock bellowing in outrage. Foulques slapped the severed head aside with his scimitar and cursed both Satan and Vignolo dei Vignoli in the same breath. Where was the Genoan? Foulques had just enough time to roll his shoulders once and assume a position with the headless corpse between himself and his new attackers before the first one came down the walkway.

Marshal Clermont had been the one who instructed Foulques in the art of fighting with two blades at once, but it was Weapons Master Glynn, the wily Scotch veteran of countless battles against both Mohammedans and English soldiers, who had trained him on how to fight over a corpse. It did not matter if the corpse was one of your own or had belonged to the enemy ranks, the key was to keep it between you and your opponent. Make your opponent be the one to step over it to attack you. When fighting, the fastest and most balanced method of moving is to keep your feet as close to the ground as possible by using a slide step. The higher you lift your foot off the ground, the slower and more unbalanced you become. As a young man, this had been so hammered into Foulques that he found himself automatically lunging with his straight sword as the next warrior raised his foot in the air to step over his fallen comrade. Foulques caught him in the stomach, and the strength of his thrust multiplied by the man's forward momentum allowed the fine point of Foulques's sword to spread the links of his mail and penetrate into his guts. He fell to one knee, but had the presence of mind to pull himself to one side of the walkway and allow others to pass by.

The next Mamluk came on with a little more caution. He traded blows with Foulques from his side of the corpse, trying to force Foulques far enough back so that he could step over the obstacle. But this was exactly the type of game

Foulques wanted to play. The enemy could only come at him one at a time on the narrow walkway. If a few of them decided to strip off their armor, they could simply jump into the water and swim over to the hut and come up behind Foulques, but he was not too worried about that happening. It was said the blood of the Mohammedans ran with the sands of the desert. They were famous for their distrust of open water, especially salt water. Eventually they would go that route, Foulques knew, but not until they had exhausted all others.

Foulques parried a straight thrust and had to stop himself from slashing the man's face with a backhand cut. It would have been a mistake to end the fight so quickly. This Mamluk was not a poor swordsman, just a predictable one. His technique was solid, his sword arm strong. But he was no match for Foulques. *The Weasel* had taught him too well. So Foulques strung his man along, and with every parry, strike, and counterstrike, it grew even easier as the Mamluk tired. Finally, the Musselman stepped back, with his mouth open and sucking in air, and a fresh warrior took his place. The new man sent a flurry of strikes against Foulques, trying to drive him back. This man was not as strong as the last, Foulques recognized, but he was much quicker. Foulques felt the stiffness of fatigue begin to creep into his arms. Recognizing his opponent as a significant threat, Foulques stopped the man's forward momentum with a direct thrust through one eye. He fell to the ground so quickly Foulques could not dislodge his sword from the man's skull in time, and the weight of the dead body yanked the blade from his hand.

"Enough!" The deep-throated command cut through all sounds of combat and sent a tremor through Foulques's abdomen. It appeared to have a similar effect on the Mamluks facing Foulques for they immediately lowered their weapons and wordlessly backed away onto the dock, where they stepped aside and bowed their heads.

The owner of the voice emerged from the darkness and approached slowly, until he stood at the opposite end of the walkway Foulques defended. Foulques recognized the Northman instantly. It was not his great height or bulk that gave him away, but rather the bare arms which glistened in the low light. His tight-fitting mail hauberk was sleeveless and the corded arms which jutted out were as thick as most men's legs.

Staring across at the imposing Mamluk, another man may have felt all hope lost at that moment. But Foulques saw only a fool before him. The Northman's arms were a target calling out to the scimitar Foulques held, and the man did not even wear a helmet. A strategy began to form in his mind and Foulques took a deep breath in preparation.

The Northman tilted his head and stared at Foulques. "I know you," he said in French. "You are the Frank that accompanied my children."

"Your children?" Foulques said, fighting to keep his voice from rising.

The Northman looked to the left and right of the half-naked man standing in front of him and his warriors. "Like everything else in this world, they belong to those with the strength to hold them. Whose do you think they are?"

Foulques gave his scimitar a swing. "Come any closer and you will find out."

The Northman reached his hands down, unclasped the buckles on his sword belt, and eased it to the ground like it was a baby.

"Where are your black robes, monk? Has your god taken them from you?" There was not a trace of mirth in his words. His thick fingers pulled at a leather tie on his mail vest near one hip. He yanked the leather through a couple dozen metal eyelets that ran all the way up to his armpit. The tie hissed as it scraped its way through the small metal rings, the sound growing longer with every pull. When he was done, the Northman shrugged his bulk out of the armor and placed it on the ground next to his sword belt with just as much care.

"Is that what happened? Are you no longer deemed worthy in His eyes since you lost your children?" He pulled his padded undershirt over his head and stood naked from the waist up in the half darkness, save for a pair of leather bracers that covered his wrists and extended halfway up his forearms. The only movement was the rising and falling of his bare, massive chest.

Foulques refused to dignify the Mamluk with an answer, but the Northman nodded his head after a few seconds of silence. "I see," he said. "I think you are a brave man to come here. But have you truly come to prove your loyalty to your god? I find that difficult to believe."

"My faith has nothing to do with why I am here," Foulques said. "I came to free these children from a lifetime of slavery."

A laugh escaped the Northman and it took him a moment to get it under control. "And what will these children do with their newfound freedom? Return to their families? Perhaps begin new lives as peddlers and merchants?"

"They will become Brothers of the Order of Saint John."

"Ah, so they will become like you. A Hospitaller. Tell me Hospitaller, do you consider yourself a free man?"

"I serve the Order because I wish to. But you are the pawn of a slave-trading whore from Marseilles. I will not take a lecture on freedom from you."

"It is true, my mistress commands me. But my life, my will, is ruled not by her or any other, nor even Allah Himself. I am a warrior. I gave myself to the Furusiyya long ago, and it is by this code that my life has been shaped." He pointed at Foulques's sword embedded in the skull of the Mamluk at the Hospitaller's feet. "Take up your sword. The Furusiyya will not let me take unfair advantage over another who follows the code."

"I care nothing for your Furusiyya," Foulques said.

"You and I both know this is not true," the Northman said. "You pronounce the word too well."

Keeping his back straight and his eyes on the Mamluk, Foulques bent at the knees and retrieved his sword with a swift yank. He wiped it on the leg of his breeches. The Northman nodded appreciatively.

"A sword like that deserves to be cared for," the Mamluk said. "Now, come to me here in the open, where we can finish this while God looks on in envy, even if, to Him, our glory lasts only for the briefest of moments."

A great calmness swept over Foulques. Gone were all traces of thoughts about strategy, Vignolo, the children, the Order and his place within it. Foulques de Villaret tossed the scimitar to the wood planking at his feet and ran his hand lightly along the edge of his hand-and-a-half sword. He stepped over the corpses in front of him and waded into the midst of the Mamluk warriors.

CHAPTER TWENTY-SEVEN

A HALF-NAKED VIGNOLO stood beside the squat
Rhodesian sailor, Vagelli, as he gripped the wheel
loosely in his sun-wrinkled, practiced hands. They were
under slow oar power only, for the moment. All the sails of
the sleek merchantman were furled.

"Easy now. Keep this heading so the wind is with us
when we need her. Nothing too jerky or we will be fishing
for a grumpy Hospitaller," Vignolo said, his breeches still
dripping with water.

"Perhaps this is something you should be telling the
donkeys," Vagelli said. He waved away Vignolo with one
hand.

Vignolo took the hint and left Vagelli alone at the wheel.
He took the few steps down to the main deck and approached the anchor rack at the rear of the ship. Another
seaman stood there holding the halter of one of the four
donkeys harnessed to the spoke and wheel anchor raising
system. The anchor itself sat on the deck a few yards away,
the rope that usually ran through its massive iron eye
noticeably absent. One end of the thick braided rope was still

attached to a huge spool built into the frame of the ship, while the other end disappeared off the back of the ship through a gap in the railing.

Vignolo checked the donkey harnesses one last time to make sure they were secure. He nodded to the seaman, stepped up onto the deck railing, and climbed down the rope netting hanging off the rear of the ship. He lowered himself back into the water and began swimming as silently as he could.

Before he was halfway back to where he had left Foulques, he heard shouts in the darkness, and moments later, the unmistakable clang of steel on steel carried across the water. Vignolo began swimming faster, no longer worried about making noise.

✠

FOULQUES REFUSED TO let his mind dwell on what would happen to him once he defeated the Northman. Most likely, the Mamluk soldiers encircling the two combatants would cut him down. He pushed that thought from his mind by stepping forward and delivering a hard thrust at the Northman's bare chest, and then followed with a quick slide-step and a powerful two-handed overhand stroke meant to split the man in two. Foulques knew the longer the fight went on the greater the chance he could be wounded. And besides, since the other Mamluks were most likely going to kill him anyway, Foulques relished the thought of humiliating their leader first. It was best on all accounts to end it now.

Perhaps if he had not been in such a hurry to end the combat, Foulques would have recognized the flaw in his strategy when the Northman stepped to the side of his thrust instead of parrying it with his own blade. The Northman had an imposing physique, and in Foulques's experience, powerfully built men approached swordplay with a bully mentality. Foulques believed it was always best to shatter these men's confidence by driving them back with an immediate head-on attack. But his blade speared empty air and the momentum dragged Foulques off-balance. He managed to check himself almost immediately, but it was enough to turn his slide-step into a stutter step and he had to twist his torso to bring his overhand attack back on target. By the time he brought his blade down, the Northman had stepped smoothly around Foulques to stand off his right side. This time Foulques was unable to catch himself and his blade carved downward to strike the wharf, gouging the wood and spitting up long slivers.

The moment his sword bounced off the planking, Foulques knew he had gravely underestimated his opponent. Out of his peripheral vision he saw the Northman calmly twist his hips as he raised his scimitar to deliver a backhand strike at the small of Foulques's back. Foulques gritted his teeth, for he was caught so far out of position there was little else he could do. The graceful curve of the scimitar was designed to cut and keep cutting once it struck. Unarmored as he was, Foulques knew the keen blade would sever his spine and lodge itself somewhere in his guts.

Foulques had dreamed of his death many times. Always

CHAPTER TWENTY-EIGHT

FOULQUES LANDED HARD on his knees yet again. Blood ran in a thin stream from his mouth and pooled between his hands on the wharf, as he willed his arms to quit shaking long enough to push himself back to his feet. He heard Marshal Clermont's voice in his head yelling at him to stop.

Rise! Do you want to die a nobody?

His arms supplied just enough strength for him to kneel. He took a moment to force air into his lungs and wipe at his mouth with the back of one hand. The blood on his hand appeared as black as the gently lapping sea that surrounded them all. The darkness of the night was kept at bay by a ring of lanterns and torches. He heard a series of muffled steps and his sword appeared on the wood planking in front of him yet again.

"Pick it up," a voice said.

Foulques looked up and saw the Marshal standing before him, his black cloak billowing in the breeze and the white cross on his chest tattered and dirty. Men called him the Mongoose but the straight sword in his hand weaved it had come while he defended a castle wall or a group of pilgrims from overwhelming enemy forces. He and several of his brothers, some dressed in the blood-red Hospitaller war tunics and others in the black ones usually worn in times of peace, stood back to back in a glorious last stand. For some reason, in his dreams, Foulques always wore the black mantle of the Order but he fought like a demon as his brothers around him were cut down, one by one. As it often was with dreams, he would wake before his own end came.

The Northman uncoiled his hips in a transfer of energy to his sword arm that Foulques could not help but admire. Just before the cutting edge of the scimitar broke the Hospitaller's skin, the Mamluk turned his wrist and the flat side of his blade slapped against the small of Foulques's back with tremendous force. Foulques cried out as his feet came off the ground, and his head and shoulders arched back from the strength of the blow. He landed hard on his hands and knees, while a white-hot, searing pain radiated across his lower back and wrapped around his sides. In his misery, with pain blurring his vision, he could just make out his sword lying several feet away.

The Northman stood over Foulques's blade, staring at it. He nudged a pointed shoe beneath it and slid it toward Foulques.

"That was for treating my future sword like a butcher's tool. Unfortunately, you will feel much worse if you do not give me your best. Fight me like an equal and I will give you a swift death; treat me like a child again and you will suffer. The choice is yours."

Breathing out the pain as best he cou[ld] his fingers around his sword handle and He tried to focus his eyes on the loomi[ng] Hashim, but the Mamluk's face blurr[ed] though he were a character in one of [Unfortunately, the pain crippling his bo[dy] very much awake. Half-naked, surround[ed] the leering faces of Mohammedans, Fou[lques] disgraced Knight of the Hospitaller Or[der] came to the sudden realization that he [was] alone.

through the air in minute movements like the head of a cobra, watching, waiting for the right moment. Foulques blinked once and the apparition shimmered. The straight sword curved, the lean form of the Marshal expanded, and his black cloak fluttered away.

"Pick it up," the Northman said again. "Die standing on your feet."

Foulques wrapped his hand around the hilt of his sword, and the feel of it gave him enough strength to stand. But he knew he had little more. His shoulders ached, beneath his breeches one thigh was purple and swollen to twice its normal size from slap after slap of the Mamluk's cruel blade. A thin line of pain burned diagonally across his chest where the Northman had cut him. Foulques tried to tell himself he had avoided a kill blow, but he knew that was a lie. The Mamluk was bigger, stronger, and quicker. Perhaps even quicker than the Mongoose himself. Not in a darting, blinding speed type of manner, but rather, the Northman's speed came from a place of balance and precision. He knew where he was at all times and where he wanted to go. Not since he was a boy had Foulques felt so overwhelmed in a sword fight.

"Are you wondering why your god has deserted you?" the Northman asked walking around Foulques in slow easy steps with his scimitar at his side. "Perhaps you blame it on your sins? Perhaps you should have gone to Rome and paid money to one of your bishops to remove those sins. Then your god would now be standing beside you."

The Mamluks encircling the two combatants had grown

bored with the fight a long time ago, but the Northman's comment brought on a few peals of laughter and a renewed interest in the contest.

"God is here," Foulques heard himself say, though his voice was hoarse and ragged. "As is Lucifer."

More laughter ensued and the Northman shook his head. "No. No, they are not. This is the realm of men. God cares little what happens here. If a stronger man decides to take something from a weaker man, all the prayer in the world, whether to Allah or your Christian god, will not prevent it."

"Those who take from the weak will be punished. If not in this life, then at the Gates of Saint Peter," Foulques said.

"Ah, but that is my point. Why wait until one is dead to punish him? The Furusiyya demands that the strong who abuse their power should be punished by those who are stronger." The Northman raised his sword and pointed it at Foulques's blood-smeared chest. "You Christians have enjoyed great power for some time. But now? Now it is time for you to be punished."

Foulques assumed a high guard with a two-handed grip. It was all he could do to keep his arms from shaking, but ignoring the pain in his leg and chest, he managed to keep the tremors at bay. The Northman recognized his struggle and nodded once, approvingly. Then he loosed a battle yell and launched himself at the Hospitaller with a flurry of hard blows. As Foulques parried the first blow, he realized with despair that the Northman was even stronger than he had previously thought. He had been toying with Foulques, prolonging the fight when he could have finished it at any time. But now he had unleashed his full fury with the intention of breaking the Christian open in a grand display before his men, to remind them why he was their Emir.

Fearing the muscles in his swollen leg would give out if he attempted to sidestep or retreat, Foulques had no choice but to plant himself firmly in place against the Mamluk's onslaught and swat aside his attacks as best he could. The men clashed together, and for a moment the Northman seemed surprised that he had failed to drive back the wounded knight. But he recovered quickly and after trapping Foulques's sword with his scimitar, brought an elbow across his temple. He attempted to bring his scimitar up for a kill stroke but Foulques, swaying unsteadily, managed to reverse the pin with his own sword and prevent the Northman from raising his weapon. The Mamluk growled, stepped in and head-butted Foulques between the eyes. Foulques's vision went dark as pain erupted from the bridge of his nose. His feet could no longer feel the ground and his arms spun in an attempt to regain balance. He hit the wharf hard on his upper back, driving the air from his lungs. The rest of his body settled around him like a blanket thrown high into the air. And then a huge pointed shoe stomped onto his midsection, pinning him to the ground.

Vaguely, like a wind blowing on the other side of a dune, Foulques could hear a voice.

"My name is Badru Hashim. I tell you this not from a source of pride, for my name means very little to me. I was born a slave. I will die a slave. No. I tell you because you fought well enough and should know the name of the man who killed you."

Blackness once again clouded Foulques's vision as he tried to will movement into his arms and legs, but the weight on his chest held him in place like an insect pinned to a board. Then, the weight was suddenly lifted.

"Turn him over."

Rough hands grabbed Foulques by his arms and legs. He was flipped onto his stomach, his cheek pressed against the cool, damp wharf.

"At first, you will want to move. It is natural to fear the pain of the knife. But death will find you, whether you fight the pain or not. However, if you embrace it, like I know you can for you have shown me your strength, I will finish the eagle quickly. All watching today will remember this moment. You will soar for many years to come. Hold him tightly."

As the Northman dragged his knife across Foulques's back, the pain brought the Hospitaller's mind back into focus. He grimaced and cried out. He tried to flail with his legs and arms, but strong hands resisted his attempts.

"Hold him!" the Northman said.

The hot pain came again. Another scream left Foulques breathless, and the cut that followed brought with it all the agony of the others, but it elicited no sound from Foulques.

"Emir!"

The pressure on Foulques's extremities suddenly released and he became aware of open space around him. His lungs attempted to drag air into his shuddering body, which resulted in a coughing fit as blood leaked down his throat from his broken nose. He turned his head to the side and, while still coughing, managed to push himself up on one elbow. With some air finally making it into his body, his head began to clear and Foulques became aware of activity all around him.

The Mamluks were yelling, shouting, and running down the wharf in the direction of the children's warehouse. Or, rather, where the warehouse had once been. It now floated twenty paces from the main dock in open water, and with every second seemed to be getting further away. Several Mamluks teetered at the edge of the dock, cringing and rocking back and forth, wondering what to do. One brave man was yelling at another to help him take off his armor so he could enter the water.

"To the ship! To the ship!" the Northman's voice boomed over the chaos.

Foulques found himself in growing darkness and thought for a moment that he was blacking out. But it was only because the men holding torches and lanterns were scrambling away to carry out the Northman's orders. Foulques collapsed onto the wharf. He cried out in pain, at first, but then welcomed the coolness of the wood as it soothed the searing cuts on his back. Then he felt a painless warmth on his shoulder.

"Now or never, Foulques. Can you walk?" It was Vigno-lo. He crouched over Foulques; his hair was slicked back and water dripped off him. "We do not have much time. Come on, now."

The way Vignolo cringed when he spoke and looked at the Hospitaller made Foulques wonder exactly how badly he was hurt. He rolled onto his side and the sudden movement shot pain throughout his entire body. He tried to curb his breathing, for he had come to associate breathing with agony.

"We have to go," Vignolo said. He dragged Foulques to his feet, and together they shuffled to the edge of the dock and sat down. Their feet dangled in the water as Vignolo fumbled with a rope looped around a deck board. "I do not suppose you can swim any better than you can walk?"

"I will do what I must to get out of here," Foulques said between clenched teeth.

"All right, then." With a few deft twists of the rope, Vignolo tied off a non-slip loop. He eased it over Foulques's head and under one arm. Foulques grabbed onto the rope with one hand and clenched his opposite arm tightly against his side. Vignolo made another smaller loop further up the rope and thrust his wrist and forearm through it. Then, they eased themselves into the black water. "Hang on," Vignolo said. "And keep your head low."

Within seconds the slack in the rope was taken up and they were being pulled slowly through the water. They passed near the spot where the warehouse had been attached to the main dock. There were only two Mamluks still there. The rest were running up the dock to the mooring bays. Foulques and Vignolo pressed themselves into the water but one of the guards noticed them and let out a shout. The two Mamluks pulled bows off their backs and nocked arrows.

"Oh, sweet Mary," Vignolo said. They were only thirty paces away and moving at a predictably easy pace. "Come on Vagelli…"

The first bowstring twanged, followed by the other. The arrows skipped across the water three feet in front of them. "Those were their range finders," Vignolo said. "The next ones are going to be a lot closer."

The men curled into balls for the next volley and the arrows hit where their feet had been. Vignolo let out a yell as water splashed up from one of the shafts into his face. As the archers drew back for their third shot, Foulques felt a vibration in the rope, like it had suddenly been put under tremendous stress.

The archers let loose their arrows.

"Hold on!" Vignolo yelled, and suddenly both men were yanked under the water. A second later they popped up and were being dragged across the water at five times their previous speed. Vignolo let out a victorious whoop as they left the archers far in the distance, their shafts arching harmlessly into the wake behind Foulques and Vignolo.

They bounced through the water for several minutes and then abruptly slowed, the rope slackened, and Foulques would have sunk if Vignolo had not supported him from underneath. They drifted there in the water for a short time, and then the rope went tight and they began moving forward again. Gradually, Foulques could make out the warehouse beginning to take shape in the darkness. Men's voices carried up to them as well.

"Come on boys! Get us in there!" Vignolo called out to

the men grunting and pulling hand over hand on their rope. Foulques closed his eyes and concentrated on keeping his ribs from not moving.

The warehouse was pulled up tight to the aft of their merchantman, which was still moving under oar power alone. The last of the children were halfway up the rope-net ladders. Vagelli leaned over the rear railing of the ship and shouted down at Vignolo and Foulques, "They have pushed away from their berth and are raising sails."

"Good," Vignolo said. "An extra dram tonight for every man! And double rations for the donkeys!"

A cheer went up from the crew and although Foulques may have been hallucinating from pain, he swore he heard a donkey bray as well. "And Vagelli," added Vignolo, "send over a plank for young Brother Foulques here. He has had a rough day and does not look like he can make the climb up."

Foulques shrugged out of his makeshift rope harness and let it fall to the narrow deck of the warehouse. "Keep your plank. I can make the climb." He limped over to the netting, wrapped one hand in it, and that was the last he remembered before all went dark.

✣

AFTER VIGNOLO LASHED the unconscious Foulques to a plank and his crew hoisted the Hospitaller up to the ship, he stepped through the broken door of the small warehouse for one last look around. A dim lantern hung from the rafters and he had to duck to pass underneath. The smell was overpowering. Most of the stench came from a dozen or so buckets, or urns, lined up against one of the walls. Vignolo guessed they had served as chamber pots, but he had no desire to get near enough to prove his theory.

However, an object in the far corner of the room did look like it warranted a closer inspection. He reached up, removed the gently swaying lantern from its hook, and walked over to what he could now see was a lockbox lashed tightly against the wall timbers. His heart skipped a beat. He blinked his eyes once to make sure he was not imagining it. He pulled out his knife and cut the ropes. The lock was a tiny, almost ornamental piece, so he pried at it with his knife until it fell open. He threw back the lid. The case was filled to the top with coins of several different denominations. Vignolo dug his hands through the box, letting his fingers revel in the coolness of the silver. All in all, he estimated there to be close to five thousand denarii in the box. Not a princely sum by any means, but more than enough to make a good deal of Vignolo's problems go away.

He put his hands together and praised Mary out loud. But, then he thought about it some more and it all made perfect sense. The Mamluks had stored their valuables all in one location to make them easier to guard.

Oh. Mamluks.

He had almost forgotten where he was. As if on cue, he heard Vagelli calling his name with a sense of urgency. Vignolo ran his hands through the coins one last time before closing the lid. He tucked the lockbox securely under one arm, grabbed the lantern off its hook, and threw it against the back wall. The lantern glass shattered and the wall exploded in a satisfying curtain of flames. Checking once again that the lockbox's lid was firmly shut, Vignolo fled the floating prison back to his ship.

CHAPTER TWENTY-NINE

T HERE WAS NO time to assemble the slaves, so Badru ordered his Mamluk warriors to the rowing deck as sailors pushed the Wyvern away from her berth with long poles. There was more than one dark look cast toward the Emir as his men stooped to go down the steps, but Badru met each man's eyes with his own. To order a Mamluk to sully himself by sitting on a galley slave's bench would have invited open riot under most Emirs' commands, but not one of Badru's men protested openly. Those few that even hinted at their discontent were kept in check by Badru's icy, gray-eyed stare. Badru did not like ordering his men to do tasks below their station, but there was no other way. At any rate, the wind was up and the Mamluks only needed to man the oars long enough to get the galley into open water. Once they cleared the port, the Wyvern's sails would take over. In the current conditions, there was no ship on the Mid-Earth Sea that could outsail her.

The drummer started his beat and the oars broke the water's surface. Badru ran to the helm where Hanif held the wheel steady as the Wyvern pulled away from the dock.

Now, not far in the distance, Badru could see the merchant-man with the warehouse pulled up tight to its stern. Every lantern on the ship must be lit, he thought, for he could clearly make out shapes scrambling about its deck.

"Hoist all sails," Badru said to Hanif. He raised an arm and Badru's command was echoed throughout the ship. Canvas fluttered to life and filled with wind. "Put us on a direct heading for that ship."

The Wyvern plowed ahead through the water, gradually picking up speed. Hanif spun the wheel to bring the bow about. His face hardened. He spun the wheel again.

"What is it?" Badru asked.

"We have lost our rudder," Hanif said.

Both men looked to port as the Wyvern crossed the merchantman's wake. The distance between them and their quarry was increasing.

"Starboard oars, full!" Badru shouted. There was a moment's hesitation before the drummer changed up his beat.

"It is no good, my Emir," Hanif said. "We cannot maneuver under oars alone. We must drop our sails!"

"I will decide what we must do," Badru said. The drum beat a furious pace but the ship was not turning to port fast enough. Somewhere ahead in the darkness, was the shallow water of the other side of the bay. If they hit that they would be wrecked upon the rocks. Hanif was right.

"Drop sails!" Badru ordered. It took some time before his skeleton crew was able to accomplish the task. Meanwhile, the Wyvern continued to pick up speed. She bounced against the waves, and the wind from their flight blew the tail of Badru's turban straight behind him.

"She is not slowing enough. We are too close!" Hanif said.

Badru had visions of the Wyvern crashing upon the rocks. He had lost the Mistress's slaves. He would not lose her ship as well.

"Port oars, hold deep!"

Hanif looked at him in horror. "Emir. The rowers could be killed."

Badru turned on him. "They are not half-starved slaves. They are Mamluk. Relay the order."

Hanif would not question him twice. He gave the order and the drum paused once again. Badru grabbed hold of the rail. He pictured the men in the cramped space below taking hold of the port oars, two men on each, as the slave-master held his stick suspended above his drum. Badru heard the first beat, the second, and on the third the rowers plunged their oars straight down below the waves, as far as the sturdy staves could reach.

The ship lurched beneath Badru's feet and his thighs crashed forward into the railing, almost flipping him over it because of his height. A series of cracks broke through the air and Badru heard the sounds of men yelling and being thrown around below deck.

Hanif scrambled over to look down along the port side. He steadied himself against the railing and let out a breath before addressing Badru. "Over half the oars are destroyed, but we have turned enough to avoid the rocks."

Badru nodded. He called over a sailor. "Check on those

below. See to any that are injured and then assemble everyone on deck."

As Badru's rudderless Wyvern floundered at the whim of the gentle waves lapping against her side, the brightly lit merchantman raised its sails and set a steady, mocking pace for the mouth of the bay. And then, the dark outline of the warehouse erupted into flames.

✠

BADRU STOOD ON deck and focused on his breathing. He watched as the darkness first surrounded the merchantman and, eventually, swallowed it up whole. The only reminder of its passage was the warehouse bobbing alone on the water, entirely engulfed in flames.

He heard footsteps approach, and then Hanif spoke. "Emir. Two of the men say they saw figures in the water as we readied the ship to sail. They loosed arrows but missed their mark."

Badru turned to Hanif. "Figures?"

"Two men. One was the Hospitaller but they do not know who the other one was."

Badru bit the edge of his cheek. He had momentarily forgotten about the Hospitaller. He closed his eyes and shook his head. He suspected he knew who the other would be. The Genoan. A man who would not show himself, yet continued to haunt Badru time after time. But it was not only Badru that he tormented. He had made fools of two of his Mamluk warriors as well. Someone would need to be punished.

"Assemble the men on the main deck. Tell the two arch-ers to bring their bows," Badru said.

There was something in Badru's voice that sent Hanif scurrying off immediately, with no thought of bothering with a reply. Minutes later the two men who had shot at Foulques and Vignolo were on their knees in front of Badru, while the rest of the Mamluks gathered around.

"How many arrows did you each loose?" Badru demand-ed.

The Mamluks looked at each other. "Three, my Emir," one man said in a small voice.

Badru nodded. "Did any find their mark? Did not one arrow draw the blood of the enemy?"

They could have lied and said the darkness prevented them from knowing for sure. But they would not dare insult their Emir in that manner. Both men shook their heads. "They were close, but I am certain none hit flesh," the second Mamluk said. He spoke up in a clear voice that everyone could hear.

"Give me your bow," Badru said to him. The man reached down in front of his knees and lifted his bow off the deck with both hands. He lowered his head, and without looking up, offered it up. Badru took the man's weapon and stepped away. The deck was lit with every available lantern, so he could see the bow clearly. It was a beautiful piece, made from a combination of maple, sinew, and horn. The core was wood but its belly, the side that faced the archer, was lined with strips of water buffalo horn, while the back of the weapon was covered with a thin layer of sinew from the leg tendons of an ox. The sinew was flexible and allowed the bow to bend, but the horn was stiff and fought against compression. Working together, they were capable of generating a great deal of power in a very short bow.

Badru held the weapon up. Its reflex tips, its 'ears', curved back to point at the Mamluks kneeling in front of him. As he hooked his thumb onto the string and pulled, the ears flexed back to point behind Badru. He did not wear a thumb ring, so he held it for only a second before allowing the string to slowly return to its starting point. It left a bloodless line across his thumb even in that short amount of time.

"Give me three arrows and your thumb ring," Badru said. The Mamluk fumbled in the quiver at his side and fished out three shafts. Then he handed Badru a thumb ring fashioned from a smooth piece of ivory. Badru tried to put it on his thumb but, of course, it was too small. He tossed it back to its owner. He reached down to a leather pocket sewn to the sheath of his khanjar and pulled out one of his own thumb rings, this one made from leather. Most Mamluks used rings made from bone, jade, ivory, or sometimes metal, but Badru had always preferred the leather types used by common soldiers. They were just as effective and it was difficult to find ones crafted from harder materials that fit his huge thumb. But the leather thumb rings were easy enough to make himself.

Thirty paces away, at the edge of the deck, was the door that led to his private cabin. Holding the bow in his left hand and all three arrows in his right, he nocked the first arrow, pulled back the string and let fly. The bow protested as it was not meant for someone with a draw length as long as Badru's, but the arrow flew true enough and it slammed into the stout wooden door. He shot the next two arrows in rapid succession with similar results.

"There is nothing wrong with this bow," he said, handing it back to the kneeling warrior. "So the fault of your failure must lie with your lack of skill."

The Mamluk fixed his eyes on the deck, while his clenched fists rested on his thighs. "Yes, my Emir. Please forgive my incompetence."

"I do not. Forgiveness should be reserved for the worthy. Stand up, both of you."

As the two men stood, all other sound coming from the onlookers ceased. When Badru drew the curved khanjar from his belt, it seemed even the sounds of the waves hitting the Wyvern's hull quieted down. Badru held the blade out and pointed to each man in turn. "Take up your bows and three arrows each." They looked at one another. The orange light of the lanterns glinted off a line of sweat as it leaked from under one man's turban, ran down the side of his face, and disappeared into his beard.

Badru turned his back on the men and walked to the far end of the deck. When he reached his cabin door, he looked at the grouping of his arrows. They were a little off, but that was to be expected. Every bow and set of arrows is matched to a particular warrior. The arrows had not been stiff enough for Badru's greater strength. He would see how well they were matched to the warrior who owned them.

He pointed at one of the Mamluks holding a bow. "Shoot for my heart."

The Mamluk hesitated. "My Emir. I do not—"

"Loose your arrow!"

He jumped, then collected himself. He realized he had no choice. He raised his bow, pulled back on the string, and released. Badru stood square-on with the short blade of his khanjar held at the edge of his chest. The arrow whistled through the air and Badru did not move at all until the arrow struck the cabin wall six inches to his left.

Badru straightened up and shook his head. He fixed the man with a venomous stare. "Shoot again. This time, if you do not aim for my heart, I will take up your bow and we shall change positions."

"Yes, my Emir."

He loosed another arrow with no further hesitation. Badru's blade swept across his chest and knocked the arrow aside. "Good. Now you," he pointed at the other warrior. The next arrow came and Badru flicked it aside as well. "One after the other. Loose!"

Arrow after arrow flew at Badru's chest and he turned them aside with his khanjar one by one. By the time all six arrows had been shot, a fine sheen of sweat covered Badru's forehead and bare arms. He took a few breaths and shook the tension from his knife arm. He gathered up the arrows and broken shafts that had collected around him, then he returned to stand in front of his men. They dropped to their knees and pressed their heads to the deck as he approached.

"If you fail me again, we will not repeat this exercise. The

Furusiyya demands I give you one opportunity to better yourselves. There will not be two."

He threw the splintered shafts on the deck in front of the prostrated Mamluks and walked away.

CHAPTER THIRTY

THE REMAINS OF two long stone buildings, which only days before had been used to house mules and sheep, were cleaned up and modified into barracks for the children. The cells were not large, but the monks' carpenters crammed enough bunks along the walls and atop one another to accommodate two dozen children in each room. Besides his cot, every boy was given a large sack for his belongings and a hook on the wall for it to hang.

The second night in their new residence, one or two hours before dawn, Thomas was awoken by the sounds of stern voices shouting out orders. He rubbed the sleep from his eyes and leaned over the edge of his bunk to see if Pirmin was awake. Lanterns outside the barracks cast streaks of dim light through the uncovered windows and gaps under the thatch. To his surprise, Pirmin and several of the older boys were on their feet, talking in hushed tones. Pirmin noticed Thomas was awake.

"Fret none, Thomi. Just visitors is all," Pirmin said.

"I hear children's voices," another boy whispered. "Many voices…"

The voices grew nearer and the sound of shuffling feet could now be heard. The door to their cell flew open and a monk entered holding a lantern at his side that momentarily blinded Thomas and he had to look away.

"Hurry now. Come in, come in!" The monk's voice was ragged and he sounded angry.

Once his eyes adjusted, Thomas looked back to the doorway in time to see child after child walk through. His heart skipped a beat when he recognized many of them. He remembered the canyon, the screams, the strangely dressed man sitting on top of Pirmin, beating him again and again, and he wondered how it was possible that these few had returned. He sat up and watched them gather behind the monk, their downward cast faces, and slow, lifeless movement betraying their complete exhaustion. There were at least twenty of them. And they stank.

"Hurry up. Get in here, all of you," the monk said, pulling the last few through the doorway. He lifted his lantern up high and waved it at all corners to make sure everyone was awake. "Now listen, everyone. You have been rejoined by your brothers. You will have to double up on your cots for the next few nights. Until other arrangements are made."

He set his lantern on the dirt floor in the middle of the room. "I will leave this here for a few minutes until you get settled. I will be back." He strode from the cell leaving the door wide open.

By the time everyone had found a bed, Thomas knew there was no sense in sleeping, for dawn was almost upon them. He twisted his head to look at the boy who now shared his bunk. He, too, was awake for he lay there staring at the underside of the thatched roof.

"My name is Thomas," he said, then realized that was only part of it. "Thomas Schwyzer."

The other boy said nothing. He continued to stare out into the darkness.

"I know your name," Thomas said, for he had recognized the boy when he had first come in with the monk. "Your name is Hermann."

The boy rolled onto his side instantly and grabbed Thomas's throat with one hand. "Do not call me that! Ever. Do you understand?"

"Eh!" Pirmin kicked the underside of their bunk. "What is going on up there?"

Hermann's grip relaxed and he removed his hand. "Ever," he said, giving Thomas one last look before rolling onto his back once again.

"Everything all right, Thomi?"

"Yes," Thomas said, which was true, for he was more puzzled than scared.

"Then go to sleep," Pirmin said.

Thomas tried to, but he could not help himself. He looked at the boy once again.

"Then, what do I call you?"

As before, the boy ignored Thomas and kept staring at something above. He considered asking him again, but thought better of it. He turned onto his back and closed his eyes. Then, in the darkness, Thomas heard the boy speak.

"Gissler. My name is Gissler."

CHAPTER THIRTY-ONE

A FTER BEING ALLOWED to sleep in late for their first day, the new group of children were subjected to a condensed version of the same tests Thomas and Pirmin's group had undergone. They were given their new names and clothing, and the very next day were rejoined with the first group.

That next day began like the last several had for Thomas and Pirmin, with the same prayers followed by the food line. The serving nuns and monks still made Thomas nervous and he stuck close to Pirmin, but he had become settled in the routine. After the meal, the boys were seated in the courtyard where the Grandmaster once again addressed the assembly. But, there was another knight there, as well. A tall, stern-looking man about the same age as the Grandmaster.

"Today you will be given your assignments. You will be divided into two groups based on the natural gifts God has seen fit to imbue upon you. One group will remain here, with Marshal Clermont, and be trained as men-at-arms to serve with a sword. The other will depart immediately to our Order's other fortresses to work in the hospices, where some of you may eventually become trained physiks. Both are noble callings. You must all praise God tonight in your prayers, and thank Him for putting you on your true path."

A murmur shot through the crowd, for the children had come through a lot together in the previous weeks, and many were fearful of being parted. Thomas did not understand everything the Grandmaster had said, but he sensed the uneasiness in his friend Pirmin, and that in itself was enough to scare the small boy. Pirmin's name was one of the first to be called, and as he stood, a terrible dread flooded over Thomas. He grabbed onto the bigger boy's leg and refused to let go until Pirmin leaned down and reassured Thomas by telling him that the monks would soon call his name, too, and then he would be able to join Pirmin on the other side of the courtyard.

But the call never came. The morning wore on, and Gissler's name was called, as were several other boys Thomas had come to know. The monk shouted name after name, but Thomas was not amongst them. He listened intently, fearful of missing his name. He looked often at Pirmin who, being one of the taller boys standing on the far side of the courtyard, was easy to pick out. Pirmin would meet his eyes and smile. Usually he would mouth something like 'soon' or 'do not worry', and it would temporarily ease the lump building in Thomas's throat. But eventually, the last name was called and then monks made the remaining boys stand, about fifty boys in all, and arranged them in marching formation. Thomas lost sight of Pirmin and had to step out of formation to see him. Pirmin bravely forced a smile and with shiny eyes held up a hand to wave farewell.

Then a man-at-arms grabbed Thomas roughly by the scruff of his neck and shoved him into the middle of the formation. Surrounded by taller boys, Thomas could see nothing. The group began marching and Thomas was carried along like flotsam. He bobbed up and down, trying to catch a glimpse of Pirmin, a suffocating presence building in his chest. He knew if he lost sight of his friend for too long, he would never see him again. As it had been with his mami and papi, and with Pirmin's dog, Zora.

In seconds, the courtyard was gone and the gates leading into the city of Acre loomed into view.

✠

FOULQUES LAY ON his stomach in the wing of the hospital reserved for nobles and other high ranking members of society. It was a small room with fewer than twenty cots, but it had large, open-air windows and the sound of the fountain outside provided a comforting sound. Normally, as a member of the Order, he would not have been placed in this section of the hospital to mend, but occasional exceptions were made for war heroes. Apparently, someone had decided Foulques was a hero.

He did not know what Vignolo had told everyone, for he could remember nothing of the return journey. The last thing he could recall was climbing out of the water and reaching for a rope net to pull himself onto Vignolo's ship. But he could remember everything else about his fight with the Northman, if one could call it that.

Shame washed over him. It was a feeling he had not had since he was a child. Shame for being so weak and unprepared. He should have trained harder. He could have, there was no doubt in his mind. Foulques had been given opportunities to better himself throughout his life that most would never receive. He had been born into privilege, yet he had still let down his Order, his God, and especially his uncle. Allowing his body to recuperate in this hall seemed to him a form of blasphemy. He had to leave.

He turned his head so he could push himself up off his stomach. Pain shot from his stiff neck up into his head. He closed his eyes and lifted himself onto his knees. More pain registered, this time from his back, and he felt the familiar sensation of stitches stretching against skin. Then, a firm hand clamped onto his shoulder.

"Take your time, Brother Foulques. No sudden movements or I will be redoing all those stitches on your back." The voice belonged to Rafi Baba, one of the physiks of the Order. Like many of the physiks and surgeons, he was not a member of the Order of Saint John, but had been hired because of his expertise. The Hospital had its pick from physiks all over the Levant, for they paid well, and the Acre facility itself was beyond compare in both its volume of patients and the quality of the equipment it possessed. Rafi, himself, was a trained hakim from the school in Damascus, and a Muslim. The Order would have preferred to employ a Christian, but often could not resist the talents and knowledge that came with a hakim trained in Arabic medicine.

Rafi was a *theorici*, a physik skilled in the use of healing herbs, as well as the analysis of bodily fluids. Many of the sergeants had taken to calling Rafi 'Master Piss' behind his back.

"Hold onto my arm. I will help you up."

Ever so carefully, Rafi assisted Foulques to swing his legs over the side of the cot and assume a sitting position. It was not until then that Foulques realized there was someone else present besides the hakim.

Grandmaster Villiers stood up from a nearby chair and approached. "How are you feeling, Foulques?"

Foulques was surprised to see him. "All right, sir, I believe. How long have I been here?"

Rafi leaned Foulques forward and pulled a blood-engorged leach from somewhere on his patient's back. Foulques felt a stab of pain as the leach refused to relinquish its hold, and then with a quiet pop it was gone. Rafi tossed the blood sucker into a nearby bowl.

"Two days," the Grandmaster said. He smiled. "You did it, son. You brought back the children."

I did nothing, Foulques thought to himself. If not for Vignolo, he would be dead. The realization that he was indebted to the Genoan made his stomach churn.

"Where is Captain Vignoli, sir?"

"The captain turned out to be far more reliable than I would have thought," Grandmaster Villiers said.

Foulques heard alarm bells go off somewhere deep inside his aching head. "Reliable?"

"Along with you and the children, he delivered to me,

personally, a chest with enough coin in it to fully outfit two Hospitaller knights, or three sergeant men-at-arms. That seems reliable enough to me."

Chest? Where did he get that? Foulques thought. He must have stolen it from somewhere in town and brought it aboard the ship on one of the donkeys. Thinking about Vignolo made his head hurt. He closed his eyes and stretched his neck from side to side.

Rafi stepped between the Grandmaster and Foulques. "Time for you to stand. Can you manage it?"

Foulques nodded.

"Good," Rafi said. "The sooner you begin to move, the sooner your humors will restore and re-balance themselves." He took hold of one of Foulques's arms, and the Grandmaster the other. The two men helped Foulques to his feet and then slowly backed away, leaving the young knight swaying there on his own.

Rafi held up a clear drinking glass. "Fill this for me the next time you feel the urge to pass water."

Foulques had suspected that was coming. "How long do I have to remain in the hospital?" He took a few tentative steps on his own, feeling steadier with each one.

Rafi shrugged. "One more night, perhaps two, if I do not like what I see in your urine." He nodded toward the door. "Someone has been waiting to see you ever since they brought you here. Shall I let her in?"

"I do not feel up to visitors today," Foulques said. And probably not tomorrow either, if he had any say in it.

"It will do you good," Rafi said. "I shall let her in, then."

He turned and walked to the door, leaving Foulques standing there wondering why he had bothered to ask him in the first place.

"I shall leave you to your recovery," Grandmaster Villiers said. He placed a hand on Foulques's shoulder. "You did well. Your uncle will be proud when he hears what you have accomplished. Godspeed, Brother Foulques." He followed Rafi out the arched doorway.

Foulques limped over to the window. The stitches on his back tugged at his skin with every step, but otherwise, he felt fairly mobile. He closed his eyes, took a deep breath of the fresh morning air, and let the sunshine warm his face.

"Foulques?"

By the time he turned, Najya had already crossed the large room. She threw her arms around his neck and he grunted in pain. But then the warmth of her began to soak in. "Oh Foulques, I have been so worried." Her voice was small and he could feel her tears soak through the thin fabric of his nightshirt. "I told you not to go after the Northman..." She smelled of honey and cinnamon, and Foulques suddenly became aware of how little he wore. The Hospitallers were not allowed to sleep in the nude, so to him, he might as well have been standing there completely naked, wrapped in an embrace with a beautiful young woman. He knew he should have been more concerned, he should have looked over her shoulder and scanned the room to see who was watching. But, instead, he pulled her in tighter to his chest, knowing God would not begrudge him this moment. It was Najya, after all.

Finally, Foulques took a deep breath and eased Najya to arm's length. She still shook with sobs, but when he used the back of his finger to wipe the tears from her cheek, she looked at him and a self-conscious laugh bubbled out. That sound did more to heal Foulques's body than a thousand physiks ever could.

"Come," she said. "The hakim told me to get you outside for a short walk." She gave his ankle-length nightshirt a once-over and shook her head. "But first, I think we will have to find you a proper robe."

NAJYA AND FOULQUES stood on a balcony with Glynn, the Weapons Master, as he watched a monk call the Schwyzer children's names one by one. The courtyard was packed so full of children, sergeants, and even a few knights, that Foulques would not have been surprised if the ground suddenly caved in under the weight and swallowed them all up. Many of the children's faces were familiar to him, since they belonged to the first group he had successfully escorted to Acre's walls, but the others' faces stirred no memories, even though he had traveled with them almost as far. It was as though his mind refused to register them until after they had come to live in the Hospitaller compound.

Foulques felt Najya touch his arm. "Look, Foulques. Every single one of those children are here because of you. You should be proud."

He shook his head. He had no right to claim credit for any of this. It was his uncle's idea from the start. And then there was the Genoan. Perhaps he had underestimated Vignolo, for he had come through for them all in the end. He had even given the Grandmaster a chest full of coin when he could have just as easily kept the money for himself. And then there were his brethren who had given their lives during the fight with the slavers.

"Others gave far more than I did to bring them here. And really, Vignolo—"

Najya put her fingers over his mouth. "Be quiet. Sometimes you have to take credit for your actions," she said, smiling. The way she looked at him, Foulques could tell she would hear nothing about letting anyone else share the stage with Foulques. He felt like a fraud, and both foolish and fortunate at the same time.

The three of them stood in silence, mesmerized by the repeated calls of the monk. Then, something odd about the whole process occurred to Foulques. He turned to Glynn, who had been unusually quiet.

"Why are you dividing them up already? I would think it is a little early to properly tell horseman from swordsman," Foulques said.

"That lot there is leaving."

"Leaving? To where?"

Glynn shrugged. "They are to become servants in hospitals throughout the Levant. The Marshal ordered me to select fifty of those lacking on the physical side and send them on to Margat today. Seems he figures we got too many soldiers here as it is." He spit over the edge of the balcony, further emphasizing his sarcasm.

"What hospitals? I know of only three that are still brave enough to fly our banner," Foulques said.

"I do what I am told. Sometimes I even have to listen to French men. But thank Mary, Mother of God that does not happen often."

They watched until the last name was called, and then Foulques decided it was time Najya should go home. She protested until he said he was feeling strong enough to escort her the short distance to the compound's gate before he returned to his bed. They said their goodbyes to the Weapons Master and set off at a less than leisurely stroll to the gate leading into Acre proper.

As they approached the gate, Foulques became aware of the sound of many shuffling feet gaining on them. Najya pulled him to the side of the road and they watched the fifty Schwyzer children close the distance. They wore forlorn and sour-faced looks. They were leaving a place, again, to go somewhere that yesterday they did not even know existed.

"It does not seem right," Najya said. "They worked so hard to get here."

"No, it does not. But they will be a welcome addition to where they are going." He spoke with more conviction than he felt. Fifty soldiers could make a difference, but fifty children? They would become kitchen scullions and stable boys. Foulques would be surprised if a single one of them would see the inside of a hospital. Maybe fifty years ago, but not now with the Order's resources stretched so thin.

They were led by an escort of brother sergeants and a handful of monks. As the line of children passed, Foulques felt his anger build and begin to crest. Men had lost their lives to get them here, and now Marshal Clermont was sending them away.

A familiar face caught his eye. It was not so much the face, but rather the long angry line of stitches down its side. He remembered how the boy had leveled a heavy crossbow at the slaver who gave him that vicious wound, and he felt his guts twist with frustration.

Najya gasped as Foulques stepped forward, pushed his way into the marching children, and grabbed the back of the boy's shirt. He lifted him clear of the others and unceremoniously plopped the boy on the ground at his feet, grunting with pain for the effort. The group continued to march by and Foulques, still breathing heavily, scanned every face as they passed.

"Where is your friend?" he asked the boy in German while searching the crowd.

When the boy did not answer, Foulques gave him a shake. "I said, where is your friend?"

He felt the boy stir and he looked down at him. His dark eyes were almost black, and wide as coins. He held one arm out at shoulder height pointing back toward the courtyard.

Foulques softened his tone, somewhat. "Good," he said. "That is where he belongs."

"Brother Foulques!" A monk scurried up to the knight holding a sheet of parchment and pointing at it. Foulques did not give him a chance to say anything further. He slapped the parchment aside.

"There has been a mistake. This one is in the wrong

group. If the Marshal has something to say about it, tell him I will be happy to discuss it with him in the Grandmaster's office." He put his hands on his knees and bent over to look the boy in the face. "Now, get back over there, boy. Go back where your friend is and be quick about it. Do you understand?"

The boy's eyes went so wide Foulques thought they might fall out of his head. Foulques turned the boy by his shoulder to give him a start and without a backwards glance he began to run, his skinny arms pumping furiously at his side. He could not be sure, but as Foulques watched him race around the side of the keep, he had the impression the boy wore a grin as wide as his eyes had been.

After Foulques saw Najya off at the gate, he made his way back toward the Palace of the Sick. As he passed near the courtyard, a voice with the force of thunder drowned out all other sounds. The Marshal addressed his new charges in High German, and Foulques could not help but listen as he limped along his course.

"The road will be hard and the years long. But that is not the only promise I can make you. When we are done with your training, you will no longer be children. You will be soldiers of the one true God. You will know His mercy, and you will know His power, and the Infidel will tremble at your approach. That is my oath to you all."

Perhaps the boy should not have been so eager to be reunited with his friend, Foulques thought. He straightened as he passed the courtyard, unconsciously masking his limp, and forced his ears to block out all further words from the Marshal's speech.

CHAPTER THIRTY-TWO

T HE VENICE HARBORMASTER eyed Vignolo and his escort suspiciously as they stepped from the skiff onto the dock. Vignolo liked to think he was the one who had caught his eye. It stood to reason, clothed as he was in his cream-colored shirt freshly tailored in the Turkish fashion, while a sapphire-blue turban wrapped his head, its narrow tail hanging down to his waist. But, he conceded, the two huge eunuchs accompanying him did draw the eyes of the locals in this part of the world. Jakeem, the man Vignolo had first met while hiding in the public bath in Acre, made an imposing figure. His massive chest was bare. In fact, the only clothing he wore on his upper torso was several arm rings that struggled to contain his fleshy arms. And he still wore the wide-bladed falchion thrust through his silk sash. Vignolo had no idea if the man was at all capable with the weapon, but that was not the point. Tucked under his arm was an ornate lockbox Vignolo had purchased for the occasion.

The other eunuch was a slightly smaller version of Jakeem, but to the populace of Venice, he was just as foreign, and just as frightening. Strange, Vignolo thought, how a people whose riches came from their colonies scattered throughout the world, could be so distrusting of those from other lands. Ah, Venetians. They wanted everything the world had to offer, but none of its people.

"Good day," Vignolo said to the harbormaster as he strode past. The man's eyes widened at Vignolo's perfect Italian. He did not have time to puzzle out the strange foreigner, however, for the eunuchs were a step behind and the harbormaster had to scamper out of their path.

Francesca Provenzano's gate servant admitted Vignolo and his entourage onto the estate grounds almost immediately, for he was wise enough to know that the exotic foreigners milling about outside on the street would only attract attention. Once in the privacy of Francesca's estate, however, he seemed in no hurry to grant Vignolo an audience with his mistress. He left Vignolo languishing in the sun for the better part of two hours. Finally, a little man wrapped in hose so tight he looked to be made of sausages, appeared and escorted the three of them into the marble-tiled antechamber of Francesca's manor house.

Francesca sat on a high-backed chair with a dozen armed men spaced around the large room. Vignolo was led up to within ten feet of Francesca, but the eunuchs were directed to stay near the door. Her chair was the only one in the room. Vignolo suspected she was not used to visitors and one look at her usually bright, inquisitive eyes revealed they had lost some of their luster. In fact, they smoldered. Vignolo had invaded her domain and she was not happy about it.

Vignolo gave a deep bow. "Lovely to see you, Francesca. My friends and I found ourselves in your part of the world and thought—"

Francesca cut him off. "I have heard disturbing things about you Vignolo."

"All of them true, I hope," Vignolo said. A man stepped forward and Vignolo glanced at his face. He recognized him immediately as the one attacker Foulques had allowed to escape from the alley behind Vignolo's inn. "Ah, good. I am so glad to see you made it out of that unfortunate situation back in Acre. Did you have a chance to tell Francesca here exactly what happened?"

The man's hand involuntarily grasped his sword hilt, but Francesca was the one who responded. "Tito provided me with a full retelling of the events."

Vignolo smiled and he looked at the man. "Everything, Tito? You told her how you soiled your leather breeches? I will give you this, it must have been awkward running for your life with all that wet leather clinging to your legs, but you did do an admirable job of it."

Tito had his sword half out of his scabbard and only the sound of Francesca yelling his name stayed his hand.

"Enough! Both of you," Francesca said. "You have cost me some expensive men, Vignolo. Give me a very good reason to not string you up in the courtyard right now and have you gutted."

"I will give you two," Vignolo said. He gestured to Jakeem to approach. A guard stepped in front of the eunuch as he started moving, but Francesca waved him away as her eyes focused on the small chest tucked under the big man's arm. Jakeem put the box on the floor in front of Francesca's chair and flipped open the lid to reveal the modest mound of coins inside. He backed away with his head lowered and returned to wait with the other eunuch by the door.

"Here is reason number one," Vignolo said.

Vignolo could tell by Francesca's look she was not impressed. "How much is there?" she asked.

"Fifteen hundred denarii," Vignolo said slowly, emphasizing each word.

"You owe me three thousand," Francesca said, shaking her head. Her mouth curled up on one side, marring her otherwise beautiful features.

"I am renegotiating," Vignolo said.

"What terms are you offering?" Her smile straightened out as she anticipated the thrill of a hunt about to commence.

"I give you fifteen hundred and we call my debt paid in full."

Francesca threw her head back in her chair and laughed. The sound made everyone in the room cringe. Everyone except Vignolo. It was his turn to smile now.

"Oh, my sweet Vignolo. I will miss you," Francesca said.

"Not as much as the Hospitallers will if anything should happen to me. Speaking of which brings up reason number two," Vignolo said. He turned to Tito. "Did you tell her what the Hospitaller said to you and your friends before he carved everyone up? 'I have need of the Genoan.' Is that not what he said?"

"You are grasping for your life, Vignolo," Francesca said, leaning forward in her chair. She blinked at him and smiled like she had just offered him a plate of biscuits to choose from.

"I believe I am stating facts. Fact number one: I have just saved the lives of two hundred future Hospitallers. Fact number two: in the process of fact number one, I also saved the life of Brother Foulques de Villaret, the very Hospitaller we spoke of a moment ago," Vignolo paused to stare at Tito's crotch before turning back to Francesca, "and fact number three: the Hospitallers have hired the unfailingly dependable Vignolo dei Vignoli yet again for a secret mission, which I cannot possibly let you in on." This last part Vignolo made up on the spot. He hoped it was not too much, but he could not resist, for he saw Francesca's shrewd mind starting to put things together and he sensed it was time to move in for the kill.

Francesca crossed her arms over her chest and narrowed her eyes.

"Now, before you say anything you might regret," Vignolo continued, "I told the Hospitallers about all my dealings with you and your organization. They know where I am right now. In fact, I sailed a Hospitaller ship here. You had a taste of what one Hospitaller Knight is capable of, imagine what three hundred of those things can do? You once told me you believed your interest charging practices were the least of your sins. I doubt my annoyingly righteous friend, Brother Foulques, would see it that way. Did I mention he owes me for saving his life?"

Vignolo could see Francesca's jaw muscles clenching and unclenching, like they were grinding her teeth into powder. Vignolo had won this day, they both knew that. But Francesca Provenzano, having risen from the slums of Milan, was a dangerous woman to have as an enemy. Vignolo did not want to think about what might happen if there came a day when she caught wind of a change in his relationship with the Hospitallers. But that was a worry for another day, for he could die a thousand deaths before that day came.

"You will leave Venice immediately. And never, ever come to my home again," Francesca said.

The tone of her voice made Vignolo shift his feet. "Well, it has been a pleasure. I suppose I had best get the Hospitallers their ship back." He bowed low, until the tails of his turban brushed the floor, and then without waiting for permission from his host—if Francesca Provenzano could ever truly be called that—began striding for the door. As he passed the eunuchs, he snapped his fingers and they fell into step behind him.

The garden gate clanged shut behind them and Vignolo found himself standing with his half-naked companions in the narrow street once again. Vignolo took in a deep breath of freedom. He was almost disappointed by how easy that had been. Remembering the look of pure animosity on her face when he informed her he was going to only pay back fifteen hundred denarii of his three thousand debt, did give him a pang of regret. He had the extra fifteen hundred, but a man needed coin for expenses. It was a trifle to someone like her. And besides, Vignolo figured he had earned a good game or two of hazard. Perhaps, even an honest one this time, if there were any such beast.

"Where to now, Vignoli?" Jakeem asked, making Vignolo jump. He did not talk often, but when he did, the low pitch always caught Vignolo by surprise. He looked at Jakeem and his companion, who was glancing nervously around with a wrinkled nose.

"You ever been to Venice before, Jakeem?"

The big man shook his head, setting off undulations in the flesh of his neck.

"Well, then I am going to take you on a float through the canals. The only way to appreciate the views of this city is while being serenaded by a gondolier. Providing, of course, we can find a gondola seaworthy enough to carry us all."

The eunuchs looked at each other with no small amount of worry in their faces. But Vignolo ignored them. This may be the last time any of them were ever in Venice, so Vignolo intended to make the best of it. He had coin in his pocket, no debts to his name, an estate on the island of Rhodes, and two eunuchs by his side. By the grace of Mary, could life get any better?

CHAPTER THIRTY-THREE

BADRU VOWED HE would sit cross-legged and motionless on the flagstone floor until he had established complete control over himself. After an hour, the pain in his legs became excruciating, but its distraction brought a welcome relief. After two hours, the agony crept into his lower back and bolts of stabbing pain shot up into his neck. The agony continued until the darkest part of the night had passed. It was during the hour before dawn that the blessed numbness of both body and mind finally found him. Just as his breathing steadied, there was a knock on the door. He could not move, so he ignored it. It came again, more urgent this time. Badru managed a grunt and the door creaked open far enough for a Mamluk's head to squeeze through.

"Forgive me, Emir, for disturbing your rest, but the Mistress's ship has docked."

Badru managed a wave of dismissal, but it took several minutes to will the blood back into his lower extremities. When he finally did move them for the first time, he screamed long and hard. Not because of the pain. No, it was to get the attention of Allah, to swear to him he had returned to the world with the sole purpose of meting out punishment to those who had wronged him.

Badru took his time when he was summoned before Madame Boulet, for he was in no hurry to discuss his failure. He climbed the curved stairway to the second floor, sliding his hand along the hundred-year-old mahogany railing and allowing it to pull him up with each step. In his other hand, he held a coiled bull-hide whip. It was a heavy, slavemaster's tool. At the end of its eight-foot length was a forked tongue embedded with tiny iron rivets designed to rip the skin and cause unbearable pain.

At the top of the stairs stood two Mamluks in front of the doors leading to the Manor's feast room. The guards bowed their heads to their Emir and pushed open the doors. Veronique sat at the furthest end of the long trestle table, but already Badru could smell the nauseatingly sweet-scented oil she used in her hair. Wine glass in hand, she wore a full-length sunflower yellow dress that set her pale skin to glowing. In front of her was her breakfast: a platter of fruit and dried meats, and a glass pitcher of wine. The platter appeared untouched. The wine level in the pitcher was below the halfway mark. To Badru's surprise, behind her stood two of her household servants. Yusuf was one of them. His eyes followed Badru as he approached.

Badru took one knee and lowered his head. "Mistress," he said.

Veronique ignored him as she picked up a grape with her delicate fingers. She squeezed until the wet ball of the fruit popped out of its skin, then she put it back on the plate.

"Stand, Badru," she said. She stared at him as she wiped her fingers on the table. He rose to his feet and looked straight ahead.

"Do you know how much I was looking forward to seeing those children?" Veronique said.

Badru kept his eyes fixated somewhere in the distance. "I failed you, Mistress. I know that, and I expect to be punished."

"I am told it was a Hospitaller and a Genoan captain that bested you?"

Badru ground his teeth. "Yes, Mistress."

"I hate Genoans," Veronique said.

I hate one, thought Badru. Though he did not even know what the man looked like.

"You have made things awkward for me, Badru. I already had some buyers for the merchandise. One was a sheik. A powerful man, with an appetite for one hundred children a year. Do you think a man like that will be happy if I simply return his gold?"

Badru knew the sheik of whom she spoke. He was a regular buyer with dark fetishes Badru would rather not think about. "No, Mistress. He will not."

Veronique nodded her head. "No. A starving man cannot eat gold."

She pointed at her glass. Yusuf leaned forward, lifted the pitcher and filled it dangerously close to the rim. As Veronique brought it to her lips, wine sloshed over the rim onto her dress at the neckline.

"You simpleton! What were you thinking?"

Yusuf's eyes went huge. "Apologies, Mistress, I did not…" he stammered.

"You did not what? Think? Pay attention? Tend to your duties? What exactly is it that you did not do?" Veronique was on her feet now, but she still clutched her glass in her hand. Her tirade sent more of the wine splashing out of her glass all over her wrist. "Oh, by the Devil's—" she wiped her hand on her dress and whipped her head toward Badru. "Emir, strike this man."

Badru and Yusuf exchanged shocked looks. "Mistress?" Badru said.

"You heard me! Strike him! He needs to be punished."

Badru recognized the fanaticism in her voice. She became like this on occasion. It was not simply a case of too much wine, or the fear of a business deal gone bad. She was a rich and powerful woman, but she had not become that way without sacrifice. There was a blackness that lived inside his mistress, feeding on parts of her that the world could not see. Sometimes, that blackness hungered for more.

There was only one thing to do. He stepped forward and backhanded Yusuf across the face. His head snapped to the side and he brought it back around slowly, his eyes wide as a buckler.

"Again," Veronique said. "Harder this time."

Badru did not hesitate. He hit Yusuf with his open hand on the other side of his face. The young man cartwheeled hard to the floor. It took some time before he struggled to his knees. When he looked up at Badru, he had tears in his eyes and blood ran from the corner of his mouth.

"Good," Veronique said. "The slave has been punished." Her chest heaved with her breathing. She stepped over Yusuf and walked up to Badru. "Now, back to the matter at hand. What are we to do with you?"

Badru tried his best to keep his sigh of relief hidden. Somehow he had succeeded in turning her ire away from Yusuf back to someone who actually deserved it.

"I should be flogged by your strongest Mamluk." He held out his whip and she took it from him like it was the most natural thing in the world.

"How many lashes?" Veronique asked.

"Until I lose consciousness. A tortured man is safe once he enters the dark embrace."

"And who would you have wield the leather?"

Badru thought for a long moment. He remembered Safir was one of the guards at the door. He was a strong warrior and would not hesitate to do the job well. "Safir," he said.

Veronique looked at Badru as her mind went over the situation. Her face was beginning to flush, not with wine, but with excitement. "Guards," she called to the doorway.

Badru pulled his tunic over his head. No sense ruining a good shirt.

"You called, Mistress?" Safir said.

"Your Emir says you can be trusted to carry out your duties?" Veronique said.

"Of course, Mistress."

"Good." She handed him Badru's whip. "Tie this man's hands around that support pillar. And remove his shirt."

Badru took a step back. Veronique was pointing at

Yusuf. What did she mean to do?

Her intentions finally became clear to his troubled mind when he saw Safir and the other Mamluk haul Yusuf to his feet and begin binding his hands around the pillar.

Badru dropped to his knees in front of Veronique. "Mistress, please. You do not understand. It was my failure. I deserve to be the one punished."

There was a tearing sound as the Mamluks ripped the shirt off Yusuf's back.

"Oh, I do understand, my Emir. It may be Yusuf's perfect, smooth skin being shredded, but I would wager you will feel it more than if it were your own back. Every time you look upon your lover, his scars will remind you of this day. Commence!"

Badru turned away from Veronique's leering face just in time to see Safir's arm fall. Yusuf bucked and screamed as the skin across his back stretched and a jagged, crimson line broke across its surface.

"Do not look at him!" Badru felt tiny fingers grab his hair and yank his head around. A sickly sweet perfume punctuated with hints of rancid oil clogged his nostrils.

"Mistress, please. Do not do this. I beg you," Badru said as he slid down to his knees again in front of her. They were almost at eye level now. Leather cracked through the air followed by another scream.

"How many was it that you said? Until he loses consciousness?"

"No!"

"No? Shall I flog him until he is dead, then?"

"Anything, Mistress. I am sorry. I will do anything. Please do not hurt him any more." Badru did not know it was possible to experience fear and panic at this level. His heart hammered so hard he instinctively put a hand on his chest to stop it from bursting through his ribs.

Veronique cupped his chin with her hands. "Oh, Badru. I truly believe you are sorry. And afraid…" Her eyes followed her one hand as it slid down his neck, over the bare skin of his shoulder and upper arm. "And angry." She lifted him to his feet with the hand under his chin. "So many emotions! I have never seen this side of you, my giant warrior." Badru heard her voice take on a flirtatious tone and if he doubted his ears for a moment, her hand fumbling with the tie on the side of his breeches confirmed it.

Another scream of agony. Badru closed his eyes. "Mistress, please…"

"You deserve a chance at redemption," Veronique said, her voice husky. Her hand slid inside his loosened breeches. "The world quakes in fear of the Mamluk known as the Northman. But it is your fear and your anger I want to feel inside myself." Her words quickened, as did the frantic ministrations of her hand. She licked his chest and leaned back onto the table, clutching at him, trying to pull him down on top of her. He resisted. Her voice became cold again. "When I feel your seed inside me, the lashes will stop. Not a second before."

The leather cracked again, Yusuf wailed, and the Northman allowed himself to be pulled down on top of his master. Veronique's alabaster face smirked in victory as she hiked her dress past her thighs and freed Badru from his breeches. She groaned and her eyes clenched shut with anticipation.

Her eyes snapped open. Then her mouth, as she realized her body was deprived of oxygen. Her tiny hands flew to her throat and pried at the massive fingers completely encircling her neck. Badru looked on as the blood vessels in her face rose and snaked across the surface of her white skin. She gave up pulling at the immovable fingers and instead raked at them, using her fingernails like they were claws. But they were not claws. She drew a little blood, but most of her nails broke off leaving her own hands bloodier than Badru's. She quaked, went still, then thrashed in a final convulsion. In the end, like many before her, Veronique Boulet found out the Northman did not bleed so easily.

Badru stumbled away from the table. He could not take his eyes off the spider-veined face of his master. He had no idea what the others in the room were doing. He did not even know for sure if they were still there. He adjusted his breeches and tried to tuck in his shirt, but realized he was not wearing one. He turned to look for it. Safir and the other Mamluk stared at him, their swords drawn. Safir's eyes darted back and forth from Veronique's body to Badru.

"What have you done?" Safir asked. The other Mamluk began to move away from Safir toward Badru's left side. They would come for him once the shock wore off. The Furusiyya demanded it. Badru was unarmed and he planned to stay so. It was the only way they would have a chance at killing him.

"Wait!" Yusuf appeared in the midst of the three warriors. He had slipped his bonds, but a strand of rope still hung off one wrist.

"Do you not see?" Yusuf turned to Safir and Badru saw the seething mess of flesh on his back. "Your master took you as far as she could. It is Allah's will that your journey continue under a new master. Do you honestly believe you were meant to follow the commands of a Frankish whore your entire life? Search your heart. You sense truth in my words, and it is not *my* truth. It is the truth of Allah."

He faced Badru, and the Northman felt his next words were for his benefit. "The great Sultan Baybairs also slew his master. He did it to liberate his people and create an empire."

Yusuf slowly dropped to his knees. He brought his hands together in front of his face, the movement bringing a cringe of pain to his fine features. "Today, our Emir becomes our master. Everything is as Allah intended. Peace be upon us." He stretched his arms out in front and pressed his forehead to the floor. "Allah is great. Long live Badru Hashim."

Safir was the first to take a knee, but the other Mamluk followed immediately. With upraised palms, they held their scimitars parallel to the floor, cutting edges toward their hearts.

"Allah is great. Long Live Badru Hashim."
"Allah is great. Long Live Badru Hashim."

The story continues in: **Mamluk** (*Hospitaller Saga* Book 2)

For more details, please go to jkswift.com or sign up for the **New Releases Mailing List** (http://eepurl.com/hTAFA). Your information will never be shared and you will only be notified when J. K. Swift publishes something new.

ABOUT THE AUTHOR

J. K. Swift recently moved into a log house deep in the forests of central British Columbia, Canada. He now has room to shoot his longbow, and when he is not busy cutting wood to survive the winter, he spends his free time making mead, riding Icelandic horses, roasting coffee, and writing historical fiction and fantasy.

J. K. Swift's website:

jkswift.com

...a message from the author:

Thank you very much for reading my work. Reviews and personal recommendations from readers like you are the most important way for relatively unknown authors like me to attract more readers, so I truly am grateful to anyone who takes the time to rate my work. If you could take a moment to rate my story and/or leave a review where you purchased it, I would greatly appreciate it. Feel free to contact me through my website with any questions or comments. Thanks very much!

All the best,
James

Sign up for the **New Releases Mailing List** (http://eepurl. com/hTAFA). Your information will never be shared and you will **only** receive notifications when J. K. Swift publishes something new.

Novels:

The Forest Knights Series:

ALTDORF (Book 1):
jkswift.com/books/altdorf

MORGARTEN (Book 2):
jkswift.com/books/morgarten

The Hospitaller Saga:

ACRE (Book 1)

MAMLUK (Book 2) Coming December 2nd, 2016

Short Stories/Novellas:

Keepers of Kwellevonne Series:

HEALER (Book 1):
jkswift.com/books/healer

FARRIER (Book 2):
jkswift.com/books/farrier

WARDER (Book 3):
jkswift.com/books/warder